SUDDEN DEATH SUDOKU

SUDDEN DEATH SUDOKU

A Katie McDonald Mystery

SHELLEY FREYDONT

RUNNING PRESS
PHILADELPHIA • LONDON

9 8 7 6 5 4 3 2 1
Digit on the right indicates the number of this printing

Library of Congress Control Number: 2008926374

ISBN 978-0-7624-3493-0

Puzzles throughout from *The Mammoth Book of Kakuro, Wordoku and Sudoku,* ed. by Nathan Haselbauer, reprinted by kind permission of Constable & Robinson Ltd., London.

Cover design by Whitney Cookman
Interior design by Maria E. Torres
Typography: Berkeley and Interstate

Running Press Book Publishers
2300 Chestnut Street
Philadelphia, PA 19103-4371

Visit us on the web!
www.runningpress.com

To Pearl

Good friend, astute critic and unflagging cheerleader

Thanks

			7	1	6		3	
6	3	8		2			1	
			3		8		4	
		2	5		9			7
5	9						8	4
7			2		4	3		
	2		9		1			
	1			4		9	7	6
	7		6	5	3			

SOLUTIONS BEGIN ON PAGE 334.

"A LITTLE HIGHER." Kate MacDonald looked up at the banner Harry Perkins was pinning to the black curtain of the VFW Hall stage. "A little lower."

Harry twisted on the ladder and gave her a look. "Kate."

Kate made a face back at him. "Try five point five centimeters lower."

Harry grinned. "That's better."

"And don't fall off the ladder."

He lowered the banner and pinned it to the curtain, then climbed down from the ladder and stood back to look at his handiwork. He turned to Kate, his face flush with excitement.

"Wicked," he said and grinned at her.

"Wicked," she agreed.

The First Annual P.T. Avondale Sudoku Challenge. Kate just wished Professor Avondale were here to see it. But he'd been mur-

dered six months before, leaving Kate a derelict puzzle museum—
and Harry.

A fourteen-year-old orphan, Harry had been the professor's
apprentice. Now, he was Kate's apprentice. He was tall for his age,
all arms and legs with a smattering of freckles across his nose and
an IQ that bordered on genius.

They stood together admiring the banner, though Kate was
looking through a haze of unshed tears. She thought maybe Harry
was, too.

She was excited, sad, and nervous as hell. What had begun as a
one-day local Saturday fund-raiser had mushroomed into a three-
day event inundated the small town of Granville, New Hampshire
with from hordes of Sudoku from fans up and down the East
Coast.

"I just hope we can pull this off."

Harry gave her another one of his looks. "Hope isn't exactly part
of the scientific method."

"Don't I know it." Kate was a mathematician, not an event plan-
ner. And she was afraid that any method beyond the scientific was
beyond her grasp.

But wasn't that why she'd left her job at the Institute for
Theoretical Mathematics to return home? She had always wanted
to be a people person, and when the professor bequeathed the puzzle museum to her, she knew what she had to do.

The hall doors opened, bringing the buzz of participants waiting in the vestibule before it closed again.

Chief of Police Brandon Mitchell strode toward them.

"Shit," Harry said under his breath.

Kate raised an eyebrow at him.

"Sorry. I meant. Oops." He started to ease toward the ladder.
One look from the chief and he stopped dead.

Kate shook her head and turned to meet the devil head on. She gave him her best smile. "Chief Mitchell. How are things going?"

He scowled back at her. "They'd be going a lot better if I had the personnel to control this crowd."

Kate gritted her teeth. She knew he'd had to borrow officers from the county sheriff's office to augment his five-man police department for the weekend. He'd even called up old Benjamin Meany to act as crossing guard. And it still wasn't enough.

But that was hardly her fault.

"And it would be better still if a certain eighth grader hadn't skipped the last three periods of school today."

Harry stepped behind Kate, even though he was taller than Kate; Brandon Mitchell towered over them both.

Kate frowned at the chief. "You mean he didn't . . ."

"No, he didn't."

"Oh."

"Oh," the chief mimicked.

They both turned to Harry, who shrugged guiltily. "I knew you wouldn't let me skip school. Nothing important was going on anyway. No tests or anything. And Kate needed me."

Chief Mitchell turned his wrath on Kate.

"I didn't condone it," she said quickly, "but I *do* need him here. I'll call the school first thing Monday and explain about the absence. And Harry will make up any work he's missed. Won't you, Harry?"

"Sure."

No hardship there. Harry was a near-genius. For him, school was not much more than babysitting. Kate could relate. She'd spent her own adolescence as a misunderstood geek.

"That isn't the point," the chief said. "I need to know where you are."

Harry jutted his chin out. "You could have called my cell."

The chief's dark eyes turned darker.

Kate touched his arm. She'd finagled him into letting Harry live with him instead of going to foster care. He was chafing under the responsibility.

"I understand. It won't happen again."

The door opened. Kate's Aunt Pru stood in the doorway, tall and thin, dressed in a red tournament sweatshirt, white knit slacks, and navy blue running shoes, in keeping with the red, white, and blue decorations on loan from the Fourth of July committee. Even her hair was blue, but it had been blue since Kate returned to Granville six months ago. The reason was still an enigma.

"Great. Just great." The chief stepped away from Kate.

Kate's hand fell to her side.

Pru scanned the room, zeroed in on the police chief, and sprinted toward them. An inveterate lady, the only thing that could make Pru move like a race car was Brandon Mitchell.

"We're ready to open the doors," she said, pointedly ignoring the chief.

"Already?" Kate barely squeaked out the word as a jolt of pre-performance jitters struck without warning. She took a deep breath. She only had to give the welcoming address and introduce Tony Kefalas, whom she had hired to emcee the weekend.

After that, all she had to do was worry about everything else.

"It's seven forty-five."

"Is Tony here?"

"Ginny Sue drove him over from the inn. He's waiting back-stage."

Kate swallowed. "Okay. Tell everyone to . . . uh . . ."

"Man their battle stations," the chief suggested.

Pru pursed her lips at him.

Kate nodded. "Let them in."

Pru hurried away, shooting a look of disapproval at the chief over her shoulder.

Kate ran her tongue over suddenly dry lips and looked around. Everything was ready.

Except Kate. She smoothed her hair. But her normally wayward curls were already gelled back into barrettes. She straightened the jacket of her black wool pant suit. Looked down at her black sling-back heels.

"You'll be fine." Chief Mitchell gave her something like a smile and strode away.

Right, thought Kate. She'd be fine.

The back doors opened. Red-shirted volunteers took their places around the room. People rushed in to fill the cordoned-off spectator area at the back of the hall. The doors to the overhead gallery opened and those seats were soon filled.

Kate took a deep breath, ran through the litany of tips she'd learned from a government speech coach. *Relax. Be gracious. Move your eyes around the room so they think you're talking to each one of them personally.*

As she reached the stairs that led to the stage, she saw Tony step from the door to backstage. *Remember to breathe.* He winked at her. Her foot caught on the lip of the first step and she stumbled. *And for heaven's sake. Don't fall up the stairs to the scaffold—uh, the stage.*

She regained her balance and managed to make it to the podium without further mishap. But when she looked over the sea of people, she panicked. Every seat was occupied. Competitors stood at the back of the room waiting for their level to be called. Rows and rows of rectangular tables filled the huge space in between.

Kate cleared her throat. This just never got any easier. The sound rumbled over the microphone and she winced. "Welcome to the First Annual P. T. Avondale Sudoku Challenge. I'm glad to see so many of you braved the elements to come here this weekend. Snow is predicted, but we New Hampshirites know how to deal with snow."

Laughter.

They thought she was joking. But she knew how easily a forecast of six to twelve inches could turn into a blizzard. She was keeping her fingers and toes crossed that it didn't happen this weekend. To heck with the scientific method; she'd stoop to anything that would ensure a successful weekend.

"The tournament is named in honor of one of Granville's most illustrious citizens, Professor P.T. Avondale, the owner and curator of the Avondale Puzzle Museum until his death last year." She had to blink rapidly before she could go on. "The professor was my mentor and friend. I know he would be pleased to see so many Sudoku fans here tonight."

She took another breath, smiled at the back wall.

"I know you're all anxious to get started, so without further ado, I'd like to introduce the moderator and emcee for the weekend. A man whose reputation precedes him . . ." This brought another round of laughter. "For those of you who may be new to the puzzle circuit, Tony Kefalas is twice Grand Master . . ." Kate listed the specifics of Tony's career, then gestured toward Tony.

Applause broke out as the renowned puzzle master took the stage.

Tony was several inches taller than Kate, about five-ten, with a slight build and black hair going to gray at the temples. He was dressed impeccably in a tweed sports jacket, tie, and v-neck sweater. A large gold medal hung from his jacket lapel by a wide purple ribbon, his latest Grand Master award.

"Thanks, Kate," Tony said, taking the microphone. "It's a pleasure to be here tonight."

Kate started to ease away.

Tony grabbed her by the elbow and pulled her back to the podium. "Kate was very generous in her accolades, but what she forgot to tell you is that not only is she the curator of the Avondale Puzzle Museum that is sponsoring this weekend, but she is also the 2004 Eastern Level A Sudoku champion."

Polite applause.

"And the only reason she didn't take nationals is that she didn't attend due to delivering a paper to the government's Institute of Theoretical Mathematics, where she was resident genius before leaving to dedicate her time to a wider range of puzzles."

Kate blushed. She'd left that life far behind. It was hard enough being accepted by her hometown after growing up as a child genius and local geek. She didn't need for them, or her, to remember just how much she didn't fit in.

Only she did fit in. This weekend was evidence of the town's support.

Individual spaces for the contestants were marked off by yellow cardboard screens. Each place was equipped with several pencils and a bottle of water, all donated by local businesses.

Red, white, and blue banners festooned the walls and stage, draped the windows and the spectators gallery. Above the stage, the numbers of a giant digital clock, paid for by Marian Teasdale, president of the museum, blinked red.

Rayette's Café was running the concession stand downstairs. The VFW had donated the use of the hall.

The event was a town effort and Kate appreciated it more than she knew how to express.

As soon as the applause began to wane, she scurried off the stage. Tony slipped on a pair of black-rimmed reading glasses and began outlining the rules for the competition.

"... two semi final rounds in all divisions. The top five winning times will advance to the finals tomorrow afternoon. All scores will be compiled to establish team rankings. Team finalists will compete in the Sudoku Smackdown, Sunday at twelve. That will give everyone time to attend the Presbyterian Church service across the street to offer up prayers for victory."

A ripple of laughter.

"Junior divisions will be held here starting at ten o'clock tomorrow morning, to be followed by—and this is my favorite part—a complimentary sticky bun and coffee breakfast, donated by Rayette's Bakery and Café on Main Street. Be sure to visit the café on your time off. I've been told she bakes the best sticky buns in town."

"In the *county*."

"In the state!"

Tony grinned. "You heard it from the folks whose motto is 'Live free to eat sticky buns or die.'"

Cheers and whistles and laughter at his play on the New Hampshire state motto.

Kate felt a little envious. Tony was so good at this. Relaxed and funny. And he kept things moving along. She had no people skills at all.

"And when you've enjoyed lunch at one of the lovely restaurants in town, please join us for a Saturday afternoon of workshops. Sudoku for Rookies, Taming the Monster Sudoku, and Breaking into Codes and Ciphers, a special presentation by Granville's own super spy, Harry Perkins."

Across the room, Harry stood at the wall, beaming with pride.

"As always, please be totally quiet during each round. And now, Level D competitors, please take your places."

A volunteer unlatched the cord that separated the competition area from the spectators and there was a rush toward the rows of tables. Chairs scraped along the floor as competitors chose their seats. Within seconds, the tables were fully occupied. The air was charged with anticipation and concentration. Volunteers began placing paper puzzles face down on the tables before each competitor. A hush fell over the hall. The red dots of the digital timer sprang to life.

"The time allowance for the first round is twenty minutes." Tony waited for the volunteers to return to the sides of the hall and the adjudicators to take their places at the end of each row of tables.

"On your mark . . . Get set . . . *Go.*"

Papers rustled as they were turned over and the contestants bent over their work. The clock began to subtract the seconds.

Kate let out a sigh of relief. They were on their way. She tiptoed along the side of the hall toward the entrance door, careful to keep her heels from clicking on the wooden floor. Even the smallest noise could be distracting to nervous puzzle solvers.

She eased the door open and slipped out to the vestibule where Alice Hinckley and five other members of the Granny Activist Brigade were manning the registration tables.

Alice looked up from her folding chair behind the A-F sign. Her rosy, paper-thin skin crinkled around her eyes as she gave Kate a thumbs up.

Alice was small, dainty, and as fragile as a sledge hammer. She lived next door to the museum and had organized her friends to block the proposed razing of the historic district in order to build an outlet mall, hence the Granny Activist Brigade, affectionately and sometimes, not so affectionately, known as the GABs.

"Haven't seen this many people in this old hall since the

or Aunt Pru—know it.

He'd been police chief since moving to Granville from Boston a year before, but he was still constantly setting off the locals with his by-the-book law enforcement. By-the-book was not the Granville way.

They'd eased up on him for a while after he solved the professor's murder. But as soon as he issued his next speeding ticket, it was business as usual. An outsider. Not one of us.

And so it would always be.

"I'll be downstairs in the canteen, if anyone needs me," Kate said and headed for the stairs.

The downstairs was half as large as the hall itself. There was a wet bar and a large counter for food service. Four green upholstered booths lined one wall. The rest of the area was filled with small round tables that Kate recognized from the bakery. High on the wall behind the bar, two small rectangular windows gave a view of the parking lot asphalt. Asphalt that was already dusted with snow, Kate noticed.

Bathrooms were located down the hallway. Across from them, a large room was filled with vendors selling an array of Sudoku-theme novelties and clothing: ties, sweaters, baseball caps, tote bags, coffee mugs, pencils. All covered with black and white grids and numbers, slogans, and graphics. Sudoku Princess. Do U Sudoku? Got Sudoku? For a Good Time Call Sudoku. Only Sissies Use Pencils.

The canteen area was crowded. Most of the tables were occupied. Knots of people stood drinking coffee and catching up on puzzle news. There was a steady stream in and out of the vendors' room.

Kate spotted Erik Ingersoll and Jason Elks sitting at one of the booths and went over to say hello. They were both members of the museum board and the Granville Arcane Masters Club. Both would be competing later that night in the A Division preliminary.

They didn't notice her at first. They were deep in conversation. Erik's bulk was wedged into the booth, and he was talking so vehemently that his cheeks wobbled. Jason leaned across the table, his bald pate reflecting the overhead light as he nodded vigorously to what Erik was saying.

Kate groaned inwardly. What could possibly be wrong already? She stopped at the booth and waited for them to see her.

Finally Jason looked up. "Katie. There's something we must tell you." He scooted over in the booth and motioned her to sit down.

Kate slid in beside him. "What is it? Is something wrong?"

Jason looked furtively around. Erik planted his chubby arms on the table and wheezed asthmatically.

"Don't look now," Jason said.

"Where?" asked Kate.

"Don't look," Erik reiterated between gasps for air.

Kate was beginning to worry about him. He was only in his mid-sixties but his weight and a tendency toward asthma concerned her.

"There's a man here," Jason said. "He's over there, standing with that group of people."

Just then laughter erupted from a group in the far corner. Kate ducked her chin and glanced in their direction.

Three men and two women stood close together. The center of attention was a tall man, in his early forties, Kate estimated. He was wearing a black turtleneck and brown corduroy slacks. He was good-looking with gold blond hair and a classic profile that would set off her Aunt Pru's husband search alarms. Pru had made it her life's work to find Kate a husband—a local man, with job security.

Kate automatically searched the room for her aunt, hoping

against hope that she hadn't spotted the Adonis in the corner. She'd set him up with Kate before he could run to the nearest exit. Hopefully he'd just flown in from Anchorage or Latvia and would soon fly out again.

Then she saw the willowy blonde standing next to him. Really close to him, molding her body to his. It was a very impressive body in its spandex pants and tight velour sweater. Kate breathed a sigh of relief. Even Aunt Pru would figure that one out.

The man was already taken. One less thing to worry about.

"Katie, are you listening?"

Kate turned her attention back to Jason and Erik.

"That's him. The one in the black turtleneck." Jason pursed his lips. "You have to disqualify him"

Kate looked back to the big blond. "Why?"

"Don't you know who he is?"

"No. Should I?"

"I suppose not. Before your time." Erik took out his handkerchief to mop his forehead.

Jason moved closer to Kate and spoke in an undertone. "That's Gordon Lott. He's a liar and a cheat and he shouldn't be allowed to participate."

Kate looked back at the man, her analysis of him suddenly tainted by Jason and Erik's dislike. There was something a little too slick about him— She stopped herself. Opinion didn't count. Just facts.

"Can you prove this?" she asked even though she knew she couldn't disqualify him without catching him in the act of cheating. It was their word against his and she certainly wasn't going to accuse him of cheating on hearsay.

"About ten years ago he petitioned to join the Arcane Masters. He lives over in Hanover. A history professor. We voted him in. He had impressive skills." Jason shook his head. "We didn't catch on right away. He was brilliant. Or so we thought."

"But he was taking liberties that the Arcane Masters don't allow." Erik tightened his lips so hard that they disappeared.

"What kind of liberties?"

"One night he came early and P.T. found him looking over the sequential we were to solve at the meeting. Lott, of course, played the innocent. Said he'd just come in and was moving the puzzles so that no one would be tempted to peek. He finished first by several seconds."

Damning perhaps, but not proven, thought Kate. Could there be a little jealousy in the men's attitude toward Lott? It was times like these she longed for the predictability of mathematics. The one thing you could say for numbers: they didn't get jealous and they didn't spread gossip.

"And when we participated in the Harvard Brain Trust Alumni and Friends puzzle weekend, I personally saw him sneak a calculator into the event." Erik snorted. "He said he hadn't realized it was still in his pocket. It was outrageous. And an embarrassment for P.T. and myself, who were alumni of the Brain Trust. Fortunately it was confiscated before the games began, but nonetheless humiliating.

"As soon as we returned to Granville we blackballed him from the Arcane Masters and sent a letter to the Brain Trust apprising them of the situation. We've heard more scuttlebutt since then. The man has no moral fiber."

"We realize this is all anecdotal," Jason said. "But we can't afford to have the integrity of our first Sudoku tournament in question. We're not the only people that know about his reputation for cheating."

"Yes," Kate said. "But we can't disqualify him without there being a valid—and provable—cause."

The two older men began to protest.

"I'm sorry. But surely you understand that. I'll post extra observers near his place at the table to keep an eye on him. At the first sign of cheating, we'll ask him to leave. Maybe he's turned over a new leaf," she added hopefully.

Erik snorted so loudly that he choked. Jason leaned over the table and slapped him on the back.

"It's the best I can do, until, or if, he's caught red-handed. Now, why don't you two forget about it and let me handle this. We don't want your concentration less than stellar. We have the Hanover and the Cambridge, Mass, teams to outscore."

Erik threw up his hands. "See. I told you she wouldn't do anything. We'll have to take care of this ourselves."

Kate was filled with an awful foreboding as she imagined Erik and Jason coming to cuffs with Gordon Lott.

"Please, gentleman. Don't do anything to jeopardize the Challenge."

"That's just what we're trying to protect. Come along, Jason. We have work to do. Excuse us, Kate."

Kate reluctantly scooted off the bench to let Jason out, then watched the two men walk away. Gordon Lott was gone and the rest of his group had dispersed. Assuming that Lott would be participating at the top-tier A-level competition, she would have a good hour to glean some solid information about him. She hurried back upstairs and checked the registration forms.

Gordon Lott. Age, thirty-seven. Occupation, history professor. Resident of Hanover, New Hampshire. He was entered in both the single A-level and the team competition as a member of the Hanover Puzzle Club.

Kate knew a couple of the other members. She could talk to

them, but it was obvious they had no qualms about Lott's honesty. And she didn't want to stir a hornet's nest. Not if she didn't have to.

When she stepped back into the hall, several of the competitors had already finished their puzzles. Runners moved through the aisles collecting puzzles. Ginny Sue Bright stood by the blackboard, stage left, and wrote down the names and times as each competitor finished.

The blackboard was on loan from the grammar school, thanks to Ginny Sue, who was a fourth grade teacher there. She was Kate's age and they'd both gone to Valley High School, but they'd only become friends since Kate had moved back to Granville. Ginny Sue was likable, with hazel eyes and a cloud of reddish brown hair that Kate envied. She was also a member of the museum board and Kate's right hand woman for the tournament.

As Kate watched, two more hands went up, and two volunteers in red sweatshirts hurried to mark the completion time and take their puzzles. Their names were added to the list.

Time was called and the few players who still hadn't finished reluctantly turned in their sheets.

Tony came back on the mike, exhorting the newbies not to lose heart. "There's always next year. Isn't that right, Kate?"

Kate jumped, then waved from the doorway. All she wanted was to get through this weekend. She'd worry about next year later.

Talking broke out while the puzzles were taken backstage where a panel of scorers would check them for accuracy.

When the official scores were finalized, Ginny Sue handed the results to Tony, who announced the finalists and handed out tournament certificates.

The tables were cleared of pencils and empty water bottles; new water bottles and freshly sharpened pencils took their place. The

Level C participants took their places at the tables.

Ginny Sue came to stand beside Kate. "Everything's going really well, don't you think?"

"Absolutely," Kate said. "Thanks to everyone's hard work. And yours especially. I haven't seen you all day. And I've been looking for you to thank you for driving to Manchester to pick Tony up."

"No problem." Ginny Sue smiled and looked toward the podium. "He's very nice."

"Yes, he is," Kate agreed. "And a sweetheart to help us out like this. He agreed to do it for expenses, no fee. But I was about to break out in hives worrying that the airport would be snowed in and his flight wouldn't be able to land."

"Not many more flights will be coming in tonight. They already had a foot of snow when we left the airport. You can stop worrying. He's here and the worst thing that can happen now is that he gets stuck in Granville for a few days."

CHAPTER

T W O

TONY TOOK THE lower D, C, and B divisions through their first round of puzzles. Between each one, the crowd burst into talking, made quick trips to the canteen and the restrooms, then came back to concentrate on the next round.

When it was time for the first round of A competitors, the highest level, Kate positioned an extra adjudicator near Gordon Lott, then went to stand at the end of the row where Gordon sat, trying to look like an interested observer, and not like the snoop she was.

Tony asked for the puzzles to be placed. When they were all face down in front of the competitors, the digital clock was reset. "Your time, competitors, is twenty minutes. Ready . . . set . . . go."

Puzzles were again turned over in the same way they had been all night. But this time there was an extra excitement in the room, more concentration from the spectators. Some of the best puzzle solvers from the East Coast were present. It would be a race to the finish.

Silence fell over the hall. Soon only the steady scrape of pencil lead on paper could be heard. The minutes ticked by. Kate kept her eye on Gordon Lott, but other than the habit of continually consulting his watch, she saw nothing unusual. Amazing what nerves could do to a person. He'd save a lot of time by just glancing at the digital clock at the front of the room.

Seconds later, Lott raised his hand. A runner stepped forward, noted the time on his puzzle, and took it away. Ginny Sue entered his name and time on the blackboard.

Nearly a minute went by before another hand rose. Jason Elks. Within the space of a few seconds, several more hands went up. Their puzzles were documented and whisked away to be checked for errors.

When the final buzzer broke through the rarefied atmosphere, fifteen names had been listed on the blackboard. Those who were still working reluctantly stopped, looks of chagrin, disappointment, self-disgust plain on their faces. Talking broke out once again.

Kate continued to watch Gordon Lott. He was leaning back in his chair, relaxed, confident. His time had been amazing, but if he had cheated, Kate hadn't detected it. Then he glanced to the spectator's gallery and gave a thumbs up. Kate followed his gaze to two of the men she'd seen in the canteen. Evidently neither of them were competing.

A few minutes later, the scores were all tallied; the winners collected their certificates and Tony announced a half-hour break. Everyone poured out the back doors. The gallery quickly emptied in a mad rush for coffee, snacks, a tour of the vendors' room, or a quick trip outside for a cigarette.

Tony left the stage and joined the migration toward the door.

Kate followed after him. She wanted to ask him what he knew about Gordon Lott.

She'd just reached the foyer when Aunt Pru grabbed her elbow.

"That man over there who just won that round . . ."

Gordon Lott stood at the head of the stairs where he was being congratulated by his Hanover teammates.

"His name is Gordon Lott."

"I know," said Kate, and she knew where this was going. "I really need to talk to Tony before the next round."

Pru's grip tightened. "He's handsome. A professor." A pregnant pause. "And he's single."

There was no question about marital status on the registration form. Her aunt had been busy. Neither rain, nor sleet, nor a pending blizzard kept Pru from her husband vigil.

"Aunt Pru. I have a thousand things to do."

"Go introduce yourself. You have so much in common. He's good at your puzzle thingies. And he has—"

"Job security," Kate finished for her. "Aunt Pru, I don't have time for this right now."

"You never have time. You're not getting any younger."

The dreaded thirtieth birthday loomed large on Kate's horizon, and even larger in Pru's mind.

"He's smart, he's got tenure. And he can commute to Hanover from here. It's only forty minutes away."

Kate closed her eyes and prayed for patience. Though it might be a good idea to introduce herself to Gordon Lott just to get a take on his personality. *Yeah.* Like she was a whiz at people reading.

She opened her eyes again and saw the blond woman Lott had been chummy with earlier sidle up to him. She rose on tiptoe and planted a kiss on his mouth. He laughed and patted her butt.

"Well, I never," Pru said. "Right here in front of all these people."

Kate breathed a sigh of relief.

"Well, it can't be said that *she* lets the grass grow under her feet." Pru clucked her tongue at Kate. "Hold your shoulders back. I'll just go find out who she is."

Kate's cell vibrated. She headed toward the windows where it was less crowded and where Pru couldn't see her.

"Just called to say I got my plow trucks standing by," said Mike Landers, whose landscaping company Kate had hired to clear the VFW parking lot. "There's a real nor'easter on its way. But don't you worry—we'll have it clean as a whistle before tomorrow's session."

"Thanks, Mike, I know I can count on you." Kate hung up, cast a quick look around for Pru, then hurried downstairs to find Tony.

The canteen was wall-to-wall people. She could barely see Rayette, who was behind the counter, handing out coffee, sodas, and cookies like the wizard she was.

She caught sight of Tony coming out of the men's room. He was frowning. He strode to the stairs and trotted up to them before she could reach him through the crush.

Kate bit her lip. What had upset him? Were they out of paper towels? Soap? Toilet paper?

The door to the men's room opened again and Gordon Lott stepped out. He was looking pleased with himself. And why not, he'd just aced the qualifying round. He turned his smile on Kate as he walked by, paused, then stepped toward her.

"You must be our lovely presenter, Katie McDonald."

Kate cringed. He must have been talking to the locals. They were the only ones who still called her Katie. "Kate," she corrected.

"Love the weekend so far." Gordon gave her the once over.

"Love the presenter."

And before Kate knew what he intended, he'd put his arm around her shoulder.

Kate smiled and wondered how she could pull away gracefully. He gave her a squeeze, his face so close to hers, she felt his breath on her cheek. "I'm not as fast at all things as I am at Sudoku. Some things are meant to be slow."

Kate didn't have to be a genius to figure out what he was talking about, and it made her skin crawl. She eased away, her smile faltering a little as she saw Jason Elks making a beeline for them.

Erik was right behind him, huffing and wheezing like he'd just finished a fifty-meter run.

Gordon saw them, too. He released Kate and casually pulled down the sleeves of his turtleneck, while he waited for both men to reach them.

"We have something to say to you, Gordon," Jason said, looking up at the taller man.

"Yes," wheezed Erik.

Kate shot both of them a pleading look. *Don't make trouble.*

Both men ignored her.

"Well, well. If it isn't my old friends. I thought I saw the two of you earlier. Come to congratulate me?" Gordon's voice was pleasant, but Kate thought she detected a hint of sarcasm.

Jason jabbed his finger at Gordon's face. "We just have one thing to say to you. If you won that round fair and square, we'll be the first to congratulate you, but if we find that you've been cheating—"

"Again," interjected Erik.

Gordon huffed out a sigh. "Ah, Katie, you'll have to forgive my colleagues." He gave her a just-between-us look. "We have a . . . history. An old story. These two self-styled puzzle masters just couldn't stand the fact that I was smarter than they were. Jealousy is such an ugly emotion. Don't you agree?"

"I—uh. Yes."

"Katie," Jason said.

Erik looked outraged.

"But so is—" she couldn't say cheating. She couldn't accuse him right here in the canteen. She had no evidence. And besides, they had attracted the attention of half the people in the canteen.

Kate bit her lip. "Our motto is play fair, win fair." *Yuck, that was so lame.* "It's the solving, not the winning, that's important." She was hopeless; people came to tournaments to win.

"How true," said Gordon and glanced at his watch. It was a gaudy gold monstrosity that probably had more bells and whistles than her computer. "I'd better get upstairs. I wouldn't want to miss the Level A semifinals."

"We mean it," Jason said. "We'll be watching you."

Gordon's demeanor finally slipped into exasperation. "This is getting boring. It was years ago and you never proved a thing. Because there was *nothing* to prove. Old news. And if you continue to harass me, I'll have you kicked out of the tournament. Read your rule books, fellas. I'm sure Katie follows all the rules."

"You—" Jason was too outraged to continue.

Erik spluttered.

"See you later, Katie." Gordon winked and headed upstairs.

Kate turned to her two board members. "You should be ashamed of yourselves."

"He cheated," Jason said angrily.

Erik nodded. "No one could have finished that Sudoku in less than six minutes. It was a bear."

The whole room had become silent. Kate pulled Jason and Eric into the hallway.

"I was watching him," Kate said. "I didn't see any signs of cheating. And frankly how could he? The puzzles were locked up until they were handed to the runners, and the runners were not allowed out of our sight from that time until they placed the puzzles on the tables.

"There's no way he could cheat. It's not a spelling bee, or a crossword. There are no external clues, just the numbers on the page and a person's own brain. Even if he'd somehow managed to find a way of relaying the integers to someone in the audience, what good would it do? They don't have access to the puzzles. Even if they did, by the time they relayed the answers back, half the other competitors would be finished. I'm afraid you're wrong in this instance. There is no way it could have been done."

Okay, she knew better than to say something couldn't be done. Because no sooner than you disproved a theory, either a new theory emerged or new data came in to prove you wrong.

"Well, I just hope you're right," said Erik. "Come on, Jason. I knew she wouldn't believe us." He hustled Jason away.

Kate stepped back into the canteen. Everyone had gone upstairs, and Rayette was dumping trash into a black plastic bag. She straightened up and pushed a strand of platinum hair from her face. "Don't let Jason and Erik push you around, hon. Those two take their puzzles seriously. Too seriously if you ask me. Sit down and take a load off. I just made a fresh batch of coffee."

Kate sank into a chair while Rayette poured out two cups and carried them over.

Rayette lowered herself into the chair next to her. "I don't know about you but my feet are killing me. Must be those extra pounds I put on last winter."

"Mine, too," said Kate and slipped her feet out of her heels. It felt heavenly. She'd wear something more comfortable tomorrow.

Providing the storm held off long enough for them to have a tomorrow. There were already two inches on the asphalt outside the window.

"It'll let up," said Rayette. "Besides, I've got ten dozen sticky buns and fifty pounds of wieners all ready for tomorrow. And no room to freeze them if they don't get eaten."

By the time Kate returned to the main hall, the second round of competition had begun, and she had no chance to speak to Tony. She spent the rest of the evening keeping one eye on Gordon Lott and the other on Jason and Erik. But there were no more confrontations.

The snow continued to fall.

Tony called for the second round of A-level competitors, and the semifinalists took their seats.

Kate once again stood at the end of Gordon's row. Ignored him when he caught her eye and winked. She spotted Jason Elks seated two rows behind Gordon. She didn't look for Erik even though she knew he was competing, too, along with the third member of the Arcane team, Obadiah Creek. She wondered what Obadiah thought of Gordon Lott.

Maybe Gordon was a cheater. Or maybe he was right, and there was more jealousy than truth in the accusation, which would be a shame. The effort of solving a puzzle really was just as important as winning. At least it was to Kate.

That was the great thing about puzzles. They held such an elementary appeal to the human mind. Everyone was enticed by some kind of puzzle.

But there was also a universal need to win. She'd just have to observe and wait.

Tony set the timer, the puzzles were placed before the competitors, and the round began. Gordon immediately consulted his watch. Obviously a nervous habit. Or a kind of talisman. People went through all kinds of rituals to ensure good luck. One man she knew wore the same tie to every tournament. One kissed his pencil for luck.

Kate always closed her eyes until she heard the word, "Go." Of course, in her case, it wasn't superstition, merely a technique to cleanse her field of vision.

Gordon consulted his watch again. Kate glanced at the digital timer. Only twenty seconds had passed. He leaned forward and Kate shifted her position in order to get a better view.

He was hunkered over his puzzle, his left forearm resting on the table as if protecting his puzzle from roving eyes, much as a school boy would do. Which was unnecessary; the partitions prevented copying.

His head moved constantly, almost as if he were consulting his watch.

Any use of electronic devises was prohibited. Not even cell phones were allowed in the puzzle area. But watches had never been outlawed. What could a watch do?

Three minutes later, Gordon's hand went up. There was an audible gasp from the spectators. At the podium, Tony put his finger to his lips, warning them to be quiet.

Gordon leaned back in his chair, looking triumphant. A volunteer rushed to his place and took his puzzle. Gordon glanced up to the spectator gallery and smiled. Kate followed his gaze, right to his three companions.

Interesting, thought Kate, her head spinning with conjecture. Then she kicked herself mentally. Ever since she'd been so foolish as to try to solve the professor's murder by herself, she'd begun seeing all sorts of meanings in the most innocuous actions. It must be a symptom of boredom. Her mathematician's brain was crying out for something more challenging than scheduling field trips and calculating ticket sales.

When Tony called time, the audience broke into talking. But this time, no one left the gallery and none of the competitors left the hall.

It would only take a few minutes for the scores to be tabulated. Although the first place winner was obvious, there were four other qualifying positions at stake. Those players would move to the final A round that would be held the following night. After that the team scores would be tallied and the top three teams would compete for the grand prize.

The tension was palpable. Some contestants paced in front of the stage as they waited for the results. Others stood off to the side biting their nails or talking in low murmurs. Others stood in front of the blackboard scrutinizing the names of the projected semifinalists.

Kate felt every emotion along with the others. She'd been in the same position many times before. It had been nerve-wracking but stimulating, fun, challenging. And she had to admit, just like all the contestants, she wanted to win.

But not enough to cheat.

Minutes passed, the crowd became restless. Kate kept watching the door that led backstage where the official scorers were double- and triple-checking the puzzles. It seemed to be taking an inordinate amount of time.

At last the door opened and Ginny Sue stepped into the hall. But instead of handing Tony the results, she looked out to Kate and motioned her over.

Something was wrong. Kate hurried toward Ginny Sue and got there just as Tony came down the steps.

Ginny Sue looked like she might cry. "We have a problem."

"The equipment?" asked Kate.

"No. Come see."

Kate and Tony followed her backstage where five scorers were huddled together. An image of a puzzle was projected on a screen with the puzzle key placed beside it.

Ginny Sue pointed to the puzzle image. "The first place competitor made a mistake."

Tony and Kate both leaned closer to the image. Kate didn't see it immediately. All the blanks had been filled in, which meant there had to be more than one mistake. Then she found it.

"Nine in the fifth row appears in the fourth quadrant and again in the sixth."

Tony shook his head. "He wrote a nine where a two should have been. Sloppy work."

"Sorry," said Ginny Sue.

Tony smiled at her. "It's not your fault the competitor didn't check his work. It happens. We're all human after all."

Ginny Sue smiled back at him.

Kate glanced back down at the screen. Level A players didn't often make those kinds of glaring mistakes. Gordon must have been in such a rush to finish that he hadn't bothered to check his work.

At least this made one thing clear. Gordon Lott hadn't cheated tonight.

Kate sighed, then looked at Tony.

"Yeah, I know. I hate to be the one to burst anyone's bubble. But in this case . . . it won't hurt so much."

Kate blinked. She'd never heard Tony make even the slightest disparaging remark about anyone. It was one of the reasons he was such a good emcee. But he'd been on the circuit for a long time and he probably knew more about Gordon Lott than most people.

Tony turned to the scorers. "Throw out the erroneous puzzle and bump up the others one place. I'll go stall."

Ginny Sue made a face. "The poor man. He'll be so disappointed."

"Yes," Tony said. "He certainly will. Oh, and don't forget to deduct points from the Hanover team's score. They're not going to be happy."

At least Jason and Erik will be, Kate thought. And whoever had been in sixth place before the error was discovered.

"Is it possible to set up the projector in the main hall? Everyone will want to see the reason for our decision."

"Sure," Ginny Sue said and began unplugging the equipment.

Tony left immediately, but Kate stayed behind to help Ginny Sue carry the projector. They set it up so that it would display on the wall next to the stage.

"Does this really happen a lot?" asked Ginny Sue.

"Not a lot," Kate said. "But it does happen." She just wished it hadn't happened at her tournament. She always felt sorry for the loser. Especially after riding high for a few blissfully ignorant minutes.

A scorer appeared in the doorway and handed the new scores to Ginny Sue, who carried them over to Tony.

"If I may have your attention . . ." It was an unnecessary request. He already had their attention.

"Unfortunately, due to a mistake in the first place puzzle of this round—"

Speculation broke out among the crowd.

"First place goes to Jason Elks of the Granville, New Hampshire, Arcane Masters with a time of six minutes forty-three seconds."

Exclamations of surprise, then applause. Kate cut her eyes to where Jason sat, looking stunned, but not as stunned as Gordon Lott.

Tony read off the other finalists. The last name on the list, the sixth place competitor who'd been bumped up because of Gordon's disqualification, was Erik Ingersoll. He pushed himself out of his chair and with a wide grin followed the other finalists to the stage.

Gordon jumped from his seat and rushed to the stage. "I question the scorers' accuracy," he bellowed loud enough to quiet the spectators.

"Oh dear," Ginny Sue said.

Oh shit, Kate thought.

Tony considered Lott for a moment, then turned toward Kate and Ginny Sue. "Miss Bright, if you will."

Ginny Sue jumped as if she'd been goosed, then switched on the overhead projector.

Gordon's puzzle and the puzzle key appeared on the wall.

"If you will observe," said Tony. "Two nines appear in the fifth row, in the second cell, and also in the eighth. The correct placement is in the second box, but the number two should appear in the eighth."

A wave of murmuring rolled across the floor and up into the gallery.

Gordon stared at the puzzle, his face pale above his black turtleneck.

"If I may have the certificates of merit," Tony continued, obviously not wanting to prolong the man's agony and embarrassment.

"It isn't possible." Gordon snatched the puzzle from the projector, wadded it into a ball and through it at Tony's feet.

Ginny Sue froze with the certificates gripped in her hand.

"That's enough," Tony said. "Don't be a sore loser." He motioned to Ginny Sue and she scuttled past Gordon to hand Tony the certificates of merit.

Tony returned to the podium, and in his usual jocular style began handing out the certificates.

Gordon whirled around and glared up at the gallery.

Gordon's companions stood up. They looked just as angry as Gordon.

A lost bet? That's the only thing that Kate could imagine that would cause such a look of mutual disgust. Betting was prohibited by the national tournament association, but Kate knew that private, "friendly" betting went on in spite of the rules.

The crowd swelled forward, engulfing the finalists. Gordon Lott was lost to view.

Kate let out her breath. Disaster avoided. *One night down, a day and a half to go.* As soon as the hall cleared, she'd change into her sneakers and jeans, oversee the cleanup, and go home to bed. Then it would start all over again—hopefully without any more emotional outbursts.

Tony came down from the stage and slipped his glasses into his pocket. "Well, I must say, I'm not sorry to see Lott get taken out. More braggadocio than skill. I always thought so." He kissed his fingers toward the exit door. "*Adios,* Signor Lott."

"Won't he come back to compete in the team trials?" asked Ginny Sue.

"With the number of penalty points he incurred with those mistakes? I doubt the Hanover team will make the team finals. Would you ladies like to have a drink somewhere?"

CHAPTER

THREE

KATE OPTED OUT of Tony's drink offer, and Ginny Sue planned to stay behind to help with the cleanup, until Kate reminded her that Tony needed a ride to the Bowsman Inn where Kate had reserved him a room. It was obvious even to Kate that the two had bonded during the drive from the Manchester airport. The Inn had a lovely bar with a stone fireplace—very romantic. The two of them would find plenty to talk about.

Really, Kate thought. A few months away from the think tank and she was thinking romance. It must be Aunt Pru's influence. Or maybe she was really becoming a people person at last.

When Kate finally locked up the VFW hall, she was surprised to see a line of cars still waiting to leave the parking lot. Huge snowflakes wafted to the ground. The pavement had turned to slush. By the time Kate had sloshed toward her Matrix parked at the edge of the lot, her sneakers were soaked and her toes were numb with cold.

She turned on her wipers and added herself to the line of cars. She'd never expected the tournament to become this big. It was going to be a huge success.

So many people had chipped in to make the event possible—the GABS, Harry, Rayette, and Ginny Sue. Izzy Culpepper, the local mailman and crossword puzzle enthusiast, was helping people into their cars. At the curb, Benjamin Meany, a retired police officer, swung his flashlight back and forth to keep everyone moving.

Kate wished the professor could be here to see what a wonderful job everyone had done. How much he had influenced their lives and how much they all respected him.

For a moment she considered going by the museum, making herself a cup of tea, and sitting in her chair by the fireplace, just to pretend that her mentor was still alive. They'd talk about the tournament, about Gordon Lott's mistakes, then they'd take out their own puzzles like they did every day, with Aloysius, the museum's Maine coon cat, kibitzing and purring from his spot on the arm of the professor's chair.

She sighed. The professor was dead and no amount of wishing would bring him back. The best she could do was honor his memory with the tournament and by making a success of his beloved puzzle museum.

Someone honked and Kate realized that she'd been daydreaming. She eased the Matrix forward. Benjamin Meany waved her into the street where another officer was directing traffic flow. Kate peered through the steadily falling snow and saw that it was Brandon Mitchell. *Good gravy*, the police chief was directing traffic. She slowed to a stop and unrolled the window.

"What are you doing out here?"

Snow had collected in the crease of his wool cap and dusted the shoulders of his police jacket. Shoulders that seemed even wider than normal under the padded jacket.

"*Freezing my*—directing traffic. What does it look like?"

Okay, he was not happy. *What else is new?*

"I'm sorry you have to stand out in the cold."

He grunted. "It's my job."

"Is Harry still here? Can I take him home for you?"

"Marian Teasdale took him."

"Oh. That's good. He's got to be back to open up for the juniors in the morning. Are you going to be able to make his cipher presentation?"

"If I can."

"He told me you were helping him with it."

The chief shook his head. "Just some basic public speaking. Nothing major."

Someone behind her honked.

"I'd better get going. Thanks for getting all this together. I know it was difficult to organize. I owe you big time."

He'd started to wave her on, but stopped. His eyebrows lifted nearly to the rim of his cap. His dark eyes lasered into hers.

"I'll buy you coffee at Rayette's or something," she added quickly. "Good night." She raised the window and stepped on the accelerator so hard that the Matrix fishtailed.

On the slow drive down the street, Kate called herself every kind of name she could think of. The chief always made her say the dumbest things. He also inspired a little thrill every time she saw him. And *that* would never do. Aunt Pru would have a conniption if she ever guessed Kate had the slightest interest in him.

She had to wait again at the corner while several cars turned left toward the Bowsman Inn. Kate could see it in the distance, where it sat on a knoll overlooking the river. The original building dated back to the Revolutionary War, but it had been updated and added to until it had become a sizable bed and breakfast and a popular banquet venue.

The inn didn't ordinarily do this much business in the winter months, mostly families who came to cross-country ski or snowmobile on the nearby mountains. But tonight it was lit up like Christmas.

Nancy and John Vance, the proprietors, had taken on extra help to accommodate the full house and to keep the kitchen and bar open late for post-tournament dining and celebrating.

They were glad to do it. They hadn't had a full house since Fall Foliage Week and welcomed the extra income. They'd even given up their suite on the first floor of the inn to guests and moved temporarily to the small apartment over the garage.

Some of the participants were staying with local families, friends, or the entrepreneurs who sometimes rented rooms at the height of tourist season.

Other cars headed straight toward Main Street, which would take them to their motels out on the highway or in nearby towns.

Kate just hoped they'd all arrive safely. She followed the cars to Main Street, but turned right at the Presbyterian church, which was dark except for the spotlit cross and the snow that covered it like a shroud.

Kate blinked tired eyes and headed slowly down Main Street toward home, an 1820s bungalow on the "new" side of town.

The small downtown looked deserted. The bank and the courthouse were dark, and only one light shone from the police station. The rest of the stores gave the impression of a ghost town.

She passed two snowplows rumbling toward her. Ordinarily they wouldn't be out until the snow let up, but with all the extra people on the streets, they'd gotten a jump on the storm.

Unfortunately, the plows hadn't reached Porter Street and Kate skidded and slid down the street to her house in the middle of the block. She pulled into her driveway, but parked close to the street where she'd have less to shovel in the morning. A good six inches had already fallen.

They were used to snow. It might delay the beginning of the tournament tomorrow, but not by much—as long as it didn't turn into a blizzard.

She shuddered just thinking about that possibility, imagining the town trying to accommodate several hundred stranded people for days on end.

Two doors down, the porch light was still on. Aunt Pru's old Buick was wedged crosswise on the driveway. It must have skidded right onto the lawn. Pru shouldn't be driving at night, especially not in heavy snow. She probably shouldn't be driving at all.

Kate would have to call and make sure Pru was okay and offer to drive her in the morning. She stomped through the fresh snow to her front porch, knocked the snow off her sneakers, and went inside. The telephone rang.

"Hello."

"Just making sure you got in safely," said Pru. "What a day."

"It sure was." She knew better than to bring up her aunt's latest car mishap. "Have you heard the weather forecast?"

"More snow. Don't you worry, I told that Chief Mitchell to be sure to have the parking lot cleared by eight a.m."

Kate cringed. Pru had never forgiven Brandon Mitchell for giving her a ticket for running the stop sign at Maple Street. People had been rolling through that intersection since the day they put up the sign a decade ago. It was the Granville way.

The police chief didn't care much for the Granville way. Which meant a lot of the residents didn't care much for him.

He was an outsider and always would be. Kate didn't even know why he stayed, but she was glad he did.

"Well, actually, I hired Mike Landers to plow the parking lot. The town is only responsible for the public streets."

"Pooh," Pru said. "He can just make himself useful."

"Aunt Pru—"

"What are you going to wear tomorrow? Sam Swyndon will be there taking pictures for the paper. You look nice for him."

"I plan on looking nice since I'm the presenter of the tournament," Kate said patiently. Actually she planned on wearing something comfortable since the morning and afternoon were junior divisions and workshops. She'd change into her pantsuit and heels for the evening festivities.

"You know," Pru said, breaking into the silence. "There are a lot of women in this town who'd give their eyeteeth to go out with Sam. He's a lovely young man."

Well-mannered with job security, Kate continued mentally. Actually she'd gone out with Sam several times. They'd had fun. But neither of them was hearing wedding bells.

She hadn't shared that bit with Aunt Pru, because Pru would merely look perturbed and start looking for the next "good catch."

"Do you want to drive over with me in the morning?" Kate asked, glad that if a car had to be snowed in it should be Pru's old Buick and not her Matrix. Pru had a Granville attitude toward the law and a short attention span, and Kate didn't think adding slippery roads would do anything to improve Pru's driving skills. "I'm leaving at six."

"No. No. I need my eight hours. Besides . . ."

"I saw the Buick."

"Darn thing. Must be those new tires Norris Edelman put on last month. Doesn't hug the road like it used to. Simon's picking me up, since he has four-wheel drive."

"Is he?" teased Kate. She had her suspicions that the semi-retired lawyer was carrying a torch for her spinster aunt.

"And several others, too, young lady. He said he felt left out not volunteering for the tournament so he's agreed to be the GAB-mobile for the weekend. Man ought do his part. Ayuh."

"Good." *One less thing to worry about.* Kate yawned. "Sorry. I'm going to bed. Good night." She hung up.

Any other night she would have built a fire and sat down with a glass of wine and a Sudoku puzzle. Tonight she was too tired, too preoccupied, too overloaded on adrenalin.

She changed into sweatpants and her "Geeks Rule" sweatshirt.

Before she crawled into bed, she looked out the window. She could barely see the next house through the curtain of snow.

She awoke several times during the night to look out the window. By two a.m., a foot of snow had accumulated. By three, another eight inches. It passed the two foot mark by four o'clock. Kate finally fell into a restless sleep until the alarm woke her at six.

The first thing she did was go to the window. The sun was shining and glistening off—Kate groaned—nearly three feet of pristine snowfall.

Would she have to cancel? Leave all those participants stranded? Had the plows managed to clear the streets? The parking lot?

She rummaged in the closet, looking for a pair of snow boots. They didn't get this kind of snowfall in Virginia, and she hadn't had time to buy real snow wear since she'd returned to Granville. She'd been too busy with museum renovations and special events and fund-raising to do much more than run from car to museum to car to home.

She knew there must be a box of old snow gear somewhere in the house. Her father had retired to Florida where he could play golf year round, but Kate knew he never threw anything away. She just hoped she wouldn't have to climb to the attic to find them.

Yawning, she padded down the hall to the spare bedroom and tried the closet. It was stuffed with hanging clothes and cardboard boxes. She pulled a few of them out and found a box at the back marked "Winter Clothes."

Eureka. She dragged, lifted, and tilted it until it fell onto the bedroom floor and its contents spilled across the carpet.

She lifted out a pink snow suit that would fit a six-year-old. Stopped for a moment as memories flooded in. Her mother always dressed her in pink even though it clashed horribly with her red hair. Her mother was killed in a car accident when Kate was ten, but she could still remember wearing this snow suit and playing in the yard while her mother watched from the kitchen window.

She folded it and placed it on the bed. She picked up a down ski parka that she remembered from high school. Of course she never went skiing. She'd never had time to learn. After her mother's death, she'd spent every waking hour at the museum with the professor.

Kate reached deep into the box and smiled when she pulled out her old quilted car coat. It was fire engine red and came down to her thighs. It didn't go with her hair any better than the pink snow suit. The hood was lined with fake white bunny fur. The "fur" had become matted over the years, but she loved it. And it was perfect for shoveling snow.

She found her favorite knit hat, long and pointed like an elf's hat and knitted in stripes of red, yellow, and orange. It had been the brunt of a lot of jokes about her needing the extra length for holding all her brains. *Katie is a ge-ek and she wears a geeky ha-at.* She stuck it defiantly on her head. Waited for the surge of embarrassment and humiliation to follow.

Nothing happened. She stood on tiptoe and looked in the bureau mirror. No wonder the kids had made fun of her. But she'd come to terms with her geekiness. No one would dare laugh at her fur and stripes now.

She went back to the closet. Leaned over the remaining boxes and came up with a pair of knee-high rubber boots.

She wouldn't make the cover of *Vogue*, but she'd be warm. And she wouldn't be getting hit by any wayward snowmobiles. She couldn't get much brighter.

She glanced at the clock. It was almost six o'clock. She needed to get a move on. She carried the bundle of outerwear out to the hall, then took a quick shower and dressed in black jeans and a cashmere sweater. She threw her evening clothes and heels in a garment bag and stopped in the kitchen for coffee.

That's when she heard the sound of shoveling coming from outside. She looked out the kitchen window. Saw nothing. Went to the front window. There was a path cleared from her porch to her car. The Matrix was free of snow and she could see someone shoveling the strip of driveway between her Toyota and the street.

She opened the front door. "Harry! Is that you?"

A head appeared from behind the car. It was covered by a billed cap with ear flaps. It could have been an old-time hunter's cap, but Kate had seen one just like it in the Gap catalogue. Hillbilly wear was the newest style. The chief and Harry had been shopping again. She waved him inside.

He scooped a last shovelful of snow and tossed it to the side, then he jabbed the shovel into the mound he'd made and trotted up to the house.

"Harry, you're a wonder! Thank you. Want some hot chocolate? Breakfast?"

"Chocolate would be good. Already had breakfast."

She went back to the kitchen while Harry got out of his boots and winter coat. His hot chocolate was ready when he got to the kitchen.

Harry was tall for his age and he'd grown two inches in the four months since she'd known him, and had begun to fill out, though he was still skinny. His hair was cut short, the chief's influence.

He'd been the professor's apprentice and had been missing when Kate first returned to Granville. She'd caught him breaking into the museum one night.

Actually Chief Mitchell caught him, and had been ready to turn him over to the authorities until she had somehow, and now she realized, miraculously, convinced him to let Harry stay with him.

They'd been uneasy roommates ever since. Things between them seemed particularly tense right now. Neither of them had volunteered why.

Harry sat down and blew on his chocolate. "It was the chief's idea."

"Brandon—Chief Mitchell asked you to shovel my driveway?"

"Ordered was more like it. But I don't mind. You have to give me a ride over to the hall though—he had stuff to do."

This was a surprise. The chief doing something thoughtful for her. He usually spent a good deal of the time exasperated with her.

"Well, I'm grateful to you even if it was his idea. I know he's busy these days."

"Yeah, thanks to you and me." Harry's face clouded over.

Kate shouldn't have said anything. For the umpteenth time, she wondered if she would ever learn to be tactful, understand how to relate to people without setting their backs up. Numbers were so much easier.

"I'm done. We should go." A big chocolate mustache covered his upper lip. He started to wipe it on his sleeve.

Kate quickly handed him a paper towel. "After you."

In the hall, they quickly dressed in their snow gear.

"Nice hat," Harry said, grinning.

"Yours, too."

Kate drove slowly down Porter Street, the ice crunching beneath the tires, the salt pellets pinging against the underbody of her car. She pumped the brakes as she approached the notorious stop sign at Maple Street.

It did her absolutely no good. The Matrix slid right out into the intersection.

"Shit!" said Harry.

As soon as she ascertained that no one was coming in either direction and there was no police cruiser waiting to ticket her, she turned on him.

"Harry Perkins, you're on your way to paying for pizza."

"Well, hel-ck, you scared the spit out of me."

"Sorry. I couldn't help it, and no one was coming."

"Well, you didn't know that when you ran the stop sign."

"I didn't do it on purpose."

"Well, I didn't cuss on purpose."

Kate grinned at him. "I won't tell if you won't. But I must say, three strikes and you buy the pizza is one of my most brilliant ideas."

"Yeah. That's all we eat these days."

Kate's mood darkened. "Things that bad?"

Harry shrugged. "It's not just when we use swear words. The chief doesn't have time to cook, and I don't know how. So it's pizza or really bad Chinese food."

"Maybe we should change the rule from the three swear words and you buy pizza rule to dinner at the Bowsman Inn."

Harry groaned. "I'll never see an allowance again."

On the rest of the drive over, they solidified last-minute details for the morning session. The junior competition would be divided into four different age groups. Each age group would work three puzzles, and the average of the two would be taken to find the winner. That way there would be less stress and more fun.

Harry would be overseeing the proceedings, though Tony had offered to emcee. Harry was much more excited about the code and cipher workshop he'd be giving that afternoon.

Kate's throat tightened, remembering his expression of gratitude and pride when she'd ask him to take such responsibility. He'd had such an unhappy childhood that she sometimes wondered if he'd ever truly get over it. When they'd first met, they'd both been grieving for their mentor. Harry had been hurt and skittish at first, but gradually he'd come to trust Kate and learned to live by the rules the chief insisted on as part of their living arrangements.

A tough kid, Harry had cleaned up his attitude and language considerably and in turn the chief had cleaned up his own language—most of the time anyway. Kate was afraid there was no hope for his attitude.

She refused to think what might happen if the chief decided he couldn't keep Harry.

Unaware of the turn Kate's thoughts had taken, Harry chatted happily about the codes he'd be introducing that afternoon.

Two plow trucks were traversing the parking lot when they arrived at the VFW hall. Piles of plowed snow created a wall of white around the asphalt. Mike Landers was standing next to his landscaping truck, drinking a cup of coffee, as he watched the progress of the two snowplows.

Kate had first met him when she'd hired his landscaping company to prune the maze in the museum's backyard. She'd chosen him because he was middle-aged, happily married, with several grandchildren. Even Aunt Pru wouldn't try to make a match between him and Kate under those circumstances.

She hadn't. But what Kate's research had failed to reveal was that one of his sons was a widower. He'd lost his wife in a car accident, the same way Kate and her father had lost her mom. They had a lot in common, said Aunt Pru. And he owned his own sporting goods store. Fortunately, it was in Oregon, so Kate was let off the hook.

Mike waved as Kate and Harry got out of the car.

"Love your outfit," he said, nodding his head at her hat and car coat. "Chief Mitchell oughta stop complaining about getting a traffic light put up at that merge on Route Twenty-six and use you instead. Save the town a wallop on their taxes."

He laughed. She laughed. Harry thought it was the funniest thing he'd ever heard.

Mike shook his head. "Don't think the chief will approve. The man has no sense of humor."

Kate had to agree, though she kept hoping.

The nearest plow truck deposited its load of snow and backed up. Then the driver lifted its plow and drove out of the parking lot, leaving the last truck to clear the last section.

The driver of the remaining truck backed up, lowered the plow, and scooped up the last load. He pushed it into the growing mound of snow. The truck slammed to a stop, jerked backward, and the engine died, the plow half lifted.

"Looks like he snagged on something. Damn," Mike said. "Hope he didn't strip any gears. We're gonna be real busy for the next few days. Excuse me."

He started toward the plow truck, but before he'd gone two feet, the truck door swung open and the driver fell out and staggered away.

Mike dropped his coffee. It splattered on the ground. "You got a cell phone? Call nine-one-one." He took off at a run.

Kate reached for her cell as she and Harry raced behind Mike. But when she reached the truck, the driver was shaking his head. "Okay. I'm . . . okay." He pointed to the truck. "There . . . plow . . . oh my *God.*"

Mike, Harry, and Kate ran to the front of the truck. There, lying half in, half out of the plow's scoop, covered in snow and chunks of ice, was a man. One arm hung over the side of the plow; the sleeve of his black ski jacket was pulled up and revealed a pale wrist above a black leather glove encrusted in ice.

A brown corduroy knee stuck up at a right angle. His face was turned into the snow, but the frozen hair was golden blond. Kate could just see the edge of a black turtleneck above the padded collar of the jacket.

And she knew in that instant that it was Gordon Lott and that he was very dead.

CHAPTER

FOUR

KATE STARED AT the body, her cell phone clutched in her hand. She made no move to check for vital signs, or call the paramedics. Visions of an earlier murder scene, that of her beloved professor, flashed in her mind and froze her in place.

Harry stood rigid beside her. She could hear his labored breathing, and she knew she should move, get him away from the gruesome scene, but she couldn't seem to activate her response system.

Someone should check the body, try to find a pulse, but even in her stupor, she knew that if Gordon Lott had been buried in the snow since the night before, he couldn't be alive. No one could withstand the cold that long.

Unless . . . Hypothermia. Didn't it slow down bodily functions? Of course it did. *Think, Kate. Think.*

Kate forced herself to take a step toward the snow plow. Made herself look at the body. And slowly her mind began to record the details.

There were pink splotches of snow encrusted on the jacket. Blood. And her own blood ran cold.

She stretched out her hand, loath to touch him.

"What are you doing?" Mike asked in a voice several octaves too high.

"Pulse."

Mike jumped. "I don't think . . . I don't think we should touch it—him—until the police get here."

"What if he's still alive?"

Mike shook his head. They both knew he wasn't.

"You'd better make that call."

Kate nodded and punched in the numbers. *Please send an ambulance. The police. The VFW hall.* It took two tries before she managed to get the words out loud. "Accident. VFW Hall parking lot. Hurry."

"Yes, ma'am. Somebody's on their way. Now just tell me what happened."

"I don't know," said Kate. "We just found him dead in the snow."

She let the dispatcher keep asking her questions, answering him with half her mind while the other half asked, *Where did the blood come from? Had Gordon slipped and fallen?* The dreaded image of a lawsuit rose to her mind. She pushed it a way; a man was dead and she was worried about being sued.

Besides, there had already been six inches of snow on the ground when they'd left last night. Even if he had fallen, the snow would have cushioned his landing. And someone would have seen and helped him.

So when had this happened? And what was he doing in the parking lot after everyone else had left? She looked again. She couldn't see blood on his head, just his chest. But that didn't mean anything. The other side of his head was hidden in the snow.

At last she heard sirens. *The Doppler effect,* Kate noted, as she listened to the whine rise in pitch as they came nearer.

Please let it be Brandon. His three patrolmen were all young and inexperienced. She needed the chief. He would be upset to find her standing over another body, but he would know what to do.

Because she was afraid—really afraid—that Gordon Lott had not died of natural causes.

She suddenly remembered Harry and turned to find him. He was standing right behind her, staring at the frozen body.

She should really get him away. Harry was still just a child in spite of his height and his savvy. He shouldn't be seeing this. None of them should be seeing this. She should send Harry inside before the chief got here. Before Harry witnessed any more. But still she didn't move.

Then the police arrived. Two patrol cars. One of them belonged to the chief of police. They screeched into the lot, sped across the cleared expanse, and stopped a few yards away.

Half a block behind them, the EMT ambulance lumbered at a slower pace.

Car doors opened and Brandon Mitchell got out, dragging his police jacket behind him. His head was bare and his dark hair and eyes seemed to absorb the early morning light.

Officers Owens and Curtis got out of the second patrol car, but stood at a safe distance from the truck, not at all happy to be there.

"Owens, Curtis, cordon of this whole section of parking lot." The chief looked down at the footprints on the icy asphalt, and Kate knew he was pissed because they'd messed up his crime scene.

Crime scene? She shivered. It was most definitely a crime scene.

The two patrolmen jumped and hurried back to the patrol car.

The chief turned to Mike and Harry. "Don't come any closer. Any of you."

Kate shook her head. Harry still hadn't moved, but he was looking at the police chief with such relief that her heart ached for him. And she knew how he felt. Brandon would take care of this.

But he couldn't make it go away.

The chief turned back to the plow, leaned over the edge, and touched the dead man's neck. Shifted his fingers once, then again, then moved them away.

He stepped back, then strode to the police car and reached inside. He was calling for backup, or the coroner, or maybe the county crime scene unit.

Kate's teeth began to chatter. It was hard to breathe. The frigid air hurt just going in.

Chief Mitchell returned, keeping his eyes riveted on the group. Kate shivered violently.

"Who was driving the truck?"

They all turned to look at the driver who had collapsed onto the running board.

"I was." He jerked his head, then buried his face in his hands.

"You didn't see him in the snow?"

"No," he moaned from between his fingers. "I would've stopped. I didn't see anything until the plow picked him up." His words rang through the still, cold air. "He was just there. Buried alive."

Brandon physically winced. "He was most likely dead before the snow covered him."

"Buried alive!" the driver repeated, his voice rising to a wail.

Brandon stepped closer, looming over him. "He was not and you'd better not spread any rumors."

The chief turned to Mike. "He works for you?"

"Ayuh."

"Then you better take him home. Unless you have something further to add."

"No, but what about Katie and young Harry here?"

"I'll see to them. You can go now."

Mike stood his ground. "I don't think—"

"It's alright, Mike," Kate said. "We'll be fine."

Mike nodded briskly and led his employee away.

Brandon lifted his chin at Harry. "Go sit in the squad car."

Harry shook his head. He looked like he might cry.

"*Now.*" The chief didn't yell, but his calm, quiet words sent an extra chill up Kate's spine.

She wished he would say something comforting, but the chief just said, "Take Kate—Ms. McDonald with you." He walked away without waiting for a reply or to see if Harry and Kate obeyed.

"Come on, Harry. Let the chief do his work."

Kate knew he would have to take their statements soon enough. And there was no way that she could protect Harry from having to relive the last hour. "It'll be warm in the squad car. And I'm freezing."

"Oh," said Harry and began walking toward the car.

Kate followed after him. She needed time to get control over her revulsion at finding Gordon's body. Time to organize the details of what she'd seen, so her statement would be coherent.

She had a photographic memory, and this was one scene she'd never forget. Just like she'd never forget the one of the professor murdered at his desk.

But she was getting ahead of herself. She didn't have enough data to start speculating. And she really wished it would turn out to be an accident. Of course, she knew how often wishes came true. They weren't high on the law of probabilities.

When they reached the car, Harry slid onto the front seat and unlocked the back doors. They both climbed in, leaving the doors ajar so they could get out again. They didn't speak, just stared forward through the metal grid trying to see what was going on outside.

And Kate thought what a frail barrier the grid was to be the only thing that separated the felons from the good guys. It didn't seem safe at all.

It felt like hours before the crime scene unit arrived, but it had probably only been thirty minutes. They weren't exactly the busiest unit in the state. There wasn't that much violent crime in the county. Not until recently.

Five men piled out of the van and went to work. Sam Swyndon arrived in his Jeep Cherokee and parked next to the chief's police car. He took his cameras out of the trunk and headed toward the yellow tape.

Kate and Sam had gone to high school together. He owned his own photography store on Main Street and doubled as police photographer when needed. Until recently the job had consisted of pictures of vandalism, robberies, and the occasional accident.

The professor's murder had changed all that. And he didn't look happy to be involved in another.

The chief nodded brusquely and lifted the tape for Sam to duck under.

"Wait here." Kate opened the door and got out of the squad car. She heard the car door slam and knew Harry had ignored her.

Kate moved cautiously toward the plow truck, trying not to slip on the thin crust of ice forming on the pavement and trying not to be seen. It wasn't just ghoulish curiosity. Their lives would be irrevocably changed because of this and Kate wanted to understand everything that was going on. It was the scientific method after all. What she knew best. What she depended on. What she thrived on. And there was no way she was going to stand back while others made the discoveries.

Harry moved up beside her. And they huddled close together.

She heard the crime scene officer talking to Brandon, his words crisp and clear. Cold air was a great conductor of sound waves. She listened unabashedly until she heard the words, "Thirty-eight caliber." She sucked in her breath. Gordon Lott had been shot.

Then Brandon walked toward her, stopped, and ran his fingers through his hair. "I thought I told you two to wait in the car. I'll question you both later, but there is no reason for you to be here. Unless you know the identity of the victim."

"Gordon Lott," she said. "His name is Gordon Lott."

"Great," he said. "Just great."

For a moment, Kate was confused. Then she realized he was pissed. And she knew why. Once more, she'd been found at the scene of a murder. She'd known both of the victims. "He's—was— a competitor. He competed last night."

"When was the last time you saw him?"

One of the crime scene investigators jogged over to them, and the interview was brought to an abrupt halt. "We've pretty much finished up here. We sifted the snow in the immediate vicinity. Nada. And there's just too much of it to go through it all; the plows have moved everything around. We passed the metal detector over it and got nothing. The photographer is finished. You can move the body."

Chief Mitchell nodded and turned back to Kate. "I'm not finished with you." Without another word, he turned, ducked under the tape and disappeared around the front of the snowplow. Without speaking, Kate and Harry moved forward.

The chief was examining the body, his hands encased in latex gloves that made a travesty of the weather. He moved slowly, methodically. Kate wished he would get on with it. The Junior Division competition was scheduled for ten o'clock. If he didn't hurry, children and their parents would arrive to crime scene tape.

Kate pushed back her coat sleeve to look at her watch. Nine fifteen. Two hours had elapsed and Gordon Lott was still hanging from the snowplow. The volunteers would be here any minute now.

She looked at her watch again, knowing the time wouldn't change just because she looked. It hadn't helped Gordon. She frowned. *Watch.* Gordon had kept consulting his watch during the semifinals.

She closed her eyes, picturing the position of the body when she'd first seen it. His arm had been sticking out of the snow. His left arm and the length of pale skin between coat and glove. His watch wasn't there.

He must have been a victim of robbery. And Kate was stunned and ashamed of the relief she felt.

At least that removed suspicion from the townspeople. Not that she thought any one of them would stoop to murder. Aunt Pru might roll through a stop sign or two. Alice Hinckley might sell a few jars of unlicensed jam. A teenager might do a little pilfering from the Market Basket. But no one in Granville would murder someone for a cheap, gaudy watch.

She hurried up to the tape to tell the chief, just as he shifted the body. It moved in one piece. Kate shuddered and thought, *It's frozen stiff.* She swallowed a bubble of hysterical laughter.

The chief lifted Gordon's jacket, slid his hand inside the back pants pocket, and pulled out a fat leather billfold.

"He was robbed," she blurted out.

"Not necessarily." He quickly slipped the wallet into an evidence bag, but not before Kate caught a glimpse of a thick wad of bills.

"He was. Check his left wrist. His watch is missing."

"And you know he wore a watch because—"

"I saw it. Half the participants at the tournament last night must have seen it. He looked at it often enough." She could hear the shrillness in her voice. She breathed out, trying to defuse her exasperation and her panic. "They didn't find it in the snow, did they? The metal detector didn't pick it up. The inspector said so."

"The investigator," he corrected her. "I'll talk to you in a minute." He turned back to the body.

Sam Swyndon ducked under the tape and stopped. He saw Kate and his mouth opened, then he strode toward her. "What are you doing here?"

"Oh, Sam."

Sam wrapped his arm around her shoulders and pulled her close. "Please tell me you didn't discover the body."

"No, but I was here."

"Well, you don't need to stay. I'll drive you home."

"I can't leave. The tournament will be starting in less than an hour. Oh God."

Sam pulled her closer and she gave in to the comfort of his warmth. He was tall and lanky, but not overbearing, like some men she knew.

"You'd better prepare yourself. The chief here might not let you continue with the tournament."

Kate pulled away. "We have to."

"There, there. Whatever happens, we'll see our way through."

She tried to smile at him, but her lips were too cold.

"When things calm down, we'll have to have dinner again. I

really enjoyed the last one."

"Me, too," Kate said. She *had* enjoyed it. They'd laughed and reminisced about high school. He made the awful things that had happened to her back then seem funny. The evening had ended in a long good night kiss. Then she'd gotten busy with the preparations for the tournament and they hadn't been out again.

In the distance a tree limb snapped and snow plopped to the ground. The chief's gruff voice broke through the ensuing silence. "Sam. You're out of here. Get those photos developed as soon as you can."

Kate added a silent, "Please," that she knew wouldn't come from the chief.

"The voice of authority speaks." Sam smiled at her. "See you at the afternoon session if Chief Mitchell allows it to go, on. I'm taking pictures for the paper."

"Sam, now, if you don't mind."

"I'm on it, Chief." He gave Kate a quick squeeze and trotted off toward his car. Kate watched him go, wondering why everyone couldn't be as nice as Sam.

"Let's continue this somewhere warmer."

She jumped. The chief was standing right behind her, looking like Vulcan to Sam's golden god. He gestured toward the VFW hall and waited for Kate and Harry to precede him across the parking lot.

"Da-arn," Kate said as they stepped into the outer hall. "I should have turned on the heat two hours ago. Harry, can you go turn up the thermostat? We need to get some heat pumping before everyone arrives."

"Wait," the chief said. "Where's the thermostat?"

"Right over there on the wall. Why?"

"Just curious. Go and come straight back."

Harry frowned at the chief, but went to turn up the heat.

As soon as Harry was finished, the three of them went into the main hall. The chief stopped at the first row of chairs and pulled out one for Kate. She sat down. He turned to Harry. "Go sit over there. I'll get to you later."

Harry flung him a defiant look and stalked to the far end of the row.

Kate turned on the chief. "Cut him a break, will you? He just saw a dead man."

"I'm well aware of that. I would have thought you'd have more sense than to subject him to a crime scene."

"If I'd known we were about to discover a body, I would have sent Harry inside."

The chief held up his hand. "Sorry. You're right. I didn't mean to—"

"Bite my head off?"

A smile flitted across his face and was gone. He sat down across from her. "Neither of you touched the body?"

"No. Of course not."

He gave her an incredulous look.

"I . . . I learned my lesson."

The chief looked even more incredulous.

"Look, Chief Mitchell. Can we get on with this? I really don't want to appear callous, but people will be arriving any minute."

He considered her, taking a breath. "Kate, I'm sorry, but you'll have to cancel the rest of the tournament."

"I can't do that! People have already *paid*."

"Kate. Let me put it straight. I'm sure you've figured it out already. Gordon Lott was murdered. Though I would appreciate it if you didn't spread it around." His eyes shot to the ceiling. He had no illusions about that fact staying secret. Granville had one of the most developed grapevines on the East Coast. "The murderer is out there somewhere. I don't have the manpower to protect the town, much less the three hundred odd extras."

So that's why he'd insisted on Harry staying close by. He was concerned for his safety. She appreciated it, but she couldn't let him close down the tournament.

"You don't understand. Everyone is depending on this weekend. Everyone. Not just me. If it was just about returning some entry fees, I wouldn't argue." *Not much anyway.* "But the museum's reputation won't be worth a hill of beans. We might even have to close down and the professor's—" she stopped, took a breath to calm down.

"Other people are dependent on the tournament, too. If we cancel, Nancy and John Vance will lose a whole weekend's worth of income, and what about the extra help they hired? They'll all lose a paycheck. And all the extra food they purchased will go to waste. And the other restaurants in town. Not to mention the huge amounts of food that Rayette ordered for the tournament canteen. I can't let them all down."

And what about her? She'd given up her lucrative government job to take over the museum and make it a success. But she'd been here since the end of the summer and she'd yet to take a salary. She couldn't live on her savings forever.

And if she were forced to abandon the museum and go back to Alexandria, how did she know that the chief would continue to take care of Harry?

"There's too much riding on this tournament," she finished.

"Kate, be reasonable."

"We can't cancel. I won't. Maybe the killer is gone. We don't know anything about Gordon Lott . . ." Except that he was accused of cheating. But she wasn't ready to open that can of worms. "It could be someone who followed him here and ran once the job was done."

"And if he didn't?"

"If he *is* still here, you'll have all the suspects in one place."

His eyes narrowed. She saw the storm brewing in his eyes.

A chair crashed to the floor. "No way we're canceling." Harry stood by the overturned chair, his fists on his hips and his eyes flashing.

"It's okay, Harry. The chief is just concerned about our safety."

"There's safety in numbers," said Harry, his eyes on the chief. "Running away won't solve the problem."

This from a fourteen-year-old former runaway. Maybe that made him an expert.

"We can't cancel the tournament. I'm giving a workshop on codes and ciphers this afternoon." Harry's voice was shrill and childlike.

Kate's throat thickened. She knew how much the presentation meant to him. It wasn't fair. Too much of Harry's young life had been touched by violence and abuse.

And for a moment she hated Gordon Lott and his slimy, cheating self and his cheap gaudy watch for bringing this down on their heads. Harry had little enough to look forward to. She'd be damned if she'd let Gordon Lott's murder take anything more from Harry than he'd already lost.

For an eon no one spoke, and Kate found herself listening to the heating vents pumping out warm air.

Reluctantly, Chief Mitchell pulled out the chair next to him. He motioned to Harry and the boy shuffled over and sat down.

The chief turned to Kate. "When was the last time you saw Lott?"

Just like that, he'd switched gears. Leaving the question of the conference unanswered.

"After the second round last night," said Kate.

Harry shrugged. "I didn't even know who he was. I was downstairs unloading supplies for Rayette most of the night."

Alarms rang in Kate's mind. Had Harry witnessed the altercation between Jason, Erik, and Gordon? Would he say anything? Kate had already decided not to divulge that unless it became absolutely necessary. Jason Elks and Erik Ingersoll were no killers.

The chief asked them a few more questions, then told Harry he could go.

"Where am I going?" Harry asked in a voice that he couldn't keep from wavering.

"You're going wherever Kate tells you to go in order to get this place ready for the next competition."

"You mean we can go on with the tournament?"

"Until further notice."

Harry's face broke into a wide grin of relief. "Thanks, Chief. You're the best. I mean. Uh . . ." He flushed.

The chief looked away. "Get going."

Harry went.

"Thank you," Kate said, meaning it from the bottom of her heart.

"Yeah. If anyone else suffers because of this, I'll probably be tarred and feathered. *Before* they fire me."

Kate smiled. "Ride you out of town on a rail."

"What?"

"The rail. It's the Granville way."

The chief groaned.

The outer door opened and footsteps sounded in the vestibule.

"Katie? Katie? Where are you? I just saw yellow tape in the parking lot. Simon went to see what happened. What's that police car doing here? Are you alright? Where are you?"

Kate braced herself as the double doors were flung open and her aunt flew inside. Pree skidded to a stop as her eyes zeroed in on the police chief. He'd managed to stand up and move several feet away from Kate before her entrance.

"Humph," Pru said, giving him a scalding look. "I should've guessed." She stood with her hands on her nonexistent hips, her feet spread, looking like Super Olive Oyl. A red ribbon was threaded through the blue curls piled high on her head. Her white down jacket puffed around her like a giant marshmallow.

"I suppose he has a reason for being in here."

"Aunt Pru—"

"Yes, he does," the chief answered for her. "A man died in the parking lot last night. I was trying to get rid of the body before the competitors arrived."

Pru's mouth fell open.

So did Kate's. Was the man without a sense of humor actually joking? Or was he just trying to shock Pru?

"Oh dear," said Pru, suddenly deflated. "I told Benjamin Meany not to stand out in the cold. Poor old soul has no business working for the police force at his age."

The chief closed his eyes.

Kate stood up. "It wasn't Mr. Meany, Aunt Pru. And you know the chief only hires him to empty the parking meters. Mr. Meany volunteered his time to help with the tournament. Just like you and me and everybody else. It was one of the competitors. Now leave the chief alone."

Pru's eyes widened.

Kate swallowed. She'd never talked back to her aunt in her life.

She darted a quick look at the chief of police. He looked just as taken aback as Pru did.

Kate steeled her nerves and focused on Pru's forehead, like the government speech coach had told her to do when she was nervous. Then for the first time since she was a teenager, Kate lied to her aunt. "He died of a heart attack. There was nothing anyone could do."

She suddenly felt very hot. Guilt probably. She unzipped her coat. "Now, I have a lot of work to do, and so does the chief. Can you please help Alice set up for the ten-year-olds?"

"Of course, dear." Pru managed to shoot the chief a withering look before leaving the room.

"Lying to a family member is bad enough," the chief said, fighting a smile. "Lying to your aunt might be a federal offense."

"Well, you weren't helping."

"I was too busy protecting my vital parts to be able to think quickly."

Kate cracked a smile. "Oh, Brandon. You're not afraid of Aunt Pru?"

"Only when I'm off duty. I don't think she'd attack the uniform." He stepped closer to her. "The real cause of death will get out. I have no illusions about that. It's probably all over town by now. But thanks for trying."

"Should I make some kind of announcement?"

"No!"

Her face suffused with heat. She'd asked for people to step forward before. It had set off a stampede of false information. Though she didn't think the locals would pull that on the chief again.

"If there needs to be an announcement, I'll make it." He smiled suddenly.

"What?"

"That." He lifted his chin toward the top of her head.

Kate's hand flew to her hair. It was probably sticking out in all directions. But what she touched was her striped knit elf hat. She'd forgotten to take it off.

"I just got the total effect."

"It's my favorite hat from high school."

"You actually wore that in high school?"

Okay, so she hadn't been your average fashion-conscious teenager. And he wasn't the first person to tease her about her hat. But it made her angry all the same. "At least I had the good sense to wear a hat. Unlike *some* people."

"Hmm . . ." he said. And before she knew what he intended, he'd pulled the hat down over her eyes and left the room.

5		1			3			
		9		4	7		2	1
	7				2	5	3	
6		5			8		1	
3			2		5			9
	4		9			8		6
	8	2	7				6	
7	6		3	1		2		
			8			9		4

GINNY SUE AND Tony arrived ten minutes before the first round of Juniors was to begin.

"Sorry we're so late," Ginny Sue said. "It's my fault. It took me forever to shovel out this morning." Her face was flushed from the exercise, Kate noted. Unless the look she shot Tony as he headed to the podium was the reason for her glow this morning.

She was wearing navy blue cords and a gold and brown sweater that brought out the highlights in her russet hair. It was a pretty color, darker, finer, and more subdued than Kate's own fire engine red mass of curls. Kate had gelled them back into two tortoise shell barrettes that morning, but between the knit hat and discovering Gordon Lott, she knew she must look like a wild woman.

Ginny Sue didn't seem to notice. She was too excited. "We heard about Gordon Lott when I went to the inn to pick up Tony this morning. The police were there asking to see Gordon's room."

"Did they?"

"See his room? No. At least not before we left. Nancy was really upset, and I hated to leave her. John had to go over to Nashua for more bar supplies this morning and she didn't know what to do. Especially after last night."

"Last night?"

Ginny Sue nodded, her eyes round. "There was an awful scene. You know how Tony invited us for a drink?"

Kate nodded.

"Well, I stopped by the inn last night before I went home, you know, for that drink? Gordon Lott was sitting at the bar. He must have gotten a head start because he was already belligerent by the time Tony and I walked in. He was complaining to a bunch of people about the competition being fixed."

That was odd. If Gordon was at the Bowsman bar last night, how did he end up in the VFW parking lot?

Ginny Sue's mouth twisted. "It made me so mad that I walked right up to him and told him to shut up. How dare he cast aspersions on our veracity."

He dared and now he's dead, thought Kate. A shiver passed over her. "Then what happened?"

"All hell broke loose. Gordon gave me attitude. And when Tony interceded, Gordon threw a punch at him. Just like that. Without any warning."

Kate quickly looked at Tony, who was taking his place at the microphone. "He looks okay."

"Gordon missed. He was that drunk. And fortunately, John and Nancy were in the bar, hobnobbing with the guests like they always do. And John told him to leave."

Ginny Sue shuddered. "Then he tried to hit John. I thought it was going to be a free-for-all. But two men he'd been drinking with took him by each arm and marched him out of the bar.

"At first I thought they were members of the Hanover team, but then I saw the other team members sitting at a table. They were staring after Gordon and they looked pissed as hell at him."

"No wonder," Kate mused aloud. "He gave the team a major setback by getting knocked out of the last round. It must have been the men he was talking to at the tournament. They must be friends of his, because they aren't competitors. Where did they go?"

"I don't know, but the Cambridge team, who is also staying at the inn, cheered and everything was alright after that."

"Whew," Kate said. "That's good, because the Hanover and Cambridge teams are serious competitors. Actually, they despise each other. They started a brawl at the Marriott bar during the 2005 Nationals. I hope they don't give John and Nancy trouble."

"They seemed congenial enough last night. But you haven't heard the best part."

Kate waited.

"You know that blonde who was hanging on him all day? As soon as Gordon and the men left, guess what she did?"

Followed them and murdered Gordon Lott?

"Turned and started flirting with the guy next to her. She left with him a few minutes later. I mean *really.*"

"Sounds like you had an eventful evening."

"Yes." Ginny Sue smiled tentatively. "And it was really nice once they were all gone. Except it took a while for Tony to calm down."

Kate, who had begun reading undertones of romance in Ginny Sue's references to Tony, went cold. "How so?"

"Well, the jerk had just attacked him. And I guess Tony and Lott have had words before. At another competition, I mean. Because Tony said he was a scumbag and somebody ought to do something to keep him off the circuit."

"Did anyone hear him say that besides you?"

"I don't know. I don't think so. We were sitting at a booth. Why?"

"Just curious." And a certain police chief might just construe that as a threat, considering that someone had killed Gordon Lott right afterward.

Kate looked over at the podium. Tony had dressed down for the junior division. He was wearing charcoal wool pants, and his grand master medal was pinned to a Sudoku U sweatshirt.

The kids laughed at something he said. He was in his element: relaxed, entertaining, enjoying his work. He didn't look like someone who had just murdered a man and left his body in the parking lot to freeze.

"What time did you leave the bar?"

Ginny Sue shrugged. "Around midnight. It took a while to get out of the parking lot. The snow was really coming down. Why?" Her eyes widened. "Are you helping Chief Mitchell pin down the time of death?"

"Good heavens, no," Kate said, nearly jumping out of her skin. "Don't even suggest that I, uh . . ."

"That you were asking questions? I won't. The chief would have your hide."

"And besides, I'm not. I'm just curious. Like everybody else."

"Does the chief suspect something?"

Kate shook her head.

"He *does!* Ohmigod!"

"No," Kate said, "he doesn't."

"Kate, you're a terrible liar. You always were. Was Gordon murdered?" Then it struck her. She snapped her head toward the podium where Tony was about to start the first round. "Don't even think it. Tony was with me. And besides, he wouldn't. He couldn't."

"Of course not," said Kate. Her attention was drawn to the adjudicators taking their places at the end of each row of ten-years-olds. While she'd been distracted by the murder and Ginny Sue's story, Harry had organized the whole shift.

He was standing on the far side of the room. She gave him a thumbs up. He grinned back.

"We're having dinner before the evening session," Ginny Sue told her. "If you'd like to join us."

Kate smiled. "Thanks. But I have other plans." Like how to keep Brandon Mitchell from jumping to the wrong conclusions. "Now, don't worry. And don't say anything to Tony or anybody else."

"But—"

Kate's cell phone vibrated. She reached into the pocket of her jeans and looked at the caller ID. "Nancy Vance," she mouthed at Ginny and held up her finger to let her know she'd be right back.

She went quickly to the outer vestibule and answered it.

"Katie. Thank goodness."

"Nancy?"

"I know you're busy, but the police were just here asking to see Gordon Lott's room."

"That's because Lott is dead."

"I know. It's all over town already. But John had to go down to Nashua to get a replacement for one of the beer taps, and he won't be back until tonight and I didn't know what to do."

"So what *did* you do?"

A nervous giggle erupted over the phone. "I told them they had to get a search warrant."

"And did they?"

"I don't know. It was Paul Curtis and Mary Owens's boy. And they went away after that and they haven't come back. But now I'm afraid Chief Mitchell will think I have something to hide."

Kate rolled her eyes—something she knew Aunt Pru hated. Pru was watching her from where she sat behind the registration desk. The morning shift of GABs were all watching her. She turned her back and moved closer to the door.

She lowered her voice. "I don't think he will suspect you of anything. When they come back—and you might as well face it, they'll probably bring the chief with them—let them into Gordon's room."

"I feel so stupid. I knew I probably should have let them in, but I just panicked. I wish John was here."

"Don't worry. Everything will be fine." Kate hung up and turned around to see six faces staring back at her, openmouthed.

"Tell all," demanded Elmira Swyndon, who was filling in for Carrie Blaine that morning. Elmira was Sam's aunt as well as the chief's secretary-dispatcher. "I knew something was up when I dropped by the station this morning on my way over. Just to check on things, you know. Dickie Wilson was there all by himself. Looking scared to death.

"I thought it odd that Chief Mitchell left him in charge. He's so young and not terribly, you know . . ." She tapped her temple. "But there he was. Said the chief had been called out. And then I get here and here's the chief." Elmira pursed her lips. "What was he doing here? Is it true that someone froze to death in the parking lot last night?"

"Does the police chief think it was murder?" Tanya asked, her eyes as round and dark as a couple of Oreos. "Did you see him? Lord, don't tell me you found him."

Kate sighed, wondering how she had become Granville's central exchange. But she knew that if she didn't give them some kind of answer, they'd make up their own.

She quickly gave them the condensed version: that Gordon Lott's body had been discovered by the plow trucks. She left out the details of how the body was hanging out over the plow. She didn't mention anything about the gunshot wound.

They'd know everything soon enough, but Kate wasn't going to be the one to tell them.

"So you think he was murdered?" Alice Hinckley asked.

"Murdered?" Kate squeaked. "No."

"Heart attack," Pru smugly informed them.

Everyone's attention turned to Kate's aunt and Kate took the opportunity to slip downstairs.

She stopped at the bottom of the stairs to mull over what she'd learned from Ginny Sue and Nancy Vance. Tony may have had a window of opportunity to kill Lott, but he'd have had to find him first, convince him to tromp through the snow to the VFW parking lot, and then shoot him. Ridiculous.

She understood Nancy's reluctance to have the police in the inn. It couldn't be good for business. But what struck her as odd was that the chief had sent Curtis and Owens to search Lott's room. Kate knew from experience that they were trained to take fingerprints. And she'd heard that the chief had been riding them pretty hard to bring the police department up to snuff. But it didn't seem like the kind of job he would leave to two inexperienced patrolmen.

So where's the chief now? And what's he doing?

"Katie, hon. Did you run out of steam?"

Kate jumped. Simon Mack was sitting at one of the small tables in the canteen, sipping a cup of coffee. He motioned Kate over. Simon was completely bald except for a fine tonsure of white hair that ringed the base of his skull. His down jacket and Tyrolean hat lay across the seat of a chair. Even in this weather and on a

Saturday he was dressed in an old-fashioned three-piece suit.

Simon would never see seventy-nine again, but he was still sharp as a tack. And he was a town favorite for his expertise and his gentlemanly manners, and especially since he could still drive at night.

He pulled out a chair for Kate.

Rayette placed a Styrofoam cup of coffee and a cranberry-orange muffin in front of her, then straightened up and brushed powdered sugar off her navy blue slacks. She waited expectantly for a moment, then Simon thanked her and waved her away. She sighed and went back to the counter.

Kate spoke in an undertone. "I guess you heard."

Simon nodded. "I saw Chief Mitchell as I came in. Not the way you want to start a weekend of festivities, is it?"

"He told you?"

Simon cut his eyes toward the canteen counter, where Rayette was energetically scrubbing the surface.

"I'm not listening," she said, clearly listening.

"He wanted me to cancel the rest of the weekend."

"He didn't order you to?"

Kate shook her head.

"Humph," snorted Simon. "The boy may be learning a thing or two after all. Ayuh."

"He said he couldn't protect everyone if there is a murderer at large. I know he's right, but I just couldn't cancel. There's so much riding on this tournament."

"I understand. And I agree. But you do need to realize that it won't be long before the details are public knowledge. You might have a panic on your hands."

"Oh," Kate said. "I hadn't thought about that."

"Well, Brandon Mitchell has. I suggest you leave everything to him. And Kate, the less said, the better." He winked at her. "Drink your coffee. And stop worrying. There's safety in numbers."

Kate looked up. "That's just what Harry said."

"Did he now? Maybe I'll take him on as a partner. How long do you think it will take him to get through law school?"

"Knowing Harry? Not long."

"He and Chief Mitchell seem to be rubbing along fine."

"I guess, but I think Harry is beginning to chafe under all the rules the chief has imposed."

"A boy needs rules."

"I know, but sometimes it seems Brand—Chief Mitchell has nothing but rules."

Simon smiled, a wisdom-of-the-ages smile. "Remember, Kate. Harry isn't the only one feeling his way in that relationship."

Kate went back upstairs to hand out the trophies for the junior events. Everyone who participated received one. The first place trophy was just a little larger than the rest.

"That went great, Harry," Kate told him as they climbed down from the stage. "You really organized that well and everyone seemed to have a good time."

"Yeah," he agreed. "And guess what? Rayette is offering free hot dogs to anyone who's staying for my workshop this afternoon."

"Very clever marketing," Kate said.

"It was my idea."

Kate laughed. Maybe she was worrying too much about Harry.

The Breaking into Codes and Ciphers presentation drew a large crowd, adults as well as kids. Harry seemed nervous and he kept looking toward the back door.

Kate's heart sank. Was he waiting for Brandon to come? Of course he was. The chief had taken the professor's place as Harry's mentor.

Kate, too, started watching the door. She knew Brandon was busy with this murder investigation. But hell, Gordon Lott was dead, and Harry was very much alive. She was about to tiptoe out to call him when the back door opened and Brandon stepped in.

Harry's face flooded with relief and Kate felt a rush of warmth. The chief looked grim, but when he saw Harry he smiled. Not a huge smile, but it transformed his face. Made him seem almost human.

She caught his eye and smiled her approval. He gave her a quick nod, then turned his attention back to Harry. Kate's cheeks suffused with another kind of heat—sheer embarrassment. It didn't pay to let the chief see her soft side.

They dealt better when he was being the clinical policeman and she approached him as she would de Morgan's *theorem of complements*. Instead, she always felt like a *dependent variable* every time he came near her.

Still, she was grateful that he'd managed to get there in time. And she would tell him so after the workshop. Chiefs of police needed positive reinforcement, too.

When Harry finished his presentation, he was immediately surrounded by people asking questions. While words like transposition, rail fence, random substitutions, and shifts bounced in the air, Kate made her way around the edge of the room to stand by Brandon's side.

"Didn't he do great?"

"Yeah." Brandon almost sounded pleased. Almost. He was a master at not giving anything away, but Kate could tell he was proud of his young protégé. Of course he would probably deny being a force in Harry's life, claim to be just an unwilling roommate until they figured out what was best for Harry's future.

It would be fine with her if they never figured it out. Then Harry could stay in Granville until college. He'd work at the museum in the afternoons after school, and go home to a good male role model instead of the abusive uncle he'd lived with for most of his life.

The professor had taken him under his wing, but he'd blossomed under the police chief's nontutelage.

When Harry finally tore himself away from his eager questioners, he hurried over to them, flushed with a sense of accomplishment.

"That was great, Harry. Congratulations." Kate was beaming almost as much as Harry.

"The free hot dogs were good, too," said the chief.

Kate frowned at him, but Harry grinned even broader.

"Maybe I should start a codes and ciphers club at the museum. Would that be okay?"

"Sure," Kate said. "An excellent idea. We just have to find a time to schedule it in." In the few months since she'd been curator, Kate had reinstituted the clubs that had fallen into disuse and added a few of her own. The museum was becoming one of the social hot spots in town.

Harry was watching the chief. He hadn't spoken again and Kate wanted to kick him into showing more enthusiasm.

A boy nearly as tall as Harry stuck his head in the door. "Hey, Harry, Rayette's got extra hot dogs. Bet I can eat 'em all before you get your skinny—" he saw Kate and Brandon "—butt downstairs."

"Not a chance." Harry took off after the boy.

"He's made a friend," Kate said happily. She knew how lonely being the school geek could be. Harry had felt that loneliness, too. She couldn't have been more pleased.

The chief just stood there.

"Aren't you excited for him?"

"Yeah."

"Then why don't you show it?"

"I am."

Kate rolled her eyes heavenward.

"I'm going to talk to Simon."

Uh-oh. The cop voice. And she hadn't breathed a word about Gordon Lott.

"About what?" She waited, knowing it wasn't going to be good.

"About whether it's possible to use some of the education fund the professor left Harry to send him to boarding school."

"No." Kate shook her head, and kept shaking it as if she could shake the chief's words right out of her head.

"Kate. He needs—"

"Someone to look up to, to care for him, to give him a good, loving home." She glanced at Brandon. *Okay, so maybe not so loving.* But she could love Harry enough for both of them.

"I realize that, but it isn't me."

"Why?"

He flinched.

She knew she sounded whiney, but she wouldn't let him just throw these last few months away. Harry would be devastated.

"I can't give him the attention he needs. I work long hours. Get called out in the middle of the night. Deal with unpleasant situations all the time. I've been thinking about this for a while, and now with this latest murder . . . I don't see any other alternative."

"Latest? You sound like it's just the beginning."

He looked at her long and hard. "Once Pandora's box is opened . . ." He trailed off and looked out toward the stage. "No boy should be witness to any kind of violence, and Harry has had way too much of it in his life."

"Brandon," Kate said, searching for an argument that would change his mind. Found none. "Please. Just wait. For a little while? At least until the end of the school year. It would be counterproductive to uproot him when he's just settling in. It isn't fair." She practically wailed the last sentence and she bit her lip to keep from getting any more dramatic.

"Wait so he can become more attached to his life in Granville? That isn't fair, either."

"Please, just wait." She'd talk to Simon. If Harry wanted to go away to school, she'd let him go. But if he didn't, she'd make Simon figure out a way to grant her custody. She wouldn't let Harry go back to foster care. "Please?"

Brandon sighed and she noticed for the first time how tired he looked. His tenure in Granville had been wearing. But Harry couldn't be that much of a burden.

"I have a murder to solve," he said. "I'll be back for the evening session."

Kate watched him leave, listened to his footsteps across the planked floor outside and the outer door open and close.

She stood for a long time after he was gone. The afternoon session was over and everyone had left. The evening's competitors wouldn't arrive for another two and a half hours.

Kate was alone in the cavernous VFW hall and she had nothing to do but worry.

9	8							2
	6		2	3		8		1
	5		8		9		3	
6		7	1	2				
		1	5		7	3		
				4	8	9		7
	3		7		1		6	
2		8		6	4		7	
5							4	9

CHAPTER

S I X

IT DIDN'T TAKE long for the word of Gordon Lott's death to spread. By the time the competitors began arriving for the night's competition, exclamations of "buried alive!" were circulating freely around the room.

Kate was inundated with questions. Had she really found the dead man? Was it murder? What did he look like? Was he really staring out from eyelids that had been frozen open? Did they have to break his bones to get him in the body bag?

At first Kate was polite and managed to avoid adding to the escalating hysteria. But when the Hanover team came en masse and asked if someone was killing off the top competitors, she knew she had to put a stop to it.

"I'll make an announcement," Tony said as he, Kate, and Ginny Sue looked over the crowd. Kate agreed. Though the chief had told her not to mention it, even he would see the need to stop the rumors. Or maybe he just hadn't wanted *her* to make the announcement.

"I guess you'd better, if you don't mind," Kate told him, glad to be able to foist the responsibility onto someone else. Besides, Tony knew how to deal with an audience.

"I'll try to refrain from saying what an annoying, cheating scum he was. So what's it to be? Heart attack?"

Kate didn't feel right about lying to the audience, but she knew better than to tell them what had really happened—all hell would break out. In less than twenty-four hours, the tournament would be over and the attendees could gossip their way home.

"Just say that he died . . . unexpectedly. No. That he, uh . . ."

"Quit this mortal plane?"

Kate jumped. Tony's eyes widened.

And there he was—without warning—looming over her like her worst nightmare.

"Chief Mitchell," Kate stammered. "Tony, this is our chief of police, Brandon Mitchell. Tony Kefalas."

The two men nodded to each other. No small talk, nothing. The chief wasn't wearing his uniform, but he didn't look off-duty. He looked ready for a showdown.

"Tony was wondering if we should make an announcement. There's a lot of speculation going around about how Gordon Lott died."

"So I've heard," the chief said dryly. "Make your announcement. Then start the competition before they have time to start talking again."

"Certainly, Chief Mitchell. What should I say?"

Chief Mitchell perused Tony before answering. "That Gordon Lott died last night. It's a sad occasion but you know that Gordon would want you to continue on with the competition. Set up a scholarship in his name or something. Give them something else to think about."

"So you can investigate unimpeded?"

Now the chief really gave Tony the once-over. "Know something you'd like to tell me?"

Normally that stare would set a person running for the hills, but it glanced right off Tony. "Only rumors I've heard. You're dealing with three hundred puzzle solvers, Chief Mitchell. They live to solve. My guess is half to three-quarters of the people out there are already piecing the facts and the rumors together, searching for the answer."

Kate was sure she heard the chief grinding his teeth. The look he gave her was accusatory.

"Then try not to give them any clues." He nodded to Tony again. A dismissal if ever Kate had seen one. "Ladies." Another nod to Kate and Ginny Sue and he walked away.

Tony winked at Kate. "He's good, if a little gruff. I'll just make that announcement."

Kate watched Tony sprint up the steps, totally unaffected by the chief's attitude.

While he put her in a quake—always.

Tony made his announcement exactly as the chief had dictated and the audience reacted just the way he had predicted.

Amazing. Simply amazing.

The rounds began in the same order as the night before, starting with D division and working up to the top A flight. Kate watched the crowd, wondering if one of them had killed Gordon Lott.

Of course it was one of them. Kate didn't really believe that someone killed him for his watch and was now hundreds of miles away selling it on the street of some big city. Why take a gaudy watch but leave that wad of bills in his wallet?

It was during one of the breaks that Kate first heard the question, "Where is Kenny?" And she flashed back to the professor, looking at her with confused, lost eyes and asking, "Where is Harry?" when Harry had been a missing person.

Now someone named Kenny Revell seemed to be missing. Kate searched her formidable memory. He wasn't a registered competitor, and he couldn't have signed up at the door. She'd cut off registration several weeks before.

So being the puzzle solver that she was, Kate did what she'd done in Harry's case. She set about learning who Kenny Revell was and if he could possibly have anything to do with Gordon Lott's murder.

The next time she heard someone ask about Kenny, she slipped into the group and asked who he was.

They all looked at her in surprise. "Kenny Revell. He's never missed a final."

She found Tony in the crowd and pulled him aside.

"Kenny Revell? He's a puzzle groupie. Doesn't compete, but he comes to every major tournament to watch. He's here this weekend. I'll point him out to you."

"Apparently he isn't here now. People are asking about him."

Tony's eyebrows knit together as he thought. "He was here last night. I saw him talking to Lott at the—" He stopped short.

"What?"

"He was at the Bowsman Inn last night. Gordon was acting like an ass, and the proprietor asked him to leave. Kenny and another man took him away." One eyebrow arched into a question. "You don't think he has something to do with Gordon's murder?"

"Shh." Kate grabbed his arm and moved him away from curious eyes and ears. "Don't say 'murder.'"

"That's what happened, isn't it? Are you forgetting that when I'm not emceeing these events, I'm also a master puzzle solver? If the cause of death had been natural, your taciturn chief of police would have said so, I would have passed that on to the audience, and there would be an end to it."

He had her there.

Tony tapped his cheek. "I wonder."

"Please don't, Tony. The chief already wants to close us down." And if Kenny Revell killed Gordon Lott and was at large . . . "What do you know about Revell? Were he and Gordon friends? Enemies?"

Tony's eyes glinted. "And they're off," he said, intoning the voice of a horse race announcer. "The puzzle-solving madness is upon her."

"No," Kate protested. "The chief will kill me if I get involved. It's just—I was wondering if Revell not being here tonight might be significant."

"I have no idea."

"Maybe not, but you're already making connections."

"It's what I do. Isn't it what you're doing?"

"Yes, but I just want to make sure if there is a connection, it's something personal, and not the beginning of a killing spree by a psychopathic puzzle groupie."

"*Whoa, girl!*"

"I know, but I'm responsible for a lot of people's safety this weekend."

"I suggest you leave that to your chief. He seems like he could handle a few psychopaths."

"Yes, but he doesn't want to."

"I can't say that I blame him, but I can't help you. I know some of the contestants, and a few of the tournament followers, but

being either an emcee or adjudicator, it would be unethical to frat-
ernize with the others. I know nothing about Kenny Revell or his
relationship, if there is one, with Gordon Lott. Just that he shows
up to a lot of competitions." Tony glanced at his watch. "Time for
the finals."

Kate went to look for Brandon. She'd just give him a heads-up
about Kenny Revell, though she was sure he'd already heard and
had pieced it together. It was harder to find him than it should be.
For such a big and formidable man, he blended very well—a useful trait in a policeman, she imagined

She went out to the registration area just in time to see him,
dressed for the elements, leading Gordon's blonde friend out the
front door. She knew the chief was probably questioning her, but
a stab of jealousy ripped through her.

Which was compounded by the fact that Aunt Pru was sitting
at the table, also watching them leave and looking smugly satisfied.

Kate backed away. Her information could wait.

She was about to return to the hall, when a "psst" stopped her.
She looked around. Jason Elks's head appeared around the corner
of the stairwell. He motioned her over, waving his hand urgently.

She walked over to the stairs and peered down at him. He
waved his hand even more urgently, then turned away.

Now what? she wondered, as she followed him down the stairs.
He went straight through the canteen, down the hall, and past the
bathrooms, the vendors' room, and the boiler room. He didn't stop
until they were at the end of the hall where a door led to the dumpster out back.

Erik was waiting for them. He was sweating. Beads of moisture
stood out on his wrinkled forehead.

"What are you doing?" Kate asked.

"Shh!" Both men put their fingers to their lips. Kate fought the overwhelming urge to laugh.

"We have information," Jason said, looking over her shoulder and peering down the hall.

"About what?"

"The murder," Erik wheezed.

Suddenly, she didn't feel like laughing anymore. The grapevine had been doing double duty.

"That sounds very interesting, but could we maybe sit down at a booth and have something to drink? It's kind of creepy down here."

They both shook their heads. "Chief Mitchell—"

"Is gone. I saw him leave a few minutes ago." *With a gorgeous blonde whose hair swooshes at her shoulders when she moves her head.* Kate unconsciously smoothed back her gelled curls.

"Oh, then that's alright." Jason pushed Erik forward and the three of them went back down the hall side by side. *Dorothy, the Tin Man, and the Cowardly Lion.*

Kate chose an empty booth and Jason slid in beside her. Erik squeezed himself into the seat across from them. They observed a tension-filled silence while Rayette placed coffee cups in front of them. She rolled her eyes at Kate and went back to stand behind the counter and listen.

Kate blew on her coffee and took a sip. "Now, what's this all about?"

Jason looked quickly around. "We were at GB and G's last night."

"The bar and grill?"

"Just to ward off the chill before driving home."

Kate nodded.

"Kate doesn't care about that," Erik said tersely. "While we were there, Gordon Lott came in with two other men."

Now she was more interested. "What time was this?" Lott must have gone to the bar and grill after John Vance kicked him out of the Bowsman bar.

"About eleven."

"We had a few words," Jason admitted.

Kate groaned inwardly. She knew where this was going.

"And the chief of police is looking for us," Erik whispered.

"But we *have* to compete in the finals," Jason added.

"Look, you two. I'm sure Chief Mitchell will be asking questions of everyone who was there. Just tell him what you saw and heard."

"No!" both men said simultaneously.

Erik kneaded his hands. "He might jump to the wrong conclusion."

"And then where would we be?" Jason's tone was plaintive.

Erik's hands slapped the table top. "In jail."

Kate was about to assure them that Brandon never jumped to conclusions, but then she remembered a time when she'd been one of his chief suspects. It hadn't been pleasant.

"So we thought we could just tell you what happened," Jason said, "and you could tell the police chief."

She looked at Jason, then at Erik. They were both grown men, intelligent, and mature, but they were acting like children right now. "He'll still need to talk to *you*. Anything I tell him will be hearsay." But even as she said it, she knew she would learn a lot more from them than they would divulge to Brandon. "Tell me what happened."

Erik shifted his eyes as he remembered. "We were just sitting there minding our own business when Gordon came in with these two other men. He saw us and marched over to where we were sitting. He accused us of colluding with you to fix the competition."

"But we didn't do or say anything," Jason added quickly, before she could react to that surprising turn.

Erik nodded. "Just took our drinks to the other end of the bar. Ayuh. So the three of them sit down at the bar and Gordon is being very vocal about losing and what a, pardon me Kate, cheesy setup this was."

Kate listened open-mouthed." That . . . I can't believe he said that."

"Don't worry, nobody believed him. Everybody was getting just a little fed up with him—"

"Jason." Erik gave him a long-suffering look.

"Then Claudine Frankel shows up."

"Who's Claudine Frankel?" Kate asked.

"You saw her yesterday. With Lott."

"Oh, the blonde?" *Who Brandon had just left with.*

"She's a . . . . particular friend of Lott's. If you know what I mean."

Kate nodded.

"At least they were the last time we saw them at the Chicago tournament, isn't that so, Jason?

"Ayuh."

"And when we saw them here, we assumed . . . . but she came into the bar with Jed Dawson—"

Jason's head bobbed. "Jed is on the Hanover team."

"Jason, if you'll just let me tell the story!"

Jason's mouth snapped shut.

"At first Lott didn't see her, and she and Jed sat down at one of the tables. Then Gordon saw her and staggered over to the table—"

"He was that drunk," Jason added.

"*Anyway,*" Erik continued. "There were words. Gordon said

something like, 'Don't think I don't know what you're up to.' He was slurring his words."

"And his sentence structure," Jason added, then shrugged apologetically. "Sorry."

"Then the two men he came in with convinced him to leave."

"Those two certainly had a busy night," Kate said. "Did one of these men happen to be Kenny Revell?"

Simultaneously, Jason and Erik's mouths dropped open.

Erik was the first to recover. "Yes. How did you know?"

"Just a wild guess." Kate sent a silent apology to logicians everywhere.

"And now Kenny has disappeared," Erik said.

"And Gordon has been murdered," added Jason.

Kate closed her eyes. She'd spent her entire day dodging questions and diffusing rumors and it hadn't made any difference. "I would be careful about making any accusations, if I were you."

"That's why we wanted to tell you instead of Chief Mitchell," wheezed Erik.

Jason nodded vigorously. "He might think we were trying to divert attention from ourselves."

"Ayuh," Erik said. "We didn't kill him, but we think that Kenny might have."

Kate put down her coffee cup. She'd been functioning solely on caffeine since late morning and her stomach was beginning to suffer for it. "Who was the other man who left with Gordon and Kenny?"

They looked at each other. "No idea. Never saw him before."

"And Claudine?"

"She was upset. Who wouldn't be? She and Jed left right after that."

Hmm, thought Kate. Claudine and Jed left the inn right after

Lott, and then again at the bar and grill. *Were they following him? For what purpose?* "What do you know about Jed Dawkins?"

"You can't think he's involved!" Jason gasped.

"Heavens, no," Erik agreed. "We've known him for ages."

How easily we forget, thought Kate. "And the other man who was with Gordon and Kenny. What did he look like?"

Jason and Erik looked at each other and shrugged.

"About medium height, not too fat, not too thin. Right, Jason?"

"Ayuh. Not fat, not thin."

"He was wearing one of those silly ski hat. The ones like a jester's hat with all those points. Looked ridiculous on a grown man."

"It was orange," Jason added.

Wonderful—a man in an orange ski hat. Like that really narrows the field. It was winter in New Hampshire.

"We stayed at the bar for another half hour. Obadiah came in and we had another round."

"I didn't," Jason said quickly. "I was driving."

"Then we left. Jason dropped me off and went straight home."

"Straight home," Jason echoed.

"Anything else?"

Both men shook their heads, their relief plain on their faces.

"Alright. I'll speak to Chief Mitchell, but he'll want to talk to you. And everyone else who was in the bar," Kate added quickly. "So stop worrying and go concentrate on winning the final."

Jason stood up. "Thank you, Katie."

"We knew we could count on you. Ayuh." Erik levered himself out of the booth.

Kate watched them climb the stairs, wondering how she was gong to explain being the official grapevine spokesperson to Brandon.

She nearly jumped out of her skin when Harry slid out of the next booth.

"Jeez—"

"Language," Harry said, grinning.

"How long have you been here?"

"Since right after you sat down. Didn't see me, did you?"

"No," Kate admitted. And Brandon would kill them both if they attempted any sleuthing.

"You shouldn't lead witnesses."

"I didn't. Did I? I didn't have a choice."

"I know," Harry said sympathetically. "They don't trust the chief. I wish everybody would just cut him a break. He's not so bad once you get to know him."

Kate heard the wistfulness in his voice and her perturbation evaporated. No way would she let Brandon send him away.

"Harry, we *really* must. Not. Get. Involved."

"Why not? We're good at it."

"We are. But we shouldn't be. I have a museum to run. You have school—"

"School's boring."

"I know. I've been there, remember? But you really, really need to make the best of it."

His excitement vanished. "Why?"

"Just because."

"He's going to dump me, isn't he?"

"No, Harry. Don't worry." She wished she could ask him what was going on between him and the chief. Or if the chief was just tired of the responsibility. He hadn't bargained for a permanent situation. Either way she would not let this boy be foisted off to a boarding school or foster care.

"Everything's going to be fine." She would make it fine—somehow.

"AT LEAST IT isn't snowing again—yet," Kate said as she and Pru stood looking out the front window of the VFW hall.

"I just can't believe it," Pru said.

"Me neither, but small blessings."

"Katie. That's no way to speak of the dead."

Kate stared at her aunt. "What are you talking about?"

"That poor Gordon Lott. Who knew someone that strong and healthy looking could have a bad heart." Pru shook her head. "And he would have been perfect for you. So no more talking about blessings. *Really.*"

"I was talking about the snow holding off."

"Oh, were you?" Pru looked out the window again. "Well, it won't hold off for long. Look at those clouds."

Kate had already seen them. Huge, black behemoths that seemed to hang over the parking lot, just waiting.

"We'll just have to keep our fingers crossed. Now, you'd better go home and change for the evening session. Wear something nice."

"I brought clothes from home. They're downstairs."

Pru sighed. "I suppose it's another one of those pantsuits. Really, Katie. As soon as this is over, we're going to go over to Lily Loves and buy you a new wardrobe. Something feminine for spring."

Spring, thought Kate. It seemed really far away. What were the chances that Pru would forget about their proposed shopping expedition by then? Kate was already the less-than-proud owner of several new outfits courtesy of Aunt Pru. A white long-sleeve polyester blouse with a huge bow at the neck. A black mid-calf-length dress that she wore to the professor's funeral and that she would never wear again. And a fuchsia double knit skirt and matching scoop neck sweater that was still in the box under her bed.

She knew Pru wouldn't be thrilled with the gray pantsuit she was going to wear tonight. It was exactly the same as the black pants suit she'd worn yesterday, professional and serious looking. As a rule mathematicians didn't go in for frills. At least Kate didn't.

And sure enough, when she came upstairs after changing, her hair regelled and pinned tightly back from her face, Pru took one look and pursed her lips in disapproval.

Fortunately the entrance hall was packed and Kate managed to thread through the crowd and get to the main hall without having to face her aunt.

The crowd was more boisterous than usual. Tournaments were always fun weekends. There were friends who'd met at a tournament and only saw each other a few times each year when they were competing. There were lots of eating, drinking, and partying. But inside the puzzle room, things became serious.

Usually talk centered around numerical versus literal puzzles, the difference between trial and error and pattern recognition, or whether the introduction of Kakuro and other spin-off games had diluted the puzzle industry.

Tonight, conversation was all about Gordon Lott.

Everyone seemed to be discussing his demise.

"I heard he was murdered."

"No, no, It was a heart attack. Poor man froze to death."

Or speculating on the whereabouts of Kenny Revell.

"He never misses a competition. He must be sick."

"I saw him Friday night and he looked fine."

"He's just dropped off the face of the earth."

"His car is still at the Bowsman Inn. What do you think it means?"

Or opining about the investigation.

"Have you seen this police force? One chief of police and a couple of boys."

"They'll have to send in someone from the state to take over. The chief of police has got to be in over his head. I mean, how many murders can a town of this size have?"

Kate almost stopped to correct their misconception of Brandon. He'd been a Boston detective before accepting the job of Granville chief of police last year. He knew about solving murders.

It would be a real slap in Brandon's face if they brought in someone over his head. And wouldn't the inhabitants of Granville love that?

Kate knew the chief would deal with that like he did with everything else, unemotionally. Nothing seemed to ruffle him, except Kate.

She watched Tony take his place at the podium. He, unlike the chief, was easy to work with. He hadn't complained once since he'd been there. He'd handled the announcement of Gordon Lott's death with aplomb and passed gracefully on to the events of the night.

Now he was joking about the weather, though they both knew it was no joke. Tony was from Minneapolis.

The D-level final began. Trophies were presented and they moved on to the C-level final.

It was during the break before the B final that Pru finally caught up to Kate and pulled her aside. "That snot-potty police chief we hired lied to you. Ayuh. Just what you'd expect from him. Gordon Lott did not have a heart attack. He was *murdered*."

"Murder" came out like the eerie voice of an old radio show announcer. "Shot." Pru went on sharply. "I told you not to trust him. Lying to honest people. . ."

Kate had been expecting this. Someone in the EMT squad or the hospital or Mike Landers was bound to let things leak out. Now she had a moral dilemma, something you didn't have to deal with in abstract numbers. Confess that she'd known it was murder, and add fuel to Pru's fire? Or continue to let Pru think Brandon had lied to her. She opted for round-about-ation. "What on earth makes you suspect that?"

"Elmira heard it from Doris Plumley, Dr. Jessup's receptionist. They called him over to County General to do the autopsy."

"If that's so," Kate said, "the chief probably didn't want anyone to know, considering how difficult everyone made his investigation last time."

"Pooh, if he can't take the heat, he should get out of the kitchen." Pru snorted. "Just wait 'til I tell the others."

"Aunt Pru! *No.* You'll be obstructing an investigation."

"Horsewaddle. And you stay away from Mr. Know-it-all. I knew no good would come from hiring an outsider. The Council insisted they'd need somebody with experience because of the new mall.

Now we don't have a mall, but we do have a persnickety police chief. They oughta just send him back down there where he came from."

"Why do you dislike him so much?"

Pru looked surprised. "Why? Because he isn't one of us. Doesn't understand how things work around here. We've had nothing but trouble since he came. If you ask me, he brought all this murder business with him."

"Aunt Pru, that isn't fair."

"Time will tell." Pru pointed a thin finger at Kate. "You just make sure he keeps his distance."

Young lady, Kate added silently.

Kate knew things would rapidly deteriorate if she didn't do something. She'd start with the GABs.

She walked with Pru back to the registration desk. "Ladies, you're doing a great job." *Always start with a compliment.* She remembered that from the Building People Skills book she was reading.

The GABs all smiled at her.

"Why, thank you, Katie," said Alice.

"Our pleasure," said Elmira.

"Is it true that Gordon Lott was murdered?" Carrie Blaine shouted from her end of the table.

"Turn up your hearing aid and stop yelling," Alice yelled back at her.

Carrie poked at her ear. "Is it true?"

Kate started to deny it, then remembered another pointer in the book. *Make others a part of your plan.*

She moved close to the group. They all leaned forward. "Yes." She didn't want them asking for details. "I don't know the details, but I need you to help me. If this gets out, people might panic and want their money back. The tournament could be *ruined.*"

Six pairs of eyes rounded owlishly.

"So if you could help me keep rumors from flying, we might just make it through the weekend without losing our shirts. I hate to ask, but—"

"Don't you worry about a thing, Katie," Elmira said. "The GABs are on the case."

"That's right," Alice said. "The man died of *a heart attack.*" She shot a pointed look at Pru.

"Oh, alright, he died of a heart attack."

"Thanks," Kate said. "I knew I could count on you."

"We'll spread the word." Alice pushed herself up from her chair. Several minutes later, Kate watched the Granny Activist Brigade separate in all directions. Carrie and Tanya to the vendor's room. Pru to the canteen. Alice, Elmira, and Maria Albioni into the main hall.

Kate wasn't sure if she'd done a good thing or a bad thing. In math, if you changed one number, a plus or minus sign, or one tiny decimal point, the results could be catastrophically different. One wrong number in a Sudoku grid would have a domino effect on all the others.

Had she disrupted the normal course of the investigation?

Maybe, but at least it might stymie the gossip. What she'd set in motion couldn't be undone. She'd just have to wait and see the results. Until now, she'd followed the chief's orders and it hadn't done one bit of good. Maybe this would.

She just hoped the chief didn't hear about it.

By the time the A Division competitors took their places, Kate was beside herself with anxiety. At least the speculation about Gordon Lott's death had seemed to die down. The GABs had done their job well.

Claudine Frankel had returned to the hall and was sitting in the gallery, watching the competition. She didn't act like a woman whose boyfriend had just died.

Kate looked around for the chief, but she didn't see him in the main hall.

Jason and Erik were sitting at their places at the table waiting for the final A round to begin. They were both intent and concentrating; not the anxious men she'd talked with that afternoon.

She hadn't seen Harry all evening. She just hoped he wasn't playing amateur sleuth. She'd been firm with him today, but teenagers didn't always pay attention. His penchant for codes and ciphers was bringing him all too close to a cloak-and-dagger attitude toward life.

When the winners of the A Division final were announced, Marian Teasdale, the museum's president, joined Tony and Kate to hand out the awards. First place was taken by Jed Dawkins of the Hanover team, though even with his win, Gordon Lott's penalty points would knock them out of qualifying for the team finals. Second place went to a Barb Huttner from the Cambridge team; Jason Elks took third.

The three of them would compete in the sudden death final on Sunday morning. Then the team standings would be announced. At least with the Hanover team docked by mistakes, Granville's Arcane Masters had a chance of being among the three highest scorers.

Kate was exhausted by the time she pulled into her driveway that night. The storm had held off, but the streets were icy and it took all of her energy to navigate safely through the town.

She dropped her clothes over a chair, pulled the barrettes out of her hair, and climbed into bed. She fell instantly into a dreamless sleep.

The telephone rang; Kate jolted upright, blinking into the darkness.

It was two a.m. according to her alarm clock. Only something dire would make someone call this late. Praying that nothing had happened to her dad or Aunt Pru, she rushed down the hall to answer the phone.

"Katie?"

"Yes?" Kate didn't recognize the voice.

"It's Nancy Vance."

"Nancy?" Kate repeatedly stupidly. Why was the proprietor of the Bowsman Inn calling her in the middle of the night? *Not another death, please.* "What is it? Has something happened?"

"There's someone in Gordon Lott's room."

Kate slumped with relief, then straightened up. *The murderer?*

"Did you call nine-one-one?"

"No."

"Then do it. Get to safety first and call them."

"I can't. I mean, I'm safe. I'm in the apartment over the garage. That's how I know someone's in there. I saw their flashlight."

"Good. Stay there. And call the police."

"I can't. John is still in Nashua. The roads were too icy to get back. I've had to do everything myself. And what with staying over the garage instead of in the inn with the guests . . . I don't know how I did it, but I left my key ring on the registration counter. I know it was stupid, but I can't call the police. What if Chief Mitchell finds me guilty of negligence or something? We might get sued. We could lose the inn. You have to help me. Please. I wouldn't ask, but with John gone—"

"Nancy, calm down."

"I'm sorry. I shouldn't have called. Forget it. I'll just go see who it is—"

"No!" Kate yelled. "It could be someone dangerous. They could be armed. Do *not* go into that house alone."

"Then you'll come? I hate to ask. But I'd feel better if you were with me. Safety in numbers and all that."

Right, thought Kate. It seemed to be the catchphrase of the weekend.

"Please, Kate. We'll just see who it is. And then if we need to, we'll call the police."

Kate sighed. She wanted to assure Nancy that the chief would understand. But he wouldn't. *He's probably never left his keys anywhere.*

Kate made one more try. "You don't have to tell him about the keys. Just say someone is in the room."

"But if he catches them and they tell him they found the keys, no telling what he'll do."

Why couldn't people just put their faith in the new police chief? He was good at his job, too good for some people's tastes. Unfortunately, he wasn't much of a people person.

And what about me? Kate thought. She hadn't trusted him to solve the professor's murder, but she wouldn't make that mistake again.

"What if I call him for you?"

"No! But you don't have to come over. I shouldn't have asked. I'm sorry I woke you up."

There was a click and Kate was listening to a dial tone.

If she went to the inn, Brandon would be angry—and hurt that she still didn't trust his abilities. But if she called him, Nancy would think she'd gone over to "the other side" and pretty soon the whole town would be calling her a traitor. Aunt Pru would never forgive her. Then she'd be on the outside looking in—again.

With a sinking heart, she dressed in jeans and her snow boots, grabbed her car coat and gloves from the closet and headed outside.

The air hit her face like slivers of glass. The windshield was covered in a coating of ice. She turned on the defroster full blast and began the tiresome job of scraping away the ice.

It was twelve minutes before she reached the inn. She parked next to the garage and got out, hoping that the intruder was long gone and she would find Nancy safe in the apartment upstairs.

Someone moved out of the shadows. Kate let out a squeak and jumped back.

"S-sorry. It's j-just me." Nancy said through chattering teeth. She pulled Kate into the shadow of the garage. She pointed to a second story window of the inn. A beam of light glanced off the pane and disappeared. "H-he's still there."

Nancy grabbed Kate by the sleeve and pulled her across the parking lot to the front door. Her hand shook so much that she could hardly unlock the door. "Not scared," she assured Kate. "Just cold."

Reluctantly, Kate slipped inside behind her. The hall lamps were lit and they cast eerie shadows over the period furnishings.

"There it is," whispered Nancy and hurried to snatch the key ring from the counter. She dropped it into her coat pocket, then looked at Kate. "Now what?"

Kate was pretty sure this wasn't the normal kind of thing friends were called on to do, but she'd gone too far to turn back. If they waited any longer, the intruder would escape, and they would only have their word that he had ever existed.

Or worse. He might catch them red-handed.

She motioned for Nancy to come closer, then whispered in her ear, "Did the police come back today with the search warrant?"

Nancy nodded. "The chief came himself. He went into both rooms—Mr. Lott's and Mr. Revell's."

Why would someone bother to break in now? It had to be a thief taking advantage of the empty room. If the chief had searched the room, any incriminating evidence would be bagged, sealed, and sitting in the state forensic lab.

"Does everyone know about the search?"

"No. They were all at the tournament when he came."

Of course, thought Kate. The man was no dummy.

But Kate had a sneaking suspicion that she and Nancy were the dummies.

Whoever was up there, burglar or murderer, they didn't know the room had been searched. She and Nancy couldn't just go upstairs and surprise them. They might be desperate. Kate didn't want to be a statistic. She wanted to run a puzzle museum.

"Is there someplace upstairs where we can hide? Where we can watch from and not have to confront the person?"

Nancy nodded, leaning close to Kate. "Broom closet." She grabbed Kate's hand and together they crept up the stairs.

When they got to second floor, Nancy pointed down the hall to a door on the right. "That's Mr. Lott's room," she whispered. She pulled Kate toward a door on the left and they crammed themselves into the closet. There was hardly room to move. The small space was filled with brooms, mops, and cleaning supplies, if they kept the door open just a couple of inches, they could see the door to Gordon's room.

"Don't make a sound," Kate whispered. "We'll identify him and make sure he's gone before we come out."

Nancy nodded. They stood squished together, afraid to move. It seemed like an eternity before the door to Gordon's room finally opened. They both jumped. A mop fell and hit Kate in the head.

She bit back an "ouch" and caught the handle before it clattered against the wall.

Across the hall, a head appeared in the open doorway. The intruder peered down the hall and cautiously stepped into the dimly lit passage.

Kate's eyes were trained on the intruder's hands, looking for a weapon. One hand held the flashlight. The other was empty. They were feminine hands. Surprised, but relieved, Kate looked up and saw the sheen of blonde hair.

"That's Claudine Frankel," Nancy gasped. "I *knew* she wasn't staying in her own room. If they were going to shack up together, they should have released the room so someone else could use it, instead of having to drive out to the highway for accommodations. And in all that snow last night."

Claudine closed the door and began to tiptoe down the hall. She was wearing a blue bathrobe, and both pockets were bulging. Kate could see the tip of a nylon undergarment hanging out of one of them. Well, at least they knew what Claudine had been searching for.

"Would you look at that?" Nancy jumped out of the closet. "Ms. Frankel."

Claudine started, looked wildly around as if she were thinking about running. Kate stepped into the hall next to Nancy.

Then Claudine recognized them and whooshed out a sigh of relief. "Christ, you two nearly scared the shit out of me."

"Just what were you doing in Mr. Lott's room?" demanded Nancy, obviously no longer afraid. Kate hoped she wasn't being premature.

Claudine put her fingers to her lips and hurried toward them. "Do you want to wake everyone up?"

"We want you to answer Nancy's question," Kate said.

Claudine bit her lip.

She's going to lie, thought Kate.

"I will, but could we go downstairs and have a drink maybe?"

Okay, maybe she wasn't going to lie. Kate really wished she could read people better; she didn't want to end up dead. But Nancy ran an inn. She must know people, and she didn't seem afraid.

"Okay," Kate said. "You go first and keep your hands where we can see them."

Claudine nodded, then preceded them down the stairs, arms held out by her sides like a tightrope walker.

When they reached the first floor, Claudine turned toward the bar.

"The kitchen," Nancy said. "I'll heat some milk."

Claudine rolled her eyes.

"Oh, alright. Back in a minute." Nancy went into the bar and Kate held the kitchen door for Claudine to enter.

Claudine hesitated. "Look, I know what you're thinking. . ."

That would be a feat, thought Kate, because she wasn't sure what to think. She motioned Claudine inside.

Nancy returned with a bottle of house wine and three glasses. Claudine started to sit down at the long farmer's table.

Kate stopped her. "I'm afraid that before you sit down, you need to empty your pockets. Slowly. Nancy, stand behind her."

Nancy looked surprised but did as she was told.

"Really, girls, this is so stupid."

"Would you rather I called the police?"

Claudine shook her head. Behind her, Nancy shook hers. Kate gritted her teeth.

"This is so embarrassing." Claudine started emptying her pockets. "You probably know that Gordy and I were—you *know.*"

Kate could guess, but she didn't answer. She just kept her eyes on Claudine's hands. Claudine might be trying to distract her while she reached for a weapon. Because if anybody looked like the grieving girlfriend, it wasn't Claudine.

Claudine shrugged. Slowly, she pulled a nylon camisole out of her pocket and laid it on the table. A red thong followed, then a pair of black lace garters.

Kate was beginning to wish she hadn't asked for this show and tell. She was really glad they hadn't called the chief.

Nancy was practically breathing down Claudine's neck to get a better look.

When one pocket was empty, Claudine pulled it inside out. "See?"

"The other one," Kate said, though she didn't want to see more.

Out came several small bottles of oil and lotions.

"What's all that for?" asked Nancy.

Claudine sputtered. "You're kidding, right?"

Nancy looked at Kate.

"I'll tell you later," Kate said quickly. *Much later, like never.* "Is that all?"

Claudine nodded. "So you can see why I didn't want the police to find them. I mean, Gordy and I used to be an item. But we are *so* over. We just hooked up this weekend because . . . well, because it was convenient. But we weren't heavy or anything.

"I mean, we were never really that close. I'm sorry he's dead and all, but hey, I hardly knew him."

Kate was getting confused. Had Claudine suddenly started talking like a valley girl?

"But still, that hunky police chief took me away for questioning. He actually implied that I had killed Gordy in a fit of jealousy. I guess he saw Gordy flirting with you last night."

"Me?" asked Kate, taken off guard.

"Yeah. He thought it might have been a crime of passion."

Brandon had noticed Gordon flirting with her? Kate hadn't even noticed that Gordon was flirting with her.

"I mean, you're nice-looking and everything, but Gordy flirted with everybody. And like if I was jealous enough to kill, hell, I'd've killed you instead of Gordy."

Nancy gasped.

Kate just stared.

"He's kind of cute, your chief of police." "Do you know if he's married?"

Kate was ready to slap the woman. Her boyfriend, ex or not, was dead and she was getting ready to hit on the chief?

"He's single," Nancy said.

Kate glared at her. They were the ones who were supposed to be asking the questions.

Claudine knocked back her glass of wine, filled her glass again and reached for the things on the table.

"You'll have to put them back where you found them," said Nancy.

"No way! It would be too embarrassing. They'll probably search Gordy's room."

"They already have." Kate had the satisfaction of seeing Claudine's face go slack.

"The police?"

"The chief of police," Nancy said.

After a moment, Claudine smiled. Slyly.

Kate didn't like the look of that at all. "We'll have to tell him that we caught you going through Gordon's things."

"If you must, you must." Claudine glanced at the items lying on the table. "I'm sure Chief Mitchell will understand." She flashed them another one of her sly smiles. "Good night." She took her wine glass and walked out the door.

"I should throw her out of the inn, right now."

"I wish you would," Kate said. "But don't. The chief will want to question her further." She looked up at the wall clock. Three a.m. "But not now."

"Katie, was that witch making some kind of double entendre about Chief Mitchell? He might rub people the wrong way, but he doesn't strike me as the type to go in for . . . that sort of thing." Nancy waved at the items on table.

Kate wasn't even going there. "If you're okay, I'm going home to bed. Promise me you'll call the chief about this in the morning."

"Katie—"

"I don't think Claudine will mention anything about the keys. I bet she used Gordon's."

CHAPTER
EIGHT

KATE WATCHED BRANDON Mitchell stride toward her, looking as dark as the storm clouds that gathered outside the VFW window. She put down her sticky bun and coffee and prepared to face the music.

"What were you thinking?" he snapped as soon as he'd reached her.

Kate frowned back at him. Which one of the many things she'd been thinking was he talking about? "That the snow is starting again?"

He glowered at her. "Nancy Vance called the station this morning."

"Oh."

"Oh," he echoed. "She should have called last night."

"I know. I wanted her to. She . . . she was afraid to."

She steeled herself for an explosion that didn't come.

"Then why didn't *you* call me? Jesus, you could have been killed."

"I know. I'm sorry. But . . . you don't understand."

He just looked at her and she had to fight the urge to squirm under his accusing eyes. He was almost as good as Aunt Pru at making her feel guilty.

He glanced past her out the window. "Unfortunately, I do understand."

This was even worse than his anger. He couldn't even look at her. He thought she had taken her stand against him.

"No. You don't."

"And I never will, because I'm not one of you. Fine, so be it. But I have a job to do and I'll do it, whether you people want me to or not."

"We're not *you people*." Kate was feeling a little angry herself. Why didn't he try harder to be liked? "Some of these families have lived here since the Revolution."

"Yeah. I know the psychology. Your aversion to strangers is almost a cliché."

"Hell, you'll never fit in with that kind of attitude."

He smiled grimly. "Got you where it hurts? Bigotry isn't exactly logical thinking, is it?"

"How dare you! We're not bigoted. Just . . . stodgy."

"So what did you learn from Ms. Frankel?" he asked, switching tactics.

Kate's cheeks, which had just begun to cool, heated up again. "Not much. At first . . ." She had to clear her throat. "She was very self-assured, assumed that Nancy and I, being women, would side with her."

"About what?"

She took a breath. "She'd taken some things out of Gordon's

room. Uh, personal things. She didn't know the police had already searched the room and she was embarrassed for them to be found. They were, uh . . ."

"I saw them."

The blood rushed to Kate's cheeks. Of course he had. He'd questioned Claudine. He'd been the one who searched Gordon's room. She glanced up at him.

He was trying not to smile.

Kate blushed hotter.

"So did you learn anything? Or is that confidential, being girl talk and everything."

She didn't miss the sarcasm. And they were attracting an audience.

"Could we please do this somewhere a little more private?"

"Get your coat."

Great. They would turn to blocks of ice while he questioned her. She retrieved her jacket from the coat check and Brandon ushered her outside.

"Where's your hat?" He was smiling again.

So glad I'm such a source of amusement. "I left it at home."

"Then put up your hood."

She did, but she noticed he didn't put on his hat. And he didn't zip up his jacket. Mr. Macho Police Chief. Probably an intimidation technique. Well, she was too cold to be intimidated.

A man hurried past them on his way inside. He was wearing an orange ski hat.

"Oh," Kate gasped.

"What?"

She shook her head. Had he talked to Erik and Jason? Their final round was coming up first thing this morning. And it wouldn't be fair for the chief to rattle them before they had a chance to compete.

"Kate."

"Yes?"

"What aren't you telling me? What did Frankel say?"

That she thought you were hunky? "Nothing much. As soon as she saw we weren't buying the 'just us girls' routine, she switched to valley girl. Said, 'you know' and 'like' a bunch of times. As if she were twenty instead of thirty-something."

"Noticed that, did you?"

Kate ignored him. She just wanted to get back inside where it was warm. "The upshot was that they weren't going together anymore and had just hooked up for the weekend out of . . . convenience." At least this time her flushed cheeks could be attributed to the cold. "And that she didn't even really like him that much. And Nancy made her leave the . . . things . . . and we let her go."

Another group of people passed. More ski hats, one with the pointed shape that Erik and Jason had described, but it was blue.

"What aren't you telling me?"

"Nothing."

His expression was hard, maybe a little hurt. "Is this going to be an 'us' versus 'him' kind of thing?"

"No. You know I wouldn't—It's just—" That she was stuck right in the middle again.

He waited.

"If you must know, Jason and Erik asked me to disqualify Gordon."

"I thought he was disqualified."

"That was after we'd found a mistake in his puzzle. They asked me to disqualify him Friday night before the competition."

"Why?"

"Because they said he was a cheater." She repeated what Jason and Erik had told her about Gordon Lott. "I told them I couldn't disqualify him without proof. Maybe I should have. Maybe he would still be alive."

"Are you saying you think Ingersoll and Elks killed him?"

"No. Of course not."

"Then what?"

She hesitated. If she had just told him about her conversation with Erik and Jason as soon as he asked, he would have dismissed it as gossip. But now that he'd had to drag it out of her, it seemed damning. Unfortunately, she had no choice but to tell him what they'd said. And she felt like a traitor. "They were upset. They said they would take care of it themselves."

She grabbed his arm. She could see what he was thinking— exactly what she knew he would think. "But they didn't mean murder him. I saw them arguing with Lott later. But they left the hall after that."

She stopped. They had also been at the bar and grill that night when Gordon came in. They'd still been there when Gordon left. Did the chief know that?

Of course he did. But she was going to tell him first, before he could accuse her of holding out on him.

"They went to the Granville Bar and Grill after the end of the competition. I guess there was a slight altercation."

"Uh-huh."

A flake of snow dropped onto his hair. Seconds later, the world turned white.

"Not yet!" moaned Kate.

"We'd better get inside." Brandon took her arm.

"You know Jason and Erik had nothing to do with murder. They couldn't."

"Because they're local boys? You seem to forget that one of your townspeople committed murder just a few months ago."

As if she could ever forget. But this was different. She turned on him. His face was blurred by a thick curtain of snowflakes. It gave her the courage to say what she felt.

"You know, Chief Mitchell, if you'd stop thinking of them as *my* townspeople and start treating them as *your* townspeople, you might get more cooperation from them. It's not a contest. We're all in this town together. And if you could figure that out, you might find a place for yourself here.

"Now, I have a tournament to run, so if you've finished questioning me." She didn't wait for a reply, but pulled away and hurried up the steps to the door.

He reached it before her. "I'm trying."

Her anger fell away. "I know." He opened the door and she stepped inside. The hall was crowded with people waiting to turn over their outerwear. Next year, they'd have to get a better system for checking coats. Downstairs maybe, or a bigger venue.

Kate pushed back her hood and unzipped her coat. She felt it lift from her shoulders. The chief was helping her out of her coat. A pleasant warmth rushed through her, then she quickly looked around for Pru. Fortunately, there were too many people between her and the registration table for her aunt to see them.

"Thank you." She handed her coat over to the teenager behind the table. Brandon kept his, but he followed her across the room. The GABs stopped what they were doing to stare.

Kate sighed.

"Why did Alice Hinckley just wink at me?"

"What?" Kate glanced over to Alice, who gave her an innocent smile. "Maybe she was flirting with you." She could have kicked herself. What a stupid thing to say.

Fortunately, the chief's reaction was strictly deadpan.

He'd once ticketed Alice for selling her homemade jams without a food handler's license. She countered by telling him that he could eat off her kitchen floor and refused to pay. She now sold them on the sly. Kate was pretty sure Brandon knew this and had decided to turn a blind eye.

Maybe he *was* trying.

Alice and the rest of the group had staunched the gossip about Gordon because Kate had asked them to, but they had helped out the chief, too.

And now Alice had winked at him. Maybe this weekend would be a turning point.

Feeling better, Kate went into the main hall. The crowd of spectators had dwindled. A lot of them had left early to beat the storm. Those who were left were sitting in rows of chairs that had replaced the tables from Saturday's larger competition.

Three huge dry-erase boards were placed on easels on the stage. They were covered by squares of navy blue canvas. The three-Level A finalists would solve their puzzles with the spectators looking on.

Tony stood at the podium that had been moved to stage right. "Welcome to the last and final round for the Top Avondale Tournament winner. Will the finalists please take their places? Mr. Jed Dawson of the Hanover, New Hampshire, Sudoku Club; Mr. Jason Elks of the Arcane Masters, Granville, New Hampshire; and Miss Barb Huttner from the Cambridge Mass Puzzlers."

The three finalists took their places in front of the easels. They were each handed a pair of soundproof headphones, just in case someone got excited and blurted out an answer.

"Take up your pens." They each picked up and uncapped one of the dry-erase pens that rested in the easel tray, then stood at the ready. A volunteer stood to the side of each easel, ready to tear away the canvas cover.

"This round will be twenty minutes long." The digital clock lit up. "Are the competitors ready?"

The three nodded.

"Then, on your mark. Get set. Go."

The canvas was ripped away. The spectators leaned forward and the finalists settled their headphones and began to scan and cross-hatch at a furious pace. For a few seconds they stayed neck and neck as numbers were hastily written in. Smaller numbers began to line up across the top of each cell, the candidates for potential placement that would be erased as their position in the cell, row, or column was ruled out.

Barb Huttner took an early lead, filling in numbers with slashes of her pen. Kate was following her progress as avidly as any of the spectators. Then she wrote in a seven in the third line of the fifth box.

Wrong, Kate thought. Barb quickly erased the seven, rewrote it in the candidate space, and went on.

Jason's pen hovered unmoving over his puzzle. Kate could practically see his mind counting and reducing, analyzing the chain of possibilities.

Then the Hanover contender, Jed Dawson, seemed to have a breakthrough. There was a flurry of writing as he entered a quick succession of numbers, nodding his head each time he competed a cell.

Jason's pen began to move again.

Kate glanced at the clock. Five minutes had elapsed. At the rate they were going, they should finish well within the allotted time.

As the grids filled up and the empty cells became sparse, the speed accelerated.

People craned their necks to get a better view. Kate moved closer. Next year, they would have to set up a projection system and display the puzzles higher for those seated in back.

Jason had taken the lead. Kate worked along with him. Then his pen faltered. *Three*, she thought. *Three in line six, cell four.*

As if he'd read her mind, Jason filled in the three.

Suddenly Kate remembered Gordon Lott looking at his watch and filling in numbers. Almost as if he'd been reading the numbers there.

It was impossible. Only a computer could have finished that puzzle as quickly as Gordon had, and there was no way to hook up to a computer and send and receive data that quickly, even if he'd figured out a way to photograph and transmit the puzzle. Besides, he'd blown the second puzzle. That had been a genuine mistake.

So why was he murdered? And where was his watch?

Barb Huttner's hand went up. She stepped away from the easel. Fourteen minutes and forty-one seconds had elapsed.

After another twenty-two seconds, Jason raised his hand and stepped back. Jed Dawson finished ten seconds later. The Hanover team was not going to go home happy.

The finalists returned to their seats. The scorers took their places before the easels. They studied each puzzle, compared it to the master copy. Checked and rechecked and finally handed a slip of paper to Tony.

Kate hurried to the stage to hand out the trophies and prize money. She took her place next to Marian Teasdale.

Marian gave her a quick smile. "We did it."

Kate let out a long breath.

"And here to present the awards to the top three individual competitors is Kate McDonald, curator of the Avondale Puzzle Museum and the tournament's organizer, and Marian Teasdale, president of the board of directors for the museum." Tony turned toward them and started the applause.

Kate came to stand behind the podium, took a deep breath, and glanced down at the names of the winners, who placed just as they had finished. No mistakes. No surprises. *Thank heaven for small favors.*

"Third place winner is Jed Dawson of the Hanover Sudoku Club." Jed came onto the stage to applause. He ducked his head while Marian placed a bronze medal around his neck and handed him a check for two hundred dollars. He shook her hand and departed.

"Second place goes to Jason Elks from the Arcane Masters of Granville, New Hampshire." Jason grinned at Kate as he trotted across the stage to collect his medal and prize money.

"And first place in the single competitor A division is Ms. Barb Huttner of the Cambridge Puzzlers." Barb took her winnings and stopped to shake Kate's hand before leaving the stage.

Tony waited for the applause to die out, then announced the team scores. As expected, Hanover had been knocked out of third place due to Gordon's mistake in the A Division. Cambridge took first place, the Arcane Masters, second. The Hartford, Connecticut, and Providence, Rhode Island, teams moved into third and fourth place ahead of the Hanover group.

"This concludes the weekend activities. Wasn't this a great tournament?"

The reaction was vocal and loud. They'd all seemed to have had a good time. Kate was pleased and relieved. From the planning to the organization to the scheduling, everything had gone exactly to plan—except for the snowstorm and the murder of Gordon Lott.

"Drive safely and we'll see you next year, if not before." Tony flicked off the mike. "Not bad for a first," he told Kate.

Kate breathed a deep sigh of relief.

"Congratulations," Marian added. "It was a huge success."

Kate nodded, watching as the crowd pressed through the back doors to retrieve coats and hats and head for home. "We'll be able to put new carpeting down now."

Marian laughed. "Not one to rest on her laurels, our Katie."

"Excellent weekend," Tony said.

"Thanks," Kate said. "A lot of the credit goes to you."

Tony nodded his thanks.

"Are you going to try to get to the airport? Ginny Sue said she'd drive you. She must be—yes, she's on her way over here. You might be able to make it before it closes down."

"Actually, I've decided to stay on for a few days. Lovely inn. Can't think of a nicer place to be snowed in."

He smiled and Kate realized he was smiling at Ginny Sue. Ginny Sue smiled back. *Good heavens, it is a romance.* Kate smiled, too. Everyone was smiling.

"Great," Kate said. Since Tony would be around for a few days, he could help her figure out how Gordon had mucked up his puzzle so badly. She just couldn't let go of the idea that his murder had been triggered by that last big mistake.

The hall was rapidly clearing out. Harry and two other boys rolled carts onto the floor and began folding up chairs and packing them away.

Izzy Carmichael and Benjamin Meany were collecting cups, paper plates, and other trash and stuffing them into big black garbage bags.

The men from the equipment rental store began rolling up cable. Everyone was in a hurry to finish before the storm really hit.

Kate followed the last of the participants into the foyer. There was still a mob around the coat check. Several GAB members were helping the two teenage girls distribute the coats. The registration table was cleared except for a cardboard box of extra forms, pencils, and hand stamps.

A vendor steered her cart of merchandise out of the minuscule elevator and zigzagged through the throng. If they really did have a second annual tournament, Kate would have to figure out better logistics for traffic flow.

Rayette came up the stairs. "The vendors are gone. I've packed up my perishables, but we'll have to leave the rest. It's coming down big time."

Kate had been watching the window and they were in a serious whiteout. It wouldn't be safe to stay any longer.

The outer door opened and snow swirled in along with Chief Mitchell.

"You'll all have to leave now." "The roads are close to impassible. I have two county vans outside to take you home."

"But what about all these garbage bags?" Alice asked.

He motioned for everyone's attention. "You'll have to leave them. Put any containing organic matter by the basement door and I'll have one of my men take it to the dumpster."

"He means foodstuffs," Alice interpreted for the others and shook her head, but she let the chief escort her to the door where Officer Curtis was waiting.

At first, Pru insisted on staying behind with Kate. But the chief for once had the final word, and she climbed into the van with the others.

Only Kate, Harry, and the chief were left in the building.

"Close up and we'll drive you home."

"I have my car," Kate said.

"You won't get it out of the parking lot. You'll have to leave it here."

Kate didn't argue, but sent Harry and the chief to make sure all the doors and windows were locked. Kate checked the bar, the vendors' room, and both bathrooms and lowered the thermostat to fifty-eight degrees before putting on her coat and going outside where Brandon and Harry were waiting.

Already the new snowfall was up to her hubcaps. There was a layer of ice beneath the fresh snowfall, and just walking without falling was an effort.

There was a black SUV parked at the base of the steps.

Brandon hurried them toward it. He opened the front door for Kate, and Harry climbed in back.

"Yours?" she asked.

"Mine," said the chief and shut the door.

Kate didn't know how the chief could see to drive. A swirling curtain of white surrounded the SUV as they crept down the street.

"This is going to be a big one," said Harry from the back seat.

Kate leaned back against the seat and closed her eyes.

"Tired?"

She turned her head to look at the chief. "A bit. I'm just glad it's over. And . . . I'm sorry that it caused you so much trouble."

He kept his eyes on the road. "Not your fault."

Kate closed her eyes again.

They arrived at her bungalow without Kate realizing it. She must have dozed off. "Thanks, Harry. You were a big help. I couldn't have done it without you."

Harry just nodded, then her door was opened and the chief loomed in the opening. Kate grabbed her bag and got out. "Get back in the car. I'll be fine."

He ignored her, of course. Just held her elbow as they made their way across what was left of the path to her porch. Kate knew Pru would be watching for her. She just hoped the snow was coming down too heavily for her to see who'd brought her home.

"Good night, and thanks," Kate said when she was standing safely inside.

Brandon dipped his chin. "I'll see to your car when the storm passes."

"Thanks. For everything." Kate watched from the door as he backed the SUV out of the driveway and onto the street. Before he'd even reached the corner, the car had disappeared behind a curtain of white.

Kate closed the door. It was over. After all the weeks of preparations, the juggling of schedules and volunteers, ordering food and equipment, the excitement, the nerves, the hurried cleanup, she suddenly felt dead tired.

She thought about Harry and Brandon snowed in together for the next few days and wondered if they would get on each other's nerves.

She would be alone—which was good. She could catch up on her sleep.

But first there was plenty more she had to do.

THE FIRST THING Kate did after shedding her coat and boots was to plug her cell phone into the charger. With the way the storm was coming in, she wouldn't have electricity for long.

The wind was gusting, hurling snow against the window panes. The windows rattled in spite of the weatherizing strips Kate had installed at the beginning of November.

This wasn't unusual weather for New Hampshire and they all knew how to prepare for it.

Kate spent the next half hour gathering up candles and flashlights and filling pans with water. She lugged the fifty-pound bag of salt to the inside wall of the mud room and covered it with a nylon tarp. If moisture got into the bag, the salt would solidify and be useless. She lined up several snow shovels next to the bag. There was a stack of dry firewood that was always kept at the ready, even in summer. She carried an armload to the living room and dropped it into the wood bin.

She laid out kindling and logs for a fire and placed the box of matches where she could find it if the lights went out. She wouldn't light the fire until it was necessary for warmth or cooking, but it was better to be prepared instead of having to rummage for wood in the dark.

When everything was ready, Kate poured herself a glass of wine and went out to the living room to work her nightly Sudoku. Funny how some things hadn't changed since she'd left her job in Alexandria. There she'd spent most nights alone with her Sudoku.

And here she was again.

She thought of Aloysius, alone at the museum. She'd left plenty of food and water for the cat, just in case she wouldn't be able to get there for a day or two. Kate knew he would be fine, as long as he hadn't been snowed out of his secret entrances to the museum.

She wished he was here, curled up beside her, but he belonged at the museum.

She turned on the television remote, looking for a weather update, and saw just what she expected to see: the northeast corridor covered by white. Somewhere beneath it was New Hampshire.

She flipped through the channels looking for an old movie, knowing she wouldn't get to see the end if the power went out.

Her hand paused on the local Portsmouth station, her attention caught by the nightly news.

"You've heard of Killer Sudoku, the puzzle craze that's sweeping the world. Well, the little town of Granville, New Hampshire, has given new meaning to the game. At the First Annual P.T. Avondale Tournament held this weekend—"

The telephone rang. Kate ran to the hall to answer it.

"Are you watching the news?" asked Pru.

"Yes," Kate said, one eye on the television. "Call you right back."

". . . Gordon Lott, history professor at . . . ." Kate sat down, absently reached for her wine. " . . . was found dead after being disqualified for the final round of the top competition. Local police chief, Brandon Mitchell, was not available for comment."

No surprise there. Brandon wasn't exactly user friendly.

"Now on a brighter note . . ."

Kate turned off the television, disappointed that the newscaster had been more interested in murder than her tournament. The museum could use some positive press. The phone was ringing again. It wasn't Pru.

"Ohmigod," said Ginny Sue as soon as Kate picked up the receiver. "I'm over at the inn. Tony and I were in the bar and John had on the news, and you'll never guess."

"I saw it, too."

"We're famous." Ginny Sue lowered her voice. "At least they didn't say anything about Lott being, you know, the M word."

Kate smiled. Ginny Sue taught fourth grade and she often lapsed into a code of half-finished words and euphemisms. "Why are you still at the inn? Does Tony have anything to do with that?" she teased, then caught herself. *None of your business*, Kate reminded herself. "Sorry, none of my business."

"Actually, Tony thought it was too dangerous for me to drive home, living on the outskirts of town like I do. And Nancy said she had some extra rooms that were just going to waste. Besides, quite a few people got stuck here and she'd already let most of her staff go home. So I offered to help out until we get plowed."

"Anybody interesting still at the inn?"

"Yes. And I'm keeping my eyes and ears open. Claudine was

checking out just as Tony and I came in. But Jed Dawson is still here. The other members of his team were already packed and left straight from the tournament. The Cambridge team took a vote and decided to stay. The Rhode Island team didn't even attempt to drive home."

"Wow. You're a storehouse of information."

"Yes. So I'm just going to stick here. They've already declared a snow day for us tomorrow. Duh. I'll take notes."

"Don't neglect Tony," Kate said.

"Oh, I won't." There was a pause. "He's really sweet. I'm so glad you got him for the tournament."

"So am I," Kate said, but for different reasons than Ginny Sue's.

Tony was the best; he was also the busiest. He was on the road a lot. He was a very charming and attractive man and met lots of women.

Ginny Sue was Kate's age and had never been married, never left Granville. Kate knew she was anxious to marry and start a family. Kate just wasn't sure that Tony was husband material.

Kate was also almost thirty and never married, but she didn't worry about things like a husband and children. She had Aunt Pru to worry about those for her.

As soon as Ginny Sue hung up, the telephone rang.

"Not available for comment. Bah. And just what was he doing that he wasn't available for comment?" Pru started right in on her favorite pastime: Brandon-bashing. "What are we paying him for, answer me that?" She didn't give Kate time to answer. "He spends all his time giving honest folks tickets for nothing, harassing grannies, when he oughta be out catching murderers."

"I imagine that's what he's doing instead of chatting with television reporters."

"Humph. And don't think I didn't see you come home in a

strange car. It looked like one of those big jeep things. Black. I know it doesn't belong to Sam Swyndon. Who does it belong to?"

"It belongs to Chief Mitchell. My car was stuck in the lot and he and Harry waited until I'd locked up the hall and drove me home."

"Well," Pru said. Which was as close as she'd ever get to condoning anything Brandon Mitchell did. "Katie, are you sure you're okay over there by yourself? Do you have everything you need? You should come stay with me. I don't know what kind of supplies Jimmy left. He doesn't have to worry about nor'easters."

Kate felt a smidgeon of envy as she thought about her father basking in the Florida sun while she was looking toward power outages and days of shoveling her way out of the house.

"I'll be fine over here. Dad left firewood and deicer, and I've got batteries."

"Did you remember to fill containers with water?"

"Yes, I did."

"Do you have food?"

Probably, thought Kate. She hadn't had much time to shop lately, but her father always kept the basement shelves stocked with emergency supplies. "Lots of food."

"Okay. But you call me if you change your mind."

"I will. You call me, too, if you need anything. Don't forget to change your cell phone. Good night."

Kate hung up and went to the kitchen. Pru's mention of food reminded her that she'd hardly eaten all weekend. She took a can of tomato soup out of the cabinet, got bread, cheese, and butter from the fridge. In a few minutes she was sitting at the kitchen table with a grilled cheese sandwich and a bowl of soup before her.

It was a meal that evoked wintry days and playing in the snow. Her mother at the stove, the windows fogged up with steam as the wind moaned safely outside. Her mother had been dead nearly twenty years, but tonight, Kate could feel her presence.

She was glad she'd moved back to Granville—even without her mother, even with her father retired and moved away. Even though she'd come too late to save her mentor.

She reached for one of her ever-present Sudoku books. Opened it to a back page where the hardest puzzles were located, and studied the grid and the preprinted numbers, the *givens*.

So perfectly logical. All the elements she needed to solve the puzzle were already on the page. The logic was built in. All she had to do was follow it. *So unlike people.*

Kate didn't understand why someone would cheat at puzzles. The whole fun of them was figuring them out. And the prize money wasn't so big that it would be worth ruining a man's reputation.

Jason and Erik's accusations against Gordon were worrisome. It was clear that neither of the men liked or trusted him. Gordon didn't seem to have any friends outside of Claudine and Kenny Revell and the man in the orange cap, who no one seemed to know.

Had he killed Gordon Lott? Had Kenny Revel?

And what about the Cambridge team? She knew they had a fierce, but usually benign, rivalry. Maybe things had passed benign to deadly. But to kill over a puzzle?

If it was over a puzzle.

Claudine had said that if she were jealous, she would have been more inclined to kill Kate than Gordon, but someone else might not be so coolheaded.

Another woman? Gordon flirted with every woman who crossed his path. Had one of them been pushed too far? A jealous husband?

The means were known: a .38 caliber. The motive was a mystery. Who had the opportunity? She wished she could ask

Brandon. She was sure he had some theories, but he wouldn't confide in her. He probably wouldn't even have time to investigate. He'd have his hands full with the storm-related incidents like stranded motorists, traffic accidents, and downed power lines.

Whereas Kate had plenty of time.

She looked down at the open Sudoku book. *What if his murder wasn't about a puzzle at all?* She needed a fresh perspective.

She went out to the hall for her briefcase, brought it back, and set it on the kitchen table. She unlocked it, and rifled through the stack of extra puzzle copies until she found sheets with empty grids.

She shoved her soup and sandwich aside and placed the blank Sudoku grid on the table. She began to fill it in, not with numbers but with darkened lines and dots. Gradually, the number grid became a map of Granville.

Of course Granville wasn't set up on a grid plan. Its streets tended to meander and dead-end for no apparent reason. Its blocks were often more like Rorschach blobs than perfect squares, but this would serve her purpose.

All the events of the weekend had taken place in the northeast section of town. She divided it into the nine boxes of the Sudoku grid. Each cell representing several town blocks—more or less.

Gordon was staying at the Bowsman Inn on the east side of town, just at the edge of the historic district, near the river. In the sixth Sudoku box, she drew a square topped by a triangle to represent the inn and wrote the initials *BI* next to it. She drew a winding river to the east of it and shaded it in.

To the west of the inn was the town park. It was a little more than one block wide and several blocks long. She filled in a diagonal area through the sixth box downward into the ninth box. She drew another "building" icon in the ninth cell of the fifth Sudoku box and penciled in *GBG*, the Granville Bar and Grill. In the fourth box, the westernmost block, she placed an icon for the VFW Hall in the northeast corner, and lightly shaded the rest of the box for the parking lot.

She looked at her "map" then put an X to mark the place where they'd found Gordon's body . . .

. . . And encountered her next puzzle. Gordon was staying at the Bowsman Inn, and left to have a drink at the bar and grill a block away. Afterward, instead of returning to the inn, he veered almost two blocks in the opposite direction to the VFW parking lot. Why?

He wouldn't have left his car at the VFW hall. He would have driven to the inn. There were no cars in the lot Saturday morning. Had he accompanied Kenny Revell and the third man back to the parking lot to get their car or cars?

No, that didn't work. Nancy had said Kenny Revell's things were still in his room. His car was parked at the inn. Had something happened to him, too? Was his body still beneath feet of snow? Or had the two men lured Gordon to the parking lot, shot him, and escaped in the car belonging to the man in the orange hat?

It sounded like an old radio show title: "The Man in the Orange Hat." Someone must know who he was, and *where* he was. Unless he was buried beneath the snow, and Kenny Revell had stolen his car and fled. Had an unknown criminal killed them all? Or—

Oh, stop it! she told herself. This was pure conjecture.

Kate sat back and picked up her congealed sandwich. She dropped it back on the plate, gathered up her dishes, and took them to the sink.

The wind was howling down her street. Not just a poetic description, she realized; Kate didn't wander into poetry very often. The wind was really howling, the lights flickering.

She shuddered as she remembered another day, another power

outage—when she was trapped in the basement of the museum. This time she was safe in her own home. If it was a little lonely, at least she was used to it.

She carried a flashlight and several candles down the hall to her bedroom, got extra blankets out from the closet, and took a really quick, really hot shower. Then she climbed into bed and turned out the lights.

Gordon Lott's face rose before her out of the darkness. She squeezed her eyes shut. She needed to turn off her brain and get some sleep. She needed it. She deserved it.

Her mind wouldn't obey. Images, like fragments of a dream, floated to her consciousness: Gordon looking at his watch. Gordon's hand sticking out of the snow. His empty wrist.

The watch was gone—someone had taken it. Otherwise the metal detector would have picked up a signal from it.

What had happened in that parking lot? An argument? A fight?

She tried to picture what might have happened. The men want the watch. Snatch it from Lott's wrist. The watchband breaks and the watch falls in the snow. Lott grabs for the watch and—

Bang.

Kate sat up. That had been a real bang. She groped in the dark until she found the lamp on the bedside table, and fumbled for the switch. Nothing. The sound she heard must have been thunder hitting the nearby transformer or routing station.

She lay back again and thought about Gordon's watch. It might be an important factor in his murder, or it might merely be an *unknown variable*, or a *confounding variable*. Or worse, it might just be the real-life equivalent of a *spurious correlation* and have nothing to do with the murder at all.

She yawned. Math-think wouldn't help solve this murder. All the equations in the world couldn't explain why humans acted the way they did.

As she finally drifted off, her thoughts turned to Brandon Mitchell. His job here hadn't been easy. In the last year, he'd gone from being the brunt of outraged citizens to being tolerated—and ignored. Until this year, there hadn't been a murder in Granville since nineteen eighty-something, then two murders in the last six months. She wouldn't be surprised if people started blaming the chief for the two that had occurred since he'd taken office.

They might even blame Kate. The murders also occurred after she'd moved back. And she'd been involved in both. This was not something she was ready to consider. She burrowed beneath the covers and forced herself to go back to asleep.

Kate awoke once during the night, long enough to spread the extra blankets over the bed and jump back beneath the covers. When she woke again, it was morning and all she saw outside was white. Everywhere.

There was still no power and might not be for days. She put on long underwear, sweatpants, and several sweaters, stuffed her feet into fur-lined moccasins and padded down the hall to the living room to light a fire. Using four blackened bricks and an old grate she found in the mud room, Kate made a makeshift oven over the wood. As soon as the fire was going, she poured water into an old aluminum coffee pot and took it back to heat over the flames.

Her cell phone was fully charged and she used it to call her aunt.

"No power, but I'm fine," Pru said. Kate assured her she was also fine and told her aunt not to attempt any shoveling.

Then she settled down with her puzzle books to wait out the storm.

By mid afternoon, she's was bored out of her mind. She'd left a message on Harry's cell that morning telling him she was staying home and asking if he and the chief had power. He hadn't phoned her back, but she tried not to worry.

He finally called around three o'clock. "Been shoveling all day. As soon as I clear a place, it snows over again, but the chief said it was my job to stay on top of it."

"Where's the chief?"

"At work."

"You're kidding. How did he manage that?"

"Snowshoes." Harry barked out a laugh. "You shoulda seen him. He looked like the abominable snowman."

Poor chief, thought Kate imagining him trudging to the station, fighting wind and snow drifts only to find the station closed up tight and the door blocked by mounds of white. She wondered if he'd realized yet that people took blizzards as a fact of life, something that couldn't be hurried or fought. Most were more than willing to stay home and sit it out.

But the chief was nothing if not dedicated.

"Do you think Al is okay at the museum all by himself?"

Kate brought her attention back to Harry. "I'm sure he is. Maine coons are snowproof, but I don't think even Aloysius will be venturing out in this weather. I left him plenty of food and water in the kitchen."

They said good-bye, neither wanting to use up batteries when they didn't know how long the land lines would be out.

Kate considered cleaning house but it was too cold to move around, so she pulled the couch close to the fire and bundled up under a pile of blankets. She didn't leave her cocoon until the next morning.

Wonder of wonders, the snow had stopped. She'd hoped for as much when she'd heard the rattle of snowplows during the night. There was still no power but that would be restored soon.

She looked out the front window. The day was sunny, with the sun glaring off the snow. There was a wall of snow at least six feet high along the curb in front of the house, though a lot of it was cast off by the snowplows.

She bundled up and dragged the bag of deicer and the two snow shovels to the front porch. She had to throw her body weight against the front door before it opened wide enough for her to squeeze through. The wind had gusted so high that even though the porch was covered, a good eighteen inches had managed to settle against the doorframe.

She started shoveling . . . and shoveling . . . and shoveling. Her father and Pru both used Mike Landers for plowing when the snow was heavy. Mike had already plowed her driveway twice that winter, but she doubted if she would see him before tomorrow. His services would be augmenting the regular town plows.

Kate started digging a path to the street. The Buick was still parked catercornered in Pru's front yard and completely covered by the snow. She might be able to dig it out.

At least it would be wheels. If she could convince her aunt to let her borrow it.

She took several breaks to go inside and warm up, eat, and start again. On one of her breaks her cell rang. It was Sam Swyndon.

"Hey," he said. "Everything alright with you?"

"Yes. There's no power and I've been shoveling all morning, but other than that, I can't complain."

"Well, don't work too hard. Main Street is clear, so if you're planning to go anywhere, use that as your main route."

"Thanks for telling me, but since my car is buried in the VFW lot and the plows dumped a huge wall of snow and ice in my driveway, I don't think I'll be going anywhere today."

"I saw Mike a while ago. He was headed east. He probably won't get to you today."

"I didn't think he would. I hate leaving the museum unattend-
ed. I'm not sure about the roof, or the state of the back stoop . . ."

"Don't worry. It'll be fine. And . . ."

"Yes?"

"I just wanted to make sure you'd recovered from the other
day."

"I'm okay."

"Good."

"I'd better go. I'm trying to conserve my cell phone."

"Good idea. Listen, I'm at the shop. This end of Main Street has
power, and I have the proofs of the pictures I took . . ."

"Pictures?" Was he offering to show her his crime scene shots?

"Of the tournament. I thought you might like to see them. And
since the inn is open for business and you're probably going stir
crazy . . . If you dig your way out to the street, how about dinner?
I'll pick you up, and we'll drive by the museum on our way."

A hot meal in a warm room, with nice company, pictures of the
weekend, and ambiance out the wazoo. It would also give her a
chance to talk to Tony and check out the other occupants before
they left. "Sure, that would be great."

They hung up. Kate put on her coat, now heavy and wet with
melted snow, pulled on her gloves and hat, and headed back outside.

It was dark by the time she finished carving out a narrow tun-
nel to the street. She spread deicer over the thin strip of ground
and called Sam. "I'm out. Give me twenty minutes."

"It'll take me that long to defrost the car and get over there."

"Just honk and I'll come out."

"No way. Pru will tell Aunt Elmira I have no manners."

"She won't be able to see you over the wall of snow."

They both laughed. Each painfully aware of what expectations they would be encouraging if they were seen at the inn together. Evidently Sam was willing to risk it.

Kate guessed she must be, too.

CHAPTER

TEN

SAM DIDN'T HONK. Kate was standing by the window when she saw his head appear over the crest of packed snow. It was followed by the rest of him as he squeezed through the narrow opening she had dug through the snowbank.

He was wearing a down jacket, scarf, gloves, and sheepskin hat with ear flaps, similar to the one Harry wore, except Kate guessed Sam's was an authentic hunting cap. A lot of New Hampshirites hunted, and just about everyone knew how to use a rifle. Kate wondered, how many could use a handgun?

True to his word, Sam drove by the museum on their way to dinner. The street had been plowed into a single lane and it was hard to see the old federal house for the mounds of snow, but the second story looked okay. The windows were intact and the gables hadn't collapsed under the weight of snow.

Kate thought about Al alone in the house. She was sure he was okay, but he'd be lonely. There was no way she could make a quick trip inside. Tomorrow, maybe.

They meandered back toward Main Street then turned right, Sam driving slowly but steadily. The parking lot of the inn had been plowed, but most of the parked cars were still covered in snow.

Sam pulled into an empty spot near the front door and reached over her to take a brown manila envelope from the glove compartment.

Nancy greeted them at the door. She looked a little tired, but her smile brightened when she saw Kate and Sam. "What a weekend. Everyone is saying great things about the tournament, Katie. Congratulations."

"Thanks." If Kate could only forget the little unpleasantness of murder, she'd be happy.

"It's hang up your own coats tonight, I'm afraid. Most of my staff couldn't make it in. So we're only serving in the bar tonight. Hope that's okay."

"That's fine," Kate said. It would give her the opportunity to see all the out-of-towners. Belatedly, she remembered Sam. She glanced at him.

"Sure," he said, helping Kate out of her coat. When he left to hang their coats, Nancy stepped closer to Kate. "People are talking. Someone started a rumor that Gordon Lott was shot. Is that true?"

Kate shrugged.

"It *is* true."

Kate grabbed Nancy's elbow. "Please don't say anything. Once everyone starts speculating, they'll bog down the investigation. And we really need this finished."

"Mum's the word," said Nancy just as Sam returned. "A group

at one of the booths is just finishing up. Why don't you have a drink and I'll come get you when it's free."

As they turned to go into the bar, Tony and Ginny Sue came down the stairs.

"Kate," Tony called out. "I was wondering if I was going to see you before I left."

"I hope you don't think you're still on duty." Kate indicated the medal that was still pinned to his jacket lapel.

"Egad zooks." He unpinned the medal and dropped it into his jacket pocket. "Forgot all about it. I don't want to turn into a dotty old man who sports his Sudoku medals while thinking they're the purple heart."

"You deserve a purple heart for this weekend."

"Not at all."

Kate introduced him to Sam.

"Nice to meet you," Tony said. "Are you two having dinner? Want to join us? Or is this a *tête-à-tête* affair?" Tony winked at Kate.

"Uh, no. I mean, yes." Kate looked at Sam.

Sam grinned. "We'd love to join you. Nancy has a booth coming up in a few minutes."

"Perfect. Why don't I buy us a round of drinks?" Tony slipped his arm around Ginny Sue and led them to the bar.

Sam's hand rested at the small of Kate's back as they followed them inside. A little shiver of pleasure skittered across her shoulders. It was a completely polite gesture, but it felt nice all the same.

The bar was a large, cozy room with a long mahogany bar, a space for ten tables, and a row of red plush booths, all of them filled. A fire was blazing in the stone fireplace.

The Cambridge Puzzlers were sitting at a table near the hearth. While Tony and Sam went to get their drinks, Kate went over to congratulate them on their victory.

One of the men stood up and nodded enthusiastically, "Barb jacked our points right up there."

Barb Huttner wiped her mouth with her napkin and stretched out her hand to Kate. "We haven't met, but I was at the Philly tournament when you won your speed record. I was still in the C Division then."

"It's nice to meet you. I hope you enjoyed the weekend." *Except for the murder,* Kate added to herself.

"Always nice to win."

Kate looked over the room. "Are the Hanover and Rhode Island teams still here? I should say hello."

"Hanover's sulking in the corner." The Cambridge man pointed to a far booth. "The Rhode Island team ate earlier. They're having a sudden death smackdown upstairs." He looked contrite and fell silent.

"Too bad about Gordon Lott," Barb said, but she didn't sound very concerned.

No one else added their voice to hers. Gordon Lott was not a popular man.

Tony and Sam joined her with their drinks and they spent a few more minutes exchanging tales from the puzzle circuit. The people at a booth got up and Kate recognized the Hanover Sudoku Club. They didn't look very happy, but who could blame them. One of their members had been killed—and they'd lost to their archrivals.

They paused at the Cambridge table long enough to congratulate the Cambridge team. Jed Dawson, the third-place individual winner, nodded at her.

Kate knew she should say something to the Hanover club members, but couldn't figure out if congratulations or condolences were in order.

"Licking your wounds, Jed?" asked the Cambridge man.

"We'll be back. So watch out, Barb. I'll be gunning for you."

Gunning? Kate nearly spilled her wine. Recovering her composure, she said, "You deserve some kudos yourself, Jed." Kate recovered and smiled at him.

Jed huffed out a sigh. "Third place."

Kate couldn't think of a thing to say, besides something inane like "third's good, too."

Tony took up the slack. He slapped Jed on the back. "You'll get a chance to pay Barb back in Philly. You all going down?"

"If we can field a third competitor from the club. Gordon managed to screw us over in more ways than one." Jed shook his head. "You emceeing in Philly?"

"I'll be there."

Jed nodded and the three members started to leave.

"Oh, Jed?"

"Yes, Kate?"

"I was just wondering. We had a bunch of things left at the coat check. One of them was an orange ski hat. Someone thought it might belong to someone in your group."

"An orange hat?"

"Multipointed like a jester's hat." Kate watched for a reaction.

"Hmm, I don't think so."

The others shook their heads.

"I can ask some of the members in the lower divisions."

"Well, we have it, and about a dozen scarves," said Kate, suddenly afraid she might be arousing suspicion. She changed the subject. "Your B Division did very well,"

"Yes, hopefully one of them will be ready for the A division before Philly. Did they find out who killed Gordon?"

Kate swallowed. What did he know? Had the chief questioned him about orange hats? She shook her head.

"The first forty-eight hours are the most important," he intoned.

Kate forced a smile. Thanks to every *CSI*-spinoff, everybody was an expert.

The Hanover team left and Nancy came to tell them that their booth was ready. She led them over and waited for them to sit down. There was a moment when Sam and Kate just stood there, both of them obviously unsure where to sit. Once again Tony took charge. He handed Ginny Sue onto the banquette and slipped in beside her.

Kate and Sam slid into the other side.

A waitress came with menus and a list of specials and a few minutes passed before they talked about anything but food. Then Kate asked Tony if he was being inconvenienced by the storm, though from his look of contentment, Kate guessed he was doing just fine.

"Lovely time," he said. "Except for this afternoon when your illustrious chief of police put me through the third degree."

"The chief questioned you?"

"Uh huh. Wanted to know about my relationship with Gordon."

"Did you have a relationship with Gordon?"

"Purely adversarial, as I told Chief Mitchell. I don't think Gordon went out of his way to win friends. He had an ego the size of Texas, but not the ability to back it up.

"I had to reprimand him for trying to sneak his cell phone into a crossword competition last spring. I probably should have confiscated it, but he said he'd been waiting for a phone call and had forgotten to take it out of his pocket."

Tony straightened his knife and spoon. "Hell, what could I do? Maybe it was just an honest mistake. On the other hand, he could have downloaded an entire dictionary onto that phone or had someone text him the answers.

"Stupid ass." "But that was Gordon through and through. He was a competitor, not a puzzler, if you see what I mean. It wasn't the process, but the outcome. I'm sorry he's dead. I'm sure his family will miss him. But the puzzle circuit won't. Even his own team was ready to kill him—oops."

Kate cut Ginny Sue a look.

Ginny Sue grimaced. "Sorry. It just slipped out."

Tony draped his arm around her shoulders. "Not Ginny's fault. I kind of figured it out, myself. Police don't usually ask the kinds of questions Chief Mitchell did if the death is natural. When I asked, Ginny Sue verified it. Besides, I'm a professional puzzle solver."

"That's okay," said Kate. "It was bound to leak out. Actually it seems to be public knowledge at this point. I just hope people don't start associating the museum's name with murder."

Tony nodded to Sam. "I take it you know, too?"

"Yes. Actually I moonlight as the police photographer. Not enough need for a full-time one. Usually."

Tony raise one eyebrow. "Interesting work?"

"Not often."

"So you have pictures of the body?"

Sam frowned. "Not with me, but I do have some of the weekend."

"Oh, let's see." Ginny Sue was overdoing the enthusiasm. But Kate appreciated it. She didn't think they should be speculating about Gordon's murder, especially with the murderer at large.

Sam slid the proof sheets out of the envelope and a magnifier out of his shirt pocket. "Haven't had time to develop any pictures, but if you see anything you like just let me know and I'll have Katie send them to you."

Tony shook his head. "You know, Kate, I would never think of you as a Katie. It's so quaint."

"Old habits," said Kate. "From the good old days."

Sam looked contrite. "Don't you like it? Everybody calls you Katie."

"It's fine." She knew she would always be called Katie in Granville. Kate smiled at him and that's when she saw Claudine Frankel come into the bar. Her eyes widened. "I thought she left."

Ginny Sue followed Kate's gaze, then nodded. "Nancy's fit to be tied. She did leave. But she peeled out of the lot without looking and ran smack into the plow truck. They had to tow her car. They're sending a rental down from Manchester as soon as the roads are safe."

"I'm surprised she even stayed after Saturday," Kate ventured. "I mean, with Gordon dead."

"Pick a man, any man," Tony said. He pulled at the cuff of his jacket. "See, nothing up my sleeve."

Was that just a trace of bitterness she heard in Tony's voice?

The noise in the bar had dropped considerably at Claudine's entrance. And no wonder. She was wearing a short black dress more appropriate for cocktails in Palm Beach than for a blizzard in New Hampshire. She had on high-high heels. Her hair was clipped back in a rhinestone clip. She tossed her head and the jewels and strands of hair gleamed in the light.

Kate was sure she heard an audible sigh among the men at the bar. Claudine sidled toward them and the seas parted to make way.

Tony snorted, but Sam was staring, his eyes wide, lips slightly parted.

Oh sure, just because Kate had on old corduroys and a sweater she'd had since high college. She owned a little black dress. A shudder passed over her. She *had* owned a black dress. She'd been wearing it when she found the professor dead at his desk. Pru had thrown it out the next day. It was covered with the professor's blood.

She took a sip of wine. It went down the wrong way. She wheezed then coughed. It seemed to break the spell Claudine had woven over Sam; he smacked her on the back.

"Are you okay?"

Kate nodded. The sea of patrons closed around Claudine.

"Highly inappropriate New Hampshire wear," Tony said archly.

"She certainly doesn't seem to be in mourning," Sam said and pulled his eyes away from the bar.

"She looks more like she's going on a hot date," Ginny Sue said. Her face suddenly went blank. "Uh-oh."

Kate looked toward the doorway. Brandon Mitchell stood silhouetted by the lobby lamps. Nancy was standing next to him. She pointed toward the bar. The chief nodded and walked into the room.

Kate slunk back against the seat. That's all she needed. For the chief to find her having dinner with Sam during a murder investigation. She'd managed to get Sam to turn over the pictures from the crime scene of the professor's murder. Actually his Aunt Elmira had convinced him—but if Brandon saw them together now, he'd assume the worst.

He didn't even glance their way, just headed to the bar. Once again the crowd parted, leaving Claudine and her little black—and backless—dress in the center.

Claudine turned, saw the chief, and smiled.

It was radiant. She was beautiful. And tongues would wag in the morning.

Kate couldn't see the chief's face, but she could imagine it. All she had to do was look around at the dopey expressions on all the other men in the room.

"Do you think he's interrogating her or taking her out to dinner?" Tony asked.

Kate shrugged. It was all she could manage. She was having trouble evaluating what she was seeing, and too worried about being spotted to be able to think straight.

Please go away. Please don't see Sam and me. Please don't be taking her out.

Kate hadn't meant to think that last thought. It was none of her business, except that Claudine might be a murderer. Okay, maybe not. Maybe Kate just wanted her to be the murderer.

Kate slunk farther into the corner of the booth. "What are they doing now?"

Ginny Sue stretched over Tony to see better. "She's flirting. He's just standing there. Oh. She's getting off the stool. They're walking toward the entrance. Where could they be going? GB and G's is the only other place that's open."

Sam was leaning on his elbow on the table, looking at Kate, his brows knit.

Kate straightened up.

"You're not embarrassed to be seen with us, are you?" asked Tony. He was joking of course, but he didn't know their history.

"She doesn't want to be seen with me."

"No," Kate said quickly. "It's just . . . well. I don't want to get you in trouble."

"Me?" Sam looked totally confused. "How?"

"He might think I was pumping you for information about the crime scene, and then you and I would both be in trouble."

"Oh, *that.*" Sam looked out to the now empty doorway. "To heck with him."

Their food arrived and for a few minutes they ate in silence.

Then Kate asked, "What do you know about her?"

"Claudine?" Tony pulled a face. "Other than the obvious? Not much. I saw her at a couple of functions hanging on Gordon's arm. Then she dropped from the scene. Until this weekend, when she shows up out of the blue. She said she was surprised to see Gordon, though I don't know why."

"She told me that Gordon was her ex."

"That wouldn't surprise me."

"Do you think she was meeting someone else?"

"Like I said, pick a man, any man. Did you have someone particular in mind?"

"Kenny Revell, perhaps."

"Katie . . ." Sam warned.

Tony chuckled. "Give it up, Sam. You can't stop a puzzle master from trying to solve a puzzle, any more than you can stop a mathematician from solving an equation. And our Kate is both."

Sam sighed.

Kate patted his forearm. "In this case, I don't even know what the equation is. But I do think it's odd that Revell disappeared and left all of his belongings and his car."

"Unless he's the murderer and he's out there somewhere." Ginny's eyes darted around the room as if she expected him to jump out wielding an ax.

"That's the real puzzle," Tony agreed. "Kenny is a regular. He never competes, just watches." He frowned. "And he takes notes. I do recall that about him. I suppose he might be some kind of journalist, but I've never really thought about him. He doesn't frequent the upper echelons, if you know what I mean."

Kate nodded. The parties that the inner cliques held. There were many different groups and the circuit could be a lonely experience if a person didn't know anyone. Of course, a lot of puzzlers were loners anyway.

That still didn't answer the question of what had happened to Kenny Revell. Unless he murdered Gordon, then panicked and fled. Or worse. If he'd been killed by the same man who killed Gordon.

And why did she assume it was a man? A woman was capable of murder. Claudine might easily have shot her lover, her ex-lover. And so could one of his disgruntled teammates, if any of them took winning as seriously as Gordon did.

Claudine didn't return to the bar, and neither did the chief.

While Tony and Sam fought over the check, Kate motioned to Ginny to follow her. "We're going to the ladies' room. Be right back."

As soon as they were in the lobby, Kate turned to Ginny Sue. "I hope Tony wasn't upset because the chief questioned him. He came to the tournament as a personal favor to me and then he becomes embroiled in a murder investigation."

"Don't worry. Tony is pretty easygoing. At least I guess he is, since I've only known him a few days. I was the one who was put out with the chief and his heavy-handed ways. Tony just shrugged it off. You don't think the chief suspects Tony?"

"I can't imagine he would." Truthfully, Kate had no idea what the chief suspected. He never shared information with her.

Nancy was sitting at the registration counter, a pair of reading glasses perched on her nose, and a copy of the *Manchester Union-Leader* opened to the food page. "Enjoy your meal?"

"Yes, thanks." Kate said.

"Delicious," added Ginny Sue.

Kate leaned over the counter and asked in a whisper, "Where did the chief take Claudine?"

Nancy leaned forward. "Upstairs."

Kate's stomach plummeted.

"I told him they could use the library."

For what? Kate wondered. But just then, Sam and Tony appeared and before she could ask anything else, Sam had bundled her into her coat and they were saying good night.

The night air hit them hard. It must have dropped ten degrees and there was a thick layer of ice on the windshield of Sam's car. While Sam scraped, Kate looked around the parking lot for the chief's police cruiser or his SUV.

She found the SUV at the end of the row. So he was here unofficially. They must be on a date. *Talk about mixing business with pleasure.* A part of her wanted to believe that Brandon would never fall for any of Claudine's tricks, but the rest of her was ready to spit nails.

She sat in pensive silence while Sam drove through the streets.

"You're not still worried about Chief Mitchell seeing us tonight, are you? I'm sure he didn't notice us."

She couldn't agree more. He'd only had eyes for Claudine Frankel. "No, sorry, just tired from all that shoveling. I'm out of shape."

"Not much snow in Virginia, huh?"

"Nope."

"I'm glad you've come back."

"Me, too." Except she was already beginning to panic at the softened tone in Sam's voice. She was really bad at this dating thing. Even with Sam who was sweet, good looking, fun to be with, and—had job security.

For heaven's sake. She sounded just like Aunt Pru.

Sam helped her through the opening in the snowbank to her driveway. It had turned to ice and they slipped and grabbed for each other in the dark until they were breathless with laughter.

There was still no power. They stood on the dark porch, suddenly quiet.

Then Sam said, "You'd better get in out of the cold."

Kate opened the door, but before she could step inside, Sam pulled her close and kissed her.

"Good night." He gave her a little push. "Light some candles so I know you're in okay."

Kate nodded. She felt her way across the entrance hall to the hall table, clicked on the flashlight, and came back to the door. "Thanks for dinner."

"My pleasure." Sam raised his hand and made his way across the dark expanse of snow to the street.

Kate watched until she heard the car drive away, then she smiled and closed the door.

THERE WAS STILL no power the next morning, though Mike Landers had plowed her driveway. He'd even managed to dig out Pru's Buick.

Kate called her aunt. "Are you going anywhere today?"

"I hadn't planned to. Why?"

"Could I borrow the Buick to go check on the museum? My car's still at the VFW Hall."

"Of course you can. Mike got it out of that darn snowdrift this morning. Cleaned it off for me and plowed the drive."

And Mike was a happily married grandfather. *Thank God!*

Kate shouldn't have allowed herself that moment of smugness. In the next breath, Pru said, "Elmira called me first thing this morning."

With a sigh, Kate looked at her watch. It was only nine o'clock.

"She said Sam took you out to dinner at the inn last night. We're both just tickled pink that you two are getting along so well. He's such a lovely young man."

And he has job security, Kate thought, ruefully remembering her own lapse into Pru-isms the night before. "We had a nice time. Could I come get the Buick now?"

"I'll just go find my keys." Pru hung up before Kate could remind her that Mike had used them to move the car, and they were probably on the hall table.

She shivered through a quick, icy sponge bath and was standing at Pru's front door ten minutes later. Pru's house was the exact same design as Kate's, though the interior had gone through a modern transformation when, according to Kate's dad, Pru had "gone off her damn rocker" a few years back. Which, Kate imagined, might also account for her aunt's blue hair.

"Here they are," Pru said as she opened the door.

"Thanks." Kate reached for them, but Pru held on.

"Now, you remember to call Sam today and tell him what a good time you had."

"The keys?"

"Don't just say 'thanks' and hang up. Give him the opportunity to ask you out again." Pru pulled a face. "I hope you didn't wear that old coat to the inn last night."

Kate shrugged. "It's warm."

"Well, when the roads are better, we'll have to go out to Burlington and get you something nicer."

Kate could just imagine Pru decking her out in Claudine Frankel-type clothes in an effort to help her snare a husband—a good local husband with job security.

She had to listen to a few more of Sam's good points before she finally got the keys.

All the lights had been restored on Main Street and two lanes had been cleared. Hopper Street was another story. In most places there was barely room for a single car.

Kate managed to park up against a mound of soot-covered snow near the museum. There was just enough room for another car to squeeze past. As long as they didn't go into a slide or spin out of control, the Buick would be fine. Actually, the Buick would probably withstand a bulldozer.

Kate was surprised to see that the walkway to the museum door was clear. She pushed open the gate and walked past the newly painted Avondale Museum sign that barely showed above the snowline. Ahead of her, the circular porch had also been cleared.

The entrance to the museum had always made Kate feel she was entering a palace, and the icicles that festooned the overhang sparkled like diamonds in the sun and added to its magic.

Even for logical Kate. The museum was like that—it brought out the best of one's imagination, introduced its visitors to wonder and awe.

The collection was beginning to draw enough visitors to help put the long-neglected museum back on its feet. With the proceeds from the tournament, she could begin on the new renovations.

She opened the door and walked into warmth.

"Al? Harry? Anybody here?"

"In the office," came the disembodied voice through the new intercom Kate had installed along with the new security system.

Kate pulled off her boots and exchanged them for sneakers. She didn't plan to open the museum today, and anyone who did manage to brave the snow to visit surely wouldn't begrudge her comfort on a day like this.

She climbed the stairs to the second-floor office. Harry was sitting at the computer desk by the window. There was a fire in the fireplace. Kate dropped her briefcase and laptop on her desk—

though she still thought of it as the professor's desk—and went over to see what he was working on.

Aloysius was stretched out along the top of the printer, his brown, grey, and black fur spread out like a feather duster over the top. He opened one eye and let out a "Yeow."

"I know. I'm in the doghouse for deserting you with only dry kibble for three days. *Mea culpa.*"

Aloysius lifted his head for Kate to scratch his neck in penance, which she did.

"Did you do all that shoveling?" she asked Harry as Al began to rumble with satisfaction.

Harry nodded, but didn't look away from the computer screen.

"No school today?"

Harry shook his head. "Power's out. Tree knocked out a transformer. Might be days."

He sounded delighted. She couldn't blame him. School could be boring when you were smarter than everyone else.

"Well, thanks for using your holiday to shovel out the museum."

Harry half shrugged. "I didn't mind. And I wanted to get to a computer. The chief's big computer has a password on it and he won't let me use it."

"How did the two of you do this weekend?"

His smile faded and Kate was looking at one troubled boy. She had every hope that things would work out. Brandon Mitchell was the exact role model a young man needed, but she should never have brought it up.

"What are you working on?" she said quickly, changing the subject. There was a Sudoku grid on the screen. "Don't tell me you've become a Sudoku convert?"

"Nope. Just checking something." He moved aside for her to see the rest of the screen.

"Why, Harry Perkins, you're using a computer cheat."

"Not me. I'm just seeing how it works."

"I've heard that one before," Kate teased.

"The chief was using one last night."

Kate's first reaction was surprise. She had no idea Brandon did Sudoku. He'd never mentioned it. Even acted dumb when she'd tried to explain it to him. "Maybe he was using it to learn how to work the puzzle."

Harry looked away from the screen long enough to give her a look that only a teenager could achieve—a "get real" expression, that made her feel ancient.

"He was cheating. I caught him at it. He clicked out of the page really fast and bit my head off." Harry shook his head, broadcasting his disgust. "I mean, why work a puzzle if you have to cheat to get the answer? Kind of defeats the whole purpose."

"There are cheat programs for almost every online game."

"I know. And the ones that help you strategize are okay, I guess."

Kate silently added the "if you're dumb enough to need one."

"But this one just gives you the answers. Look."

Cheats were just one of the reasons no electronics were allowed in the competition room, and why they were still using paper and pencil or erase boards instead of computerized puzzles. Kate was well aware of how they worked, but she let Harry explain it to her.

Harry clicked on a fresh puzzle grid. "So here are the whatever."

"Givens," Kate supplied.

"Yeah, the givens, then you just apply the cheat and *voilà*." The puzzle blipped, then appeared with all the numbers filled in. "I mean, okay, if you want extra weapons or extra lives in a video game, you at least have to do some work. But all you have to do for this is press 'enter' and it's done for you! That's so bogus."

Kate was glad to see Harry's reaction. Cheats were another kind of given in the world of video games. She'd never even downloaded one, though she'd used computers all day long at the institute. They were used to work complex equations or to check out provinces that were beyond the human mind, but the results were dependent on the intelligence of the person inputting the data. A working relationship, not cheating.

"He cheated."

Kate frowned at him. "Who?"

"The chief."

"Oh." For a moment Kate had thought he meant Gordon Lott. Which at this point was academic. The man was dead. It no longer mattered what he had done in his life. Or did it?

She pulled up a chair and sat down. "Are you sure the chief was cheating?"

Harry scowled at her. "What else would he be doing?"

"Analyzing." *Or taking an interest in Claudine's interests.* Though Kate didn't think Sudoku was the reason Claudine came to tournaments.

Harry narrowed his eyes at her. "What's to analyze? The program figures out the answer and fills it in for you."

"I know, but—"

"And besides, it only works on the programmed puzzles." Harry slumped back in his chair with a sigh. "Do you think he was trying to figure out if Gordon Lott was cheating?"

"I'm sure he was doing something that involved his investigation. You don't really think the chief is a cheater, do you?"

"I guess not. But he was pretty pissed that I caught him at it."

"Probably because he was working." She looked back at the screen. Did Brandon think Gordon's murder was precipitated because of his cheating? In a little tournament in a little town in a little state? Except that the event had grown out of proportion as soon as they began advertising. It would have continued to grow if Kate hadn't closed the registration. People were hungry for more Sudoku venues.

There was something special about gathering actual bodies to compete; much more intense than a faceless web opponent in internet play.

"You think someone killed him because he was cheating?" asked Harry.

And would you stop making conclusions as quickly as I do? You're just a kid. "It's possible, but we'll leave it to the chief. We have a museum to run."

"We could run the museum *and* solve a murder."

"Harry. . ."

"Come *on*, Kate. We helped the chief last time. Not that he'd ever thank us for it."

"No, and he wouldn't thank us for interfering in this one." Kate sensed there was something more to Harry's desire to investigate than just the puzzler's compulsion to know the answers.

She wished Harry would just tell her. Then she remembered her own teenage years, how isolated she was from everyone except the professor. If only he were here now.

It was a fruitless wish. She had to place her confidence in Brandon Mitchell and hope he would come through for Harry the way the professor had for her.

"Harry, is something wrong between you and the chief?"

Harry shook his head. An automatic response. He wasn't going to talk.

"There might be times when things aren't always, you know, easy, when you live with someone else." How would she know?

She'd never lived with anyone since she'd left home after high school. She'd tried her freshman year in college, but her roommate was always wanting to talk, and Kate had to study. "I'm not exactly an expert, but I realize that you and the chief might have some stuff to work out."

"He treats me like a kid."

"I hate to break it to you, but you are a kid." As soon as she said it, Kate knew that she'd made a mistake. "By law, that is. I know that you're big and strong and smart. I know that you can take care of yourself.

"But the chief needs—wants—to make sure you're taken care of, provided for—" She stopped after that. Harry was provided for. At least his education was. The professor had seen to that. She had no idea what the chief wanted—or needed. She just knew he was considering sending Harry away to school, which she was afraid might have the same impact on Harry as being sent back to the foster care system.

Did Harry know the chief's plans for him? Was that why he said the chief was going to "dump" him? Had they talked about the possibility? She wouldn't dare ask and risk making a mess of an already tense situation.

"Okay. What do you think?"

"About what?" Harry had lost interest; his question was barely mumbled.

"About whether Gordon Lott cheated or not."

In a flash, Harry straightened up. "What I can't figure out is how he could interface the written puzzle with a cheat. He might have concealed a cheat cartridge in a Blackberry or cell phone."

"That's why we don't allow them."

"Right. But he might have sneaked something in. We didn't set up a metal detector or anything."

"It was a puzzle tournament, not an airport."

"Still, I think we should next time."

"You're probably right."

"That still doesn't solve the problem of how to enter the paper puzzle into a blank grid in a program that was connected to a cheat. Do you know how long that would take?"

"Longer than six minutes and some odd seconds," said Kate, alluding to Gordon's finish times. "Besides, I was watching him. He kept both hands in sight. He wasn't secretively entering numbers into a computer. Just kept consulting his watch."

"The missing watch?"

Kate nodded, staring absently at the computer screen as she thought. She didn't see how cheating on such a small scale could lead to murder. She was still hanging onto the thwarted lover scenario, which was totally not scientific. Or the missing Kenny Revell scenario.

Then something Tony had said made her breath catch. He thought Kenny was a journalist. Journalists were keen observers. Maybe Kenny had seen Gordon cheat. *And what? Got so angry he shot him? Tried to blackmail him? And when Gordon refused, shot him? Ridiculous. Maybe.*

And who was the guy in the orange hat? Was he still here or had he fled with Kenny Revell.

"Harry, do you remember seeing a guy in an orange ski hat? One of those multipointed jester-looking hats."

"About a hundred. No, seriously, maybe ten? Though they all might not have been orange. Why?"

"Because Gordon Lott was last seen with a man named Kenny Revell, who has disappeared, and another man nobody seems to know, who was wearing an orange ski cap."

"Yes!" Harry pumped his hand in the air. "We *are* going to help the chief."

Kate made a quick inventory of facts. One man dead, one missing, one missing, one unknown, most of the competitors gone, and the others would be leaving within a couple of days. Should they try to help? Kate turned the situation around, looking at it for flaws, couldn't find a way that a little inquiry could possibly lead to harm.

"In a purely theoretical, armchair way. A puzzle to solve." She nodded, pleased with the way she'd handled that. "In the meantime, we need to check all the windows and make sure no moisture got into the puzzle rooms."

"I already did."

"And there's vacuuming to be done."

"I already didn't," Harry said emphatically.

"And dusting."

"I'll vacuum."

By noon, the museum looked decent enough to welcome visitors. Someone from the Granny Brigade came once a week to clean, but Kate wouldn't call them out in this weather.

They decided to walk over to Rayette's and have lunch. Aloysius followed them to the door, and looked put out when he wasn't allowed to come.

"He knows we're going to lunch," Harry said.

"Probably," Kate said at the same time they heard an angry yowl from the other side of the door.

"We should bring him something back."

"We should keep him to a strict diet. He's getting fatter than ever."

At the end of the block, they turned left onto Main Street. The plow trucks had been through again, and now the north side of the street was cleared for parking. Not that there were a lot of cars.

Most people were still digging their way out.

Rayette's was virtually empty. There was no one working at the bakery bar. Kate and Harry went through to the recent extension, a quaint bistro-style room, with round tables and a huge espresso machine.

Rayette was standing by the antique cash register, reading a paperback.

She looked up and swiped two menus.

"Quiet today. I don't mind," said Rayette, leading them to a table by the window. "My stock is low and the delivery trucks are just beginning to show up."

Izzy Carmichael was sitting at a nearby table, his mailbag occupying the opposite seat. He waved to Kate and Harry. Kate detoured to thank him for his help with the tournament.

"Glad to do it, Katie. Just sorry we had to have somebody die. But that's life for you."

Kate agreed, told him that yes, the crossword club was still scheduled for Wednesday night as long as it didn't snow again, and went to join Harry.

They were eating clam chowder and cranberry cornbread when the door opened and Jason Elks and Erik Ingersoll walked in.

They stopped, looked at each other, and made a beeline for Kate and Harry.

"Guess you both got plowed out," Kate said, making conversation.

"Guess we did," Jason said, unwinding his scarf. "And guess where we spent the morning?"

Kate shrugged. Jason was looking downright bellicose.

Erik whipped his cap off his head, leaving the sparse strands sticking straight up. "The police station. Ayuh."

Kate put down her spoon. "Why?" Though whatever the reason, it couldn't be good. They didn't much care for the "new" chief, even though Jason should have been sympathetic. He was still considered a newcomer and he'd lived and worked in Granville for fifteen years.

Jason's face reddened. "Because that—that—chief of police heard we had an argument with Gordon Lott."

Erik snorted. "Just wonder where he heard about that?"

Kate was aware of Rayette coming toward them with menus. Izzy had looked up from his lunch and was watching them.

"A lot of people were in the canteen at the VFW and also at the bar and grill, right?"

"But only a traitor would have ratted on us." Jason's face had darkened to a frightening color and his mouth was so tight he could hardly form the words.

Kate's cheeks reddened, not from anger but from embarrassment, and she could have kicked herself. If Jason and Erik hadn't yet guessed who had been the traitor, her reaction must have given her away.

"We'll probably be taken away in the night," Erik complained. "I wouldn't put it past that whippersnapper. And it's your fault, Katie." He finished the sentence wheezing.

"That's not fair," Harry snapped.

"You two going to eat or just flap your lips at the air?" Rayette shoved menus at them.

Jason took the menus. "You stay out of this, Rayette."

"It's my place, my business. Two grown men acting like children. I'm bringing you clam chowder, so sit down." She pointed to a far table. "Over there."

The two men shot dark looks at Kate and Harry, but did as they were told.

Izzy finished his lunch and lugged his bag over his shoulder.

Izzy was just five feet three. It was always amazing to Kate that such a small man was expected to carry such a heavy load, but he'd been mailman for as long as Kate could remember. He was older, slower, but he still got the mail to you, rain or shine.

He detoured over to where Kate and Harry were sitting. "Don't let those two upset you, Katie. They can't stand it that things are changing. Ain't your fault and it ain't the chief of police's fault. See you Wednesday then."

Izzy had joined the chief's side. Kate was glad for it, but she hated seeing the town always at odds.

They said good-bye and Izzy hauled his bag to the door.

"Another traitor," Erik mumbled under his breath.

"I heard that, Erik Ingersoll. Don't expect any letters or magazines this week. Good chowder, Rayette. See ya tomorrow."

Kate let out her breath. Her face was still burning. Rayette came back and pulled up a chair, but not before shooting a warning look toward Erik and Jason. "Don't mind them. Everybody's short-tempered. Going stir crazy 'cause of the snow."

"They're mad because I told the chief about their fight with Gordon Lott down in the canteen."

"Is that all? Hell." Rayette looked over to the other table. "Hey, you two, stop picking on Kate. I'm the one who told Chief Mitchell about your fight."

Kate's mouth dropped open. Jason and Erik looked stunned. Then they went back to eating.

"Did you really tell Brandon about the fight?" she whispered.

"Nope. But I woulda if he'd asked me. God knows he's been asking questions everywhere."

"He has?"

"Sure has. One thing you can say for the chief—the man's got guts. His way or the highway—all the way."

"But not the Granville way," said Kate.

"Don't mention 'the Granville way' to the chief," Harry said quickly.

"Don't you two worry. Just let the chief solve this one by himself. It'll give him some points with locals."

"He already solved the professor's murder," Kate pointed out.

"Yeah, but you caught the murderer."

"Just on a fluke. And it nearly got me killed. The chief solved it methodically. That's the only way it made it to trial."

"Maybe so. But folks around here like their heroes homegrown."

Al was waiting for them by the front door when they returned to the museum. Harry was carrying a plastic baggie of tuna tartar that Rayette had sent along. "Too old to serve to patrons," she'd said, "but somehow I don't think Aloysius will mind."

Al didn't mind at all. His radar picked up the contents of the bag and he streaked toward the kitchen and his food bowl.

Harry laughed. "Not bad for a fat cat."

Al still moved like a hunter, but if he kept gaining weight he'd probably have a heart attack. Kate dumped the tuna into his bowl and went up the stairs to put on water for tea.

Harry came up a few minutes later. He stoked the ashes of the fire they'd banked before going to lunch, added a couple of logs, then sat down in his wing chair by the fireplace and took a pencil from the pencil caddy on the side table. He picked up a book and began filling in the page.

Kate finished steeping the tea, then carried two cups to the fire. She sat down in the other wing chair and opened a Sudoku book.

It was a tradition. Hot drinks and puzzles by the fire. Mentor and apprentice. The professor and Kate. After Kate had left for college, the professor and Harry. And now that the professor was gone, Kate and Harry.

Who would come next, she wondered, looking over at the lanky fourteen-year-old and trying to imagine him as curator of the museum.

Harry deciphered his first code and gave a satisfied sigh. But instead of starting another, he just gazed into the flames. "Kate?"

"Hmm."

"Why does someone resort to murder?"

2					1		4	8	9
6			8		2			
9			4	7	5			
	6		7		8	9		
8		7				1		3
		9	6		1		5	
			9	2	4			5
			5		3			1
5	3	4		6				2

CHAPTER
TWELVE

KATE THOUGHT ABOUT it. "Anger, fear, greed, revenge . . ." She was more concerned about why this particular murder had been perpetrated during her tournament than with Harry's seemingly theoretical question.

"And jealousy," added Harry. "You forgot jealousy."

"Yeah, I did," Kate said. "I guess I just can't imagine someone killing over a Sudoku title and a cheap medal." She sighed. "Or even a watch."

Harry gave her a look.

"Not in Granville, anyway. I know people murder for all sorts of insignificant things, but to steal a watch in the middle of a blizzard and then murder the victim? Too weird."

"What about Claudine Frankel?"

Kate stared at him. "How do you know about Claudine Frankel?"

"I have eyes and ears, don't I?"

Yeah, but Kate didn't think a fourteen-year-old boy should be paying attention to a woman like Claudine Frankel. On the other hand, she was just the kind of woman an adolescent boy would notice. And probably fantasize about.

"What if she was cheating on somebody with Gordon?"

"*Harry!*"

"*Kate.*" His expression was half defiance, half amusement, and the heat rushed to Kate's cheeks.

"You're embarrassed," he said, triumphantly.

"I am not."

"Don't you treat me like a baby, too. Don't patronize me. It's the twenty-first century and guys my age know stuff. Lots of stuff."

Kate shuddered inwardly. She hesitated, wavering between talking to Harry about sex or talking about murder. She opted for murder. It seemed the lesser of two evils. She'd leave it to Brandon to give Harry the talk about sex.

"Okay. Claudine Frankel said Gordon was her ex, uh, boyfriend."

"They were lovers," Harry interjected. "I heard people talking about it. But he couldn't keep his—he, uh, flirted a lot so Claudine dumped him."

Kate was teetering on the verge of a nervous giggle—it was bouncing around her throat and she couldn't seem to swallow it. She couldn't believe she and Harry were discussing someone's sex life in an almost disinterested way.

Was this normal for a teenage boy? Shouldn't he be sneaking peeks at *Playboy* on the drugstore newsstand? Was it possible that she was really this out of touch with the ways of the world?

She cleared her throat. "She told me the same thing. Not about the, uh—She said they'd just . . . hooked up for the weekend."

"So maybe she was seeing somebody else, who saw her hanging all over Gordon and went ape sh—went crazy. And plugs Gordon."

Kate just stared at him. One of the rules Brandon had imposed on Harry was to clean up his language. After four months he was still having to self-edit. And so was Brandon. Harry had convinced him that rules worked both ways.

Kate was pretty sure that if Brandon knew they were talking about other people's sex lives, that would go on the not-to-do list of rules, too.

"I don't know, Harry. I don't think puzzle geeks carry handguns to weekend tournaments. A sharp pencil maybe."

Harry laughed. "You are so naïve."

"Me?"

Harry nodded. "Do you know how many people own hand-guns?"

Kate shook her head. She didn't really want to know.

"One out of five. And that's only the people who admit it. So out of two hundred and sixteen registered competitors and another—I don't have the figures—but say, another two hundred spectators, that's eighty-three point two people carrying at the tournament this weekend."

"Not a large enough base for comparison," Kate said, trying not to thinking of eighty gun-wielding Sudoku enthusiasts, many of whom were still at the Bowsman Inn.

"No. But it stands to reason that whatever is lost in the size of the control group is made up for by the fact that this is New Hampshire."

"And we like our guns," Kate added. "But there were a lot of out-of-staters."

"Do you know how easy it is to buy a gun? Hell, I could prob-ably find a store that would sell me one."

"Don't even try it."

"Nah. I'd never shoot anybody. Too easy." Harry tapped his temple. "I'd outsmart them."

"Brains or no brains, don't confront anybody. There's a killer out there."

Harry jumped up.

"Where are you going?"

"Just to the computer."

Kate followed him over to the computer desk.

Aloysius jumped to the top of the printer.

"So there you are. Did you enjoy your treat from Rayette?" she asked.

"Yeow," said Al and spread himself across the printer's surface.

Harry began tapping keys while Kate absently scratched Al behind his ears.

A spreadsheet appeared on the screen. Harry quickly adjusted the cell and column sizes to make a five-by-five-celled chart.

"A giant." Kate said.

"Huh?"

"A five by five grid. It's called Go Duko."

"Oh, Sudoku," Harry said, unenthusiastically. He'd never been won over to Sudoku. He didn't like solving something that was already solved. He was more interested in decoding and creating codes. He was a spy in the making. "It's just that five squares fit the page. If you move to six, you don't have enough room to type in anything."

"Very practical. So what are we typing in?"

Harry's fingers moved efficiently over the keyboard. Not bad for a boy who until last fall had been living in a trailer without electricity.

Gordon Lott's name appeared in the first box.

"What do we know about him?"

"He's a history professor."

Harry typed in unrecognizable words.

"Harry."

He grinned back at her. "Don't tell me you can't decipher this. It's simple."

"I have no intention of taking the time right now. Use standard abbreviations please."

"Boring."

Maybe so, thought Kate, but he seemed to be having fun—at least his face was cleared of that troubled epression he'd been wearing for days. What harm could a little armchair sleuthing do?

Kate was sure that Brandon was way ahead of them in the game. She doubted if she and Harry would find anything that would lead them into danger.

Harry ran a Google search. Gordon's name appeared as the author of several published history papers. He'd won a few small Sudoku and crossword tournaments, but nothing really big. He'd placed in the Philly competition several times, but wasn't even mentioned in the Stamford or Chicago tournaments.

That was about it—no academic awards, no society page announcements.

Next Harry searched for Claudine Frankel.

The screen changed to show several different sites. All of them fit on one page. She was listed on the employee roster of a software company called MKD Technologies. Further links provided her position: receptionist.

"*Eesh.*" Harry clicked on her MySpace page. A thumbnail picture of Claudine popped up. Smiling at the camera, wearing a skimpy tank top and low rider jeans, and looking sultry.

Harry whistled.

"Hmm," Kate answered. "Favorite movies, favorite television shows, favorite music . . ." She snorted. "Favorite pastimes: playing and dancing the night away. Oh, yuck."

Harry clicked to make the picture larger. "Definitely hot."

Kate groaned. Even Harry was enslaved by Claudine's charms. "Can we get back to the grid? Just fill in 'hot secretary for MKD who loves to party.'"

Harry shrugged and pulled up his spreadsheet.

At that point the telephone rang and Kate went to answer it.

"Katie? It's Alice Hinckley. Tanya Watson just called. She was driving by the VFW hall. They were clearing the parking lot. We're all going over in the morning to finish cleaning. You don't need to come. The GABs'll take care of everything."

"Are you sure you don't want to wait a few days?" Kate asked her, imagining twelve senior ladies slipping on the ice and breaking their hips.

"No, no. I called the vets, they'll have somebody salt the walkway and turn up the heat before we get there."

Of course Kate would go. She hadn't opened the museum for business since the storm and one more day wouldn't matter. She hung up and went to look out the window. From where she was standing she couldn't tell if Alice's walk had been shoveled. She turned to Harry.

"Time to get physical," she told him. "Let's go see if Alice needs to be shoveled out."

Harry groaned. He quickly typed in one last thing. "I've locked this folder. It's named AEGLT."

Kate raised her eyebrows. "I suppose that's code for something."

"Yep. But too difficult to explain right now, if we have to shovel."

Kate gave him a look. "Something to do with mobile agent software by any chance?"

Harry grimaced. "Yeah. And Gordon Lott. See the GL in the center?"

"You misspelled aglet."

"No I didn't. It's a simple scramble code."

"I'll take your word for it. What's the password?"

"I'll never tell."

"Harry Perkins, this is a perfect example of bureaucratic behavior. The chief locks you out of his files, so you think you should lock me out of yours. Don't even think it. I have friends who can break any password." She gave him her most sinister frown. "You wouldn't like them when they're angry."

Harry burst out laughing, a sound that had been way too infrequent lately. "It's SUIS."

"Another codeword?"

"Oh, Kate." Harry shook his head like a disappointed school teacher. "It's the last four letters of Aloysius spelled backward."

"I knew that," Kate said and strode out the door so he couldn't see her chagrin.

They were just finishing Alice's front walk when a police car drove up and stopped at the curb.

"It's six already?" moaned Harry.

"Must be." Kate watched the car door open. Brandon Mitchell unfolded himself from the front seat.

"Hi Chief," Kate said and leaned on her shovel, trying to look relaxed—and not like someone who was dying to ask what had happened between him and Claudine, or if he'd gotten any leads.

Unfortunately, she only managed to break off a big chunk of snow. The snow crumbled, the shovel slipped, and she fell on her butt on the sidewalk.

Harry started laughing. The chief shot him a quelling look, but when he turned to help Kate up, the corner of his mouth was twitching.

"Not funny," she said, brushing off her jeans.

"Where's your hat?" he asked, now grinning unabashedly.

"In my coat pocket, just in case there were any chiefs of police driving by who might make fun of it."

"All is vanity," he said. "Come on, Harry. It's time to go."

He and Harry saw Kate inside the museum and then left for home.

Kate shrugged out of her coat and went back upstairs to the office. She glanced at her watch: six twenty. She might as well go home, too.

Instead, she sat down at the computer. She kept thinking about Gordon looking at that stupid watch. Maybe if he'd paid more attention to solving the Sudoku instead of worrying about the time, he wouldn't have made those fatal mistakes. And maybe he'd still be alive.

And maybes are not scientific, she reminded herself.

She just couldn't figure out why anyone would want to steal *that* watch. It was huge and cumbersome, larger than most sports watches. Covered with gadget buttons. Very showy. It might tempt someone, but enough for someone to follow him into a snowstorm and shoot him for it?

Kenny Revell and the man in the orange hat were probably the last people to see Gordon alive. Kenny had disappeared. Did he have the watch? Did Orange Hat?

Where were they?

Kate went back to the computer. She typed in the password to the AEGLT folder and stared at the spreadsheet.

The square next to Kenny Revell was still blank. She Googled him. There wasn't much. He wasn't a journalist as Tony had suggested, but a software developer. A software developer who never missed a Sudoku tournament. Yet there was not one mention of Sudoku in the first five sites she pulled up.

On the fifth site, she found a picture of him with three other men at a launch party for a new fighter pilot game developed by MKD Technologies.

Interesting. He and Claudine worked for the same software company. MKD. That might explain how Kenny knew Gordon.

Gordon was a history professor, Kenny was a video game designer. They both liked puzzles. At first glance, it seemed a benign enough connection. Could it have led to more?

Kate wished Harry were still there. She needed a sounding board. Even though he groused that crosswords and ciphers required thinking, while Sudoku only required processing, his preference was just a matter of intellectual taste. He was more than adept at solving both.

Sudoku depended on sequential steps. Eliminate all the number candidates until you were left with the correct ones. When you were finished, all the grids would be filled. Computer games also encompassed a sequence of events; in the case of Kenny's fighter pilot game, eliminate the enemy planes and you won.

But the internal logic didn't hold true for both.

With Sudoku, if you made a mistake you simply erased it, corrected it, and continued on. In fight simulation, if you made one wrong move, the game could be over. Sudoku was based on mental acuity, the computer game on quick reflexes and eye-to-hand coordination.

So what's the connection?

She pulled up the MKD site and clicked on their merchandise page. Hundreds of games, tip sheets, and cheats appeared. Slowly she began to scroll through the list, clicking on games and seeing if the individual designer was named. Kenny Revell's name appeared on many of them. Even more often, his name was coupled with that of Isaac Walsh, a codesigner.

She added Walsh's name to their spreadsheet and copied and pasted in the video games they had designed together. Walsh might have heard from Kenny, or at least could provide a clue as to why he was at the tournament.

Of course, she couldn't just call and ask him—that would be interfering in a police investigation. Surely Brandon had come up with the same information; he was a computer geek.

She saved the new input and put the computer in sleep mode.

She was tired. Her *brain* was tired. She didn't even know if Kenny was still missing. The chief might not keep her abreast of his investigation, but Elmira would. Kate didn't think much came or went through the police station that Elmira didn't know about.

Kate made a quick call to Elmira at home. "Still missing," she said when Kate asked her about Kenny Revell. "Never heard of the other guy, but I'll keep my eyes and ears open."

Kate thanked her and hung up, thinking that if only the residents would as eagerly share information with the police chief as they did with Kate, the chief's job would be a whole lot easier.

She leaned back in the desk chair and heard a thunk that told her Al had jumped from his favorite perch on the top shelf of the bookcase and would soon be appearing on her desktop. She waited for him to scramble up her lap and spread himself across the ink blotter.

It was a ritual they went through at least four times a day. She scratched his ears and he flopped to his back so she could tickle his stomach.

"Oh, Al, too bad people can't be as straightforward as cats."

::

Kate was happy to see that the lights on Porter Street had been restored. She returned the Buick to Pru's driveway, then knocked on her door to return her keys.

"Come in and have some soup," Pru said, taking the keys.

Kate hesitated. All she really wanted to do was take a long, hot shower, work her Sudoku puzzle, and go to bed. But her aunt had been stuck at home for several days, and Kate knew she must be lonely.

"So tell me all about your dinner with Sam the other night," Pru said as she placed a bowl of beef barley soup in front of Kate.

"We went to the inn."

"What did you wear? It's always hard to juggle snow boots and high heels."

"It is," Kate agreed. Which was why she'd not bothered with high heels. Of course, she didn't need to tell Pru that. Or that she'd worn corduroy pants and an ancient sweater. Sam didn't mind, but she knew Pru would.

"Alice called. We're going over to the VFW hall in the morning. Don't know what the rush is. We got out all the perishable garbage before we left, but you know Alice. Woman has to be in charge."

"She called me, too," Kate said. "I'll drive over with you, if I may. See if my car will start."

Pru's eyes sparked. "Well, if it doesn't, we'll just call Endelman's Garage. I'm sure Norris will be happy to come give you a jump. Such a nice man."

And such job security, Kate added silently. He also liked to bowl, which had been one of Kate's favorite pastimes when she lived in Alexandria. But bowling with Norris and his friends didn't have quite the same appeal as bowling with mathematicians who analyzed, theorized, and gambled on every aspect of the game.

Sometimes Kate missed her colleagues. She was glad she'd come back to Granville. The museum was important to her. Most of the time, though, she still felt like a stranger in a strange land.

Or possibly just a geek.

She finished her soup and Pru stood on the porch to watch while Kate ran shivering up the street and onto the front porch of her own bungalow.

"Pick you up at nine-thirty," Pru called before Kate closed her door.

CHAPTER

THIRTEEN

PRU HONKED FOR Kate the next morning at exactly nine thirty. They drove down the icy street, Pru chatting away and not paying very much attention to where she was going. She cruised through the Maple Street stop sign like she always did and headed for town.

"Sooner or later, you're going to get another ticket," Kate warned her. "Not to mention you might have an accident."

"Pooh," Pru said. "Nobody ever stops at that stupid sign. Never have, never will. Don't know why they don't take it down. Don't know why they put it *up* in the first place."

Kate bit her tongue. There were some battles she'd never win. She kept quiet for the rest of the short drive, half the time with her eyes squeezed shut.

The plow trucks had cleared the VFW parking lot and Kate's Matrix sat alone, perched on a doily of snow in the middle of the asphalt.

Someone had brushed it clean and Kate made a mental note to call Mike Landers and thank him.

The engine caught on the first try. Pru stood nearby with her lips pursed, clearly unhappy not to have an excuse for calling Norris Endelman. Kate let it idle for a few minutes, trying not to comment on Pru's evident disappointment.

The other GABs began to arrive. First Tanya's Subaru station wagon with Alice and Carrie Blaine in the backseat. Tanya was followed almost immediately by Rayette, who wasn't a granny, but who'd volunteered to drive. Maria Albioni was her only passenger.

"Elmira's working and Beatrice has a cold," Alice informed Kate. She was muffled in an ankle-length, black down coat with a hood drawn tight around her face, a diminutive Darth Vader with rosy cheeks. "Chop, chop," she ordered. Everyone filed down the newly deiced sidewalk, Carrie sounding out the pavement with her ebony cane before each step. It was slow progress and Kate and Rayette kept watchful eyes on the group as they toddled up the steps to the hall.

True to their word, the vets had turned on the heat, and the vents were pumping out warm air. They were also pumping out the musty smell of dust and dead air.

Kate looked around the empty foyer. It was hard to believe that only a few days before it had been filled with people. There were papers left on the registration desk, a mitten on the floor. Several scarves, forgotten by their owners, were draped over the counter in front of the coat check.

Alice bustled the others to the coat rack where they hung up their coats, scarves, and hats while Alice organized them into teams.

Pru and Rayette went downstairs to pack up the canteen. Alice took a broom to the vendors' room, while Tanya, Carrie, Maria, and Kate went into the main hall to gather up papers and programs and whatever else had been left behind.

Harry had only managed to store half the chairs before they'd had to leave the building. Tanya and Kate took that job, letting Maria and Carrie do the lighter work.

The hall gradually grew warm, and Kate and the others began to shed their outer layer of sweaters. Unfortunately, the heat hadn't dispelled the stale air. It actually seemed to grow stronger.

"What's that smell?" Tanya asked, wrinkling her nose.

Kate shook her head. "I hope it isn't a gas leak."

"Nope. Not gas. More like garbage. We must've left a bag behind by mistake. Good thing it isn't summer."

Rayette stuck her head in the door, sniffing the air like a hunting dog. "It's up here, too. But not as bad."

"Smells like we left a bag of garbage behind," Tanya told her.

"Nope. It's real nasty downstairs, and Pru and I have been looking. We didn't leave anything. Come see for yourself."

Kate and Tanya followed Rayette outside and down the stairs, leaving Carrie puttering about with a garbage bag. They met Maria, who was just coming back from the ladies' room.

"What's that nasty smell?" she asked.

"That's what we're trying to find out," Rayette said.

Maria fell in step with the others. "It's a good thing we got here when we did. Can you imagine the Vets walking into this? They'd never let us rent the hall again."

When they reached the canteen, Pru was just climbing down from a stepladder. The high, narrow window was open, and though it was mostly covered with snow, a cold breeze wafted in.

"I know it's a waste of good heat, but I could use the fresh air."

Pru looked a little pale and Kate empathized with her. The smell was much worse down here.

Rayette was still sniffing the air like a hunting dog, which would have been funny if the smell wasn't so overpowering.

"Maybe one of the bathrooms backed up," volunteered Tanya.

They checked each bathroom. Everything seemed in order.

Alice met them at the door of the vendors' room, holding a broom and wearing a lace-edged handkerchief tied over her nose.

"I think someone must have left a garbage bag inside the back door," she said, her words muffled by the handkerchief. "I was just going to check."

Without discussion they all walked down the hall. At the very end, a locked door led up cellar steps to the dumpster. There was no garbage bag near it, and Kate began to get a terrible feeling.

"It's strongest here," Tanya said, covering her mouth and nose with her hand. She was standing at the door of the boiler room.

"Rats," Maria said. "Came in to die. Always do during a cold snap. Nasty things." She pointed to the door of the boiler room, with a dramatic gesture right out of Italian opera.

"Rats?" Kate's stomach lurched.

"If you had a husband," Pru whispered, "*he* could take care of it for us."

"We'll call the exterminator," Kate said, ignoring her aunt. She had no desire to bag and toss a decaying rodent.

Tanya pushed them aside. "*Please.* I grew up in the country. Dead rats don't scare me."

"You grew up half a mile outside the town limits," Alice reminded her.

"Like I said, in the country." Tanya reached for the door knob.

The door opened and a putrid smell burst out of the boiler room. Kate's stomach lurched. Someone groaned. Pru yanked the collar of her turtleneck up over her nose.

They all just stood there as warm fetid air surrounded them.

"Probably sped up the decaying process, cause of the boiler making the room overly warm," said Tanya. She took the broom out of Alice's hand. "Somebody get me a couple of those big garbage bags." She stepped inside and was immediately engulfed in shadows.

The others huddled in the doorway, except Kate, who, feeling responsible for the group, took a step inside the door. She stretched out her foot and, not encountering anything, took another step. Finding nothing, she groped along the wall for a light switch and flipped it on. A single overhead lightbulb glared yellow in the gloom and cast the room into strange shadows.

Kate peered around the boiler room. It was ten feet square, with concrete block walls, a cement floor, and one small rectangular window high on the wall. An ancient furnace took up most of the space. Two straight-back chairs faced each other across a steamer trunk that was placed near the furnace. *A makeshift table, used by the custodians,* Kate guessed.

"See anything?" she asked Tanya, trying not to look for herself.

"No," came the muffled reply and Kate realized Tanya was holding her breath.

Kate stepped completely into the room and was hit by a cold current of air. She looked toward the gray patch of window. It was covered by the snow and barely let in any light.

But it was letting in snow. Kate moved closer. Something crunched beneath her foot. Glass. The window was broken. There were shards of glass on the floor amid a pool of water and ice.

"That's how the rat got in," said Tanya. "Now, if it just didn't get into the walls before it died . . ."

Kate shuddered. Rayette and Pru had joined them and were looking around tentatively, though it was obvious that they were not anxious to find anything.

Pru pointed to the steamer trunk. "What's that? Sticking out of the trunk."

With a feeling of foreboding, Kate steeled herself and stepped toward the truck, just as Tanya lifted the top.

Belatedly, Kate screamed, "Don't!"

The top fell back revealing not a rat, but a man, still dressed for outdoors arms, and legs folded up and wedged inside. His black knit cap tilted at a rakish angle and his eyes were wide open.

There was a moment of horrified silence. Then Tanya screamed. There was a mad dash for the door. Kate backed away, the smell forgotten.

There was a dead man in the boiler room.

"Kate, get away from there!" Pru called from the hallway.

Kate nodded and backed out the door, slamming it behind her.

"What's all that noise?" Carrie Blaine was hobbling down the hall toward them, her cane clacking on the concrete floor. "And what's that darn smell? Makes me gag."

"A dead man," wailed Tanya, whose *sangfroid* seemed to stop with small furry animals.

"Where? Let me see."

"No!" shouted Kate.

"Can't hear you," Carrie lied, using her cane like a cattle prod to get through the group. "Got my hearing aids turned off." She puttered past and opened the boiler room door. "Merciful heavens, it's a dead man. Whew! Reeks like the dickens." She shut the door.

Rayette, who until now had been standing like a statue, suddenly sprang to life. "I'll call the chief."

"That young beans for brains?" said Alice. "I say we let Kate solve this, like she did the last time."

"I didn't solve the last one," Kate insisted. "Chief Mitchell *did*. And saved my life in the bargain."

"Aw, pshaw," said Alice. "I was there and that man was a day late and a dollar short."

Kate shook her head. In spite of Alice's bravura, the GABs suddenly looked fragile, frightened, and close to being sick. "Rayette, please call. The rest of us are going to wait outside. *Way* outside." She rounded the seniors up and herded them toward the stairs while Rayette went for her cell phone.

"Two murders," said Alice as Kate helped her up the steps. "That makes three, counting the professor. What's this town coming to?"

"Things haven't been the same since we got that new police chief," Pru said. "When Roger Blanchard was the chief, nothing ever happened. Nobody got killed and nobody got traffic tickets."

"Probably because Roger was too busy fishing to notice," muttered Tanya.

"You just name me one—"

"Aunt Pru, please." Kate wanted to shake her aunt but she was too busy trying to keep on her feet and help the others. "You'll be blaming me next. All of the murders happened since I came back to Granville."

Pru stopped on the stairs long enough to gape at her. "That has nothing to do with it."

Only because Kate was one of them and the chief wasn't.

Kate shooed them along, stars beginning to dance behind her eyes. She needed fresh air and so did the others.

"They're on their way," Rayette said, as she joined Kate. "And Pru McDonald, stop talking beans. It's probably just some poor old tramp who climbed in to get out of the storm and died."

"Humph."

Rayette and Kate exchanged looks. They both knew it wasn't some vagabond who chose the wrong place to die—they'd seen the blood clotted on the man's face. Unless he'd bashed himself on the head, it was going to be another case of murder.

"It's possible," Kate said slowly. "He broke the window to come inside where it was warm, looked into the trunk for a blanket or something, and the top fell and hit him on the head . . ."

"Honey," said Tanya, "That man didn't hit his head, then climb into the trunk for a snooze. Someone offed him. Lord, Lord, Lord."

"Amen," Alice said.

"Amen," said the others.

When Chief Mitchell arrived, along with his two additional squad cars, Kate and Rayette were waiting for him. Maria had been sick and Kate had made everyone get into Tanya's car with the engine pumping out heat.

The chief was tight-lipped and merely nodded to Kate and Rayette before saying, "Where?"

"The boiler room."

"Stay here."

"But—"

"I'll find it." He motioned to Officers Wilson and Owens, who looked anxiously toward the building. Reluctantly, they shuffled toward it. Paul Curtis followed them, the forensic case banging against his thigh as he walked.

Suddenly the car doors opened and five granny activists crowded around the chief.

"Ladies—" he began. He closed his mouth, opened it. "Not now." He turned on his heel and followed his officers inside.

"Well, of all the cheek," Pru said. "Just what you'd expect. Leave a bunch of traumatized senior citizens to fend for themselves . . . in the cold . . . all alone."

Alice snorted. "You're finally calling yourself a senior citizen?

You and your dyed hair and crazy outfits. Me, I'm a senior citizen and proud of it."

"Then why did you want me to join this granny group?" Pru fisted her hands at her hips.

"Because you're too big for your britches. Your spandex, made-for-teenagers jogging britches. Not that I've ever seen you jog as far as the mailbox."

"Why—"

Kate didn't even try to stop them. As long as they were sniping at each other, they wouldn't be thinking about what they'd seen. She wished the chief had told them to go home. They might be feisty, but they weren't hardy enough to withstand this cold, and she didn't think she could get them to leave by herself.

And besides, the chief would have to question them, wouldn't he? She looked over the group. The GABs were a force to be reckoned with. She didn't envy the chief.

She took Rayette aside. "I'm going to ask Chief Mitchell if they can go home. Keep them here."

Rayette lifted her eyebrows, but nodded.

Kate took a breath and headed toward the hall.

Officers Wilson and Owens were standing guard at the door of the boiler room. Wilson glanced at the open door. He didn't move, just called for the chief.

Kate stopped halfway down the hall, knowing that the chief wouldn't like her being there. He stepped out of the boiler room, hands at his sides and covered in latex gloves.

Wilson pointed down the hall toward Kate.

The chief's countenance was grim. The smell, now that Kate knew what it was, was overpowering. She didn't know how he could stand being in the small space with the source of it.

He walked toward her, but instead of stopping when he reached her, he continued down the hall. Kate had no choice but to follow him.

When she caught up to him, he was pulling off the latex gloves. He dropped them in the trashcan and turned to face her.

"Isn't the crime scene unit coming?" Kate asked.

"Can't get through. Slide covered the highway with snow. Is that why you ignored my orders to come down here? To make sure I wasn't mucking up—"

"I came down to see if it would be okay to send the GABs home. They're cold and frightened."

"Wilson, Owens."

The two bounded forward as if they'd been shot from a cannon. They were both pale. Dick Wilson, the younger of the two, looked like he might faint. Paul Curtis appeared from the boiler room. He closed the door and hurried after them.

"You finished in there?"

"Yes, sir," Paul said. His face was tinged with green.

"Then let's go upstairs and question some witnesses."

"Yes, sir," they said in chorus and scrambled up the stairs.

The chief watched them go, then shook his head. "After you." He gestured for Kate to precede him.

The GABs crowded around them as soon as they stepped outside.

"Ladies," the chief said. "Just a few questions please, and then you can go."

Pru set her chin stubbornly in the air. Alice pursed her lips and scowled past her dimples at him.

"What's he saying?" yelled Carrie.

"He wants to ask us questions," Tanya yelled in her ear.

"I'll try to be quick. Did any of you touch the trunk or the deceased?"

He was met with stubborn silence.

Kate made a face at Pru.

Pru ignored her.

The chief heaved a sigh. "Take them all downtown and print them."

His three officers stared back at him, wide-eyed, as a burst of outraged voices split the air.

"*Brandon,*" Kate said under her breath.

"You don't think one of us murdered that poor man," Pru demanded.

The chief flinched. "It's merely procedure. In order to distinguish your prints from any others that might be there."

"You'll be helping the investigation," said Rayette, jumping in. "You might even get your names in the paper—"

The chief gave her his winning scowl.

"—And *afterward*, the officers will drive you to the café for lunch." Rayette grinned at the chief. "As Chief Mitchell's guests."

Round-eyed astonishment from the GABS competed with barely concealed exasperation from the chief.

"Why would he do that?" Alice asked suspiciously.

"To show his appreciation for your cooperation."

"And the chief of police is paying?" yelled Carrie Blaine.

"Deaf as a post except when it comes to someone else's nickel," whispered Pru.

"Yes." Rayette turned to the chief. "I'll put it on your tab."

Brandon looked startled, but merely said, "Certainly," then he turned and went back inside.

"Does he have a tab at the café?" Kate asked Rayette under her breath.

"He does now. Come along ladies, I have a nice potato soup and crab cakes special today."

Kate was wondering if he meant for her to go with the others, when she heard a sharp, "Ms. McDonald."

She had her answer. "Yes, Chief Mitchell."

"Since your fingerprints are already on file, would you mind answering a few questions?"

Kate's cheeks burned. He'd tricked her into leaving her fingerprints when she'd been his number one suspect in the professor's murder. It still rankled.

"Certainly." She walked toward him, but hesitated at the steps.

"I don't suppose you want to go back inside."

Kate shook her head, though she didn't want to stand out in the cold, either.

The chief reached inside his shirt pocket for his pad and pen. He wasn't wearing a coat and his knuckles were already turning red from the few minutes he'd been outside.

"I guess the outer hall will be okay," she said.

The chief nodded and practically pushed her up the steps to the door.

"Jesus, it's cold," he said as soon as they were in the foyer.

"This is nothing. It's been a mild winter."

"Oh, great." He pulled a folding chair near the door and motioned for her to sit. Kate noticed that he'd left the door ajar for the fresh air and she silently thanked him for it.

He pulled another chair over and sat down across from her, his ankle crossed over the other knee, his pen poised.

He didn't have to ask her questions—she'd done this before. "We came to clean up and right away noticed an unpleasant smell." She swallowed. "But it got worse as the heat kicked in. We thought we must have left garbage since we didn't have time to finish cleaning Sunday."

She went through the morning. Why they decided to look for

the source of the smell. How they followed the smell downstairs to the boiler room door. Who opened the door. What happened when she turned on the light.

The chief just wrote, not asking any questions, occasionally holding up his hand for her to wait while he caught up.

"I noticed the broken window, and Tanya—Tanya Watson—she thought a rat must have gotten in and died."

The chief grimaced.

"Yeah," said Kate. "I wanted to call the exterminator." Her voice broke, something between a laugh and a sob.

"You're doing fine. Just a bit more."

Kate closed her eyes, exhaled. "Then Pru saw a piece of fabric, it looked like dark blue or black nylon caught on the edge of the trunk. Did I tell you that the trunk was partially opened?"

The chief nodded. "Just keep going."

"Pru opened the lid and there . . . there he was like one of those marionettes stuffed in the trunk. And his hat—" Tears clogged her throat. "Why are two men dead? And at my tournament?"

"What about the hat?" he asked gruffly.

It was the perfect tone to bring her back from a fit of near-hysteria.

"It wasn't orange."

"Ah, yes, the man in the orange hat."

"But this man's hat is black. Who is he? What's he doing there?"

"I think, Kate, that you've just discovered the whereabouts of Kenny Revell."

6								8
		5	9		6	3		
	4	9		1		6	5	
	7			8			6	
			2		4			
	6			7			1	
	9	7		3		1	8	
		3	6		7	4		
4								2

"I WAS PRETTY sure that's who it was," Kate said. She felt raw, inside and out. She wanted to go home and take a long hot bath, scrub away the smell, the horror, the memory. A photographic memory was her curse as well as her blessing, and she knew that Kenny Revell's staring, bloated face would haunt her for a long time.

"Anything else?"

"What? No. It's just . . ." She heaved a sigh. "Why now and here?"

"Kate."

She thought she detected an undercurrent of gentleness beneath the exasperation in the chief's voice, but she was probably mistaken. "I know. But . . . it couldn't be because of the competition, could it? Did my tournament cause the death of two men?"

"It might have been the catalyst, but I imagine the seeds were planted before."

"I should have known you wouldn't say anything comforting."

"I wouldn't patronize you."

Kate glanced up at him. He was stony faced, in police chief mode. "Thanks. I guess."

The outer door swung wide and Sam Swyndon burst through, lugging his camera cases. "Katie? Are you alright?"

The chief stood up.

Sam nodded curtly. "Chief Mitchell. Sorry I couldn't get here sooner. Family portrait."

"This way." The chief started toward the stairs.

"Surely there's no reason for you to keep Katie here."

"It's okay, Sam," Kate interjected "The chief is just doing his job—"

"If the chief were doing his job, I wouldn't be here photographing another murder."

"Sam, that isn't fair," Kate said, blushing with embarrassment for both of them.

The chief merely gave him a bland look, then turned around. "Kate, you can go for now. I may have questions later."

Kate nodded, stunned. He and Harry were the only ones who called her Kate. Everyone else in town still called her Katie, much to her professional chagrin. The chief never called her anything but Ms. McDonald in front of other people.

His "Kate" was obviously a challenge to Sam's "Katie."

At another time she might have found it amusing, even flattering, but at the moment she just felt sick. She stood up.

Saw stars. Sat down again.

Sam knelt by her chair. "Wait here. When I'm finished, I'll take you home."

"Sam, if you please." The chief's voice was all business.

Sam's eyes flashed, but he patted Kate's knee and followed the chief downstairs.

As soon as they were gone, Kate stood up again, this time more slowly. She made her way to the door, pushed it open, and gulped huge breaths of the cold brisk air. Her head cleared but the stench seemed to have taken up permanent residence in her nostrils. She drove home for a bath and change of clothes before driving to the museum.

Kate was sitting at the office computer desk when the newly installed buzzer alerted her that someone was at the door.

She went downstairs and found Alice Hinckley standing on the porch.

"Didn't know if you planned to open. But it's my day, so I came over right after lunch." She held out a plastic bag. "Rayette sent you this. Said as long as the chief was paying, you might as well eat in style."

Kate took the bag and stepped aside for Alice to come in.

"How did things go at the station?"

Alice began pulling off her gloves. She held up one hand. "Look at this."

Kate could see the residue from the fingerprint ink.

"I've never been fingerprinted in my life."

Great. Another grudge for the old guard to hold against the chief. "It's just because they need to be able to compare your prints to any fingerprints they find at the scene."

"Helen Greer and two ladies from the garden club were at Rayette's when we got there." Alice sighed contentedly. "They were positively green with envy. And when they found out Chief Mitchell was footing the bill? Well, you should have seen their faces. Wicked cool."

Kate blinked.

"And I can tell you, the girls didn't scrimp on lunch."

Somehow Kate couldn't imagine Alice and the others chowing down lunch after what they'd witnessed. It had certainly killed Kate's appetite.

Shouldn't Alice be home, lying in a dark room with her smelling salts nearby? Instead she was crowing about pulling one over on the chief *and* making her friends jealous. Kate would never understand people.

"And," Alice's sharp blue eyes twinkled with merriment. "Rayette served my homemade jam. Isn't that a kicker? The police chief aiding and abetting a felon."

"I don't think selling jam without a license makes you a felon . . . " Kate began.

"Little you know. But if that southern boy thinks he can butter us up . . ."

Here we go again. Back to square one. Would they ever learn to accept him?

Kate got Alice settled at the reception desk and went back upstairs. She'd barely sat down when the private phone line rang. She checked caller ID and saw it was Sam.

"Why didn't you wait for me?" he asked as soon as Kate said hello.

"I'm sorry. I meant to call and leave you a message but I got busy."

"I've been worried sick. You didn't answer your home phone. I called your Aunt Pru, but she didn't answer."

Kate cringed. *Small favors.*

"So I drove over to make sure you were okay."

"I came to work."

"I figured that out."

"You shouldn't have worried."

"Well, I do worry. That's what friends do. Take care of each other. I thought—"

Kate cut him off. It seemed like everybody was trying to tell her what to do. "Sam, I appreciate your concern, but I'm fine and I really do have work to do."

Silence at the other end of the call. Kate knew she'd hurt his feelings, but she was edgy and her patience, what little she had to begin with, was wearing thin. "I'll talk to you later, okay?"

"Sure. Fine. Bye." He hung up.

Kate held the receiver for a few seconds, not understanding exactly what had just happened, but assuming it was her fault. She knew Pru would think so.

She'd thanked him, reassured him, offered to talk later, and he'd practically hung up on her. She just didn't get it.

And now she had another murder to cope with. She should probably be doing something to staunch any bad press associated with the museum's tournament, but she didn't have a clue as to what to do. She might make things worse.

So here she sat, clueless.

The intercom buzzed; Alice's voice warbled through the speaker. "Tony Kefalas is here."

"Great," Kate answered. "I'll be right down."

With all that had happened, she'd been remiss about Tony, though she guessed he hadn't minded being handed over to Ginny Sue.

She hurried down the stairs and found Tony and Alice.

"Well," Tony said, after giving Kate a kiss on the cheek. "I must say. This is the most eventful competition I've ever been to."

"Alice told you about this morning?"

"Yes. It's too bizarre to contemplate."

"I'm sorry you've gotten sucked into all this. I really thought it would be an easy and fun weekend for you."

Tony smiled at her. He was so charming and lovely to look at. No wonder Ginny Sue was smitten. "You know I was happy to do it. But two murders? I'll dine on this story for months. No wonder you left the think tank. This has got to be more exciting than sitting around arguing about numerical possibilities that will never have any usable application."

Kate frowned a little at that. Was that what she had spent her life doing? Playing with useless numbers? "I could use a tad less excitement."

"I sympathize. Do you think he was lying there during the whole tournament?"

Kate had tried not to think about it at all. "Possibly."

"But how did he get there?"

"A window was broken. It's just big enough for a man to squeeze through."

Tony puffed out air. "So did he climb in, or did the murderer climb out?"

"He must have climbed in," Kate said. "There was glass on the floor."

"My goodness," Alice piped in. "I didn't think about how he got there. Katie, you are so clever. I knew you'd be able to solve this."

Kate shook her head.

Tony raised both eyebrows at her. "I confess, I'm a little slow on the uptake here. A man breaks a window and crawls into a boiler room where someone is waiting to kill him? Does the killer climb out of the broken window? Or go out through the door?"

"I don't know," admitted Kate. "I was too busy trying to figure out if it had anything to do with the tournament."

"You think two people were murdered over a puzzle?" Tony

barked out a laugh. "Sorry, but that's a new one. Jealousy can be pretty rampant at these things, but Gordon Lott lost. Competitors are generally *happy* if the competition loses. They don't run around killing each other."

"Of course not," Kate said.

"And Kenny Revell wasn't even competing."

Kate froze. "How did you know it was Kenny Revell?"

Tony's eyebrows lifted. "Alice told me."

"Oh."

"Don't give it another thought. The tournament isn't culpable. Now, why don't you show me this museum of yours."

Glad to be off the subject of murder, Kate led him to the room opposite the reception area. "This is the Jigsaw Room."

"Love it," said Tony, gazing around with enthusiasm. "Especially how you've got the spherical ones hanging like the planets. Absolutely magical."

"The professor did that. The kids love it." Kate smiled, proud to be carrying on the professor's life work.

"He sounds like an extremely special person."

"He was. Actually, I sometimes think he's still here."

"The ghost of the puzzle museum?"

"Not a ghost, but—I don't know—a presence."

"I like the new you."

"Me?" Kate asked in astonishment. "Am I different than I was before?"

"More . . . whimsical. It suits you."

Kate laughed. "I've never been called whimsical in my life."

Tony shrugged and they went across the hall to the mechanical puzzle room. Tony was delighted with all the exhibits. They walked from room to room, Kate showing him her favorites and telling him stories about the acquisitions. She forgot about the murders as the museum worked its magic.

Tony was just the audience she needed right then. He was first and foremost a puzzle lover, highly appreciative of the scope of the exhibits, and entertained by her anecdotes.

She had to practically drag him from P.T.'s Place, the interactive room, named after her mentor. Tony had zeroed in on a new three-dimensional Sudoku cube and might have sat there for hours if the downstairs buzzer hadn't rung and the sound of children's voices carried up the stairwell.

"Wednesdays are field trip days," Kate explained.

Tony reluctantly put down the puzzle and they went to the office where Kate made tea.

"Actually, Tony, if you're not in a rush, I'd like to pick your brain about a few things."

Tony glanced at his watch. "I have some time. Ginny Sue is meeting me at the inn for dinner. Then we're going barhopping. Though she tells me there are only two in town and one isn't the kind of place we'd care to go to. She's a nice girl."

"We went to school together. She's been a godsend to me and the museum."

"She told me. Not about being a godsend—she's very modest—but a lot of fun. She's driving me to Boston tomorrow to catch my flight to Chicago, just so I could spend an extra day in Granville."

"Sounds serious."

"Just a good time."

Kate wasn't sure Ginny Sue saw it the same way. She considered asking Tony what his intentions were, but decided against it. She had no business mucking around in other people's affairs; she couldn't even handle her own—or lack of them.

Tony held up one of Harry's cryptogram books. "Going into spy mastering?"

"They're Harry's."

"Indeed? Clever boy, your Harry."

"Yes he is. Photographic memory, but only an almost-genius, according to him. I have my doubts."

Tony chuckled.

The dumbwaiter door behind the desk swung open. Tony stepped back and watched in amazement as Aloysius padded into the room. He stopped to give Tony an appraising look.

"Good God, I thought it was a raccoon. Is this the famous Maine Coon cat?"

"Infamous is more like it," Kate said. "He runs the place." She leaned over to stroke his head. "Don't you, Al?"

Al chirruped and passed on to Tony. He rubbed up against Tony's trouser leg and Tony bent down to scratch him under the chin. Al flopped onto his back, paws splayed out to the side. Tony tickled his stomach, which Al enjoyed for a bit, then, assured of his new conquest, he rolled to his feet and continued on his path to the windowsill.

Tony stood up and brushed his hands off. "So what do you want to pick my nongenius brain about?"

Kate handed him a cup of tea. "I thought you might be able to help Harry and me figure something out."

"Sure, if I can."

"He should be here soon. He comes every day after school. I can bring you up to speed before he gets here."

"I'm intrigued."

They sat down in the wing chairs and Kate began to tell him what she and Harry had learned so far.

Harry burst into the room a few minutes later. "Everybody on the bus was talking about the new murder," he said, throwing his backpack into the corner. "And I missed it! You'd think that living with the police chief would give me an in."

"Trust me. You didn't want to be there."

"Yeah, I did. But instead, while you were discovering a *body*, I was taking a test on the Hundred Years' War. Boring. Hi, Tony."

"Good to see you, Harry."

"How'd you do on your test?" Kate asked.

Harry gave her a look. "Name, dates, battles. *Duh.*" He rolled the computer chair over and sat down. "Tell me everything."

"Another obsessive puzzle solver," Tony said and raised his mug to salute Harry.

A curse as well as a blessing, thought Kate. She gave Harry the expurgated version of finding Kenny Revell's body.

"Wow. So did you and Tony come up with any theories about what happened?"

"Not yet."

"Not even a guess?"

"Harry," she said with mock censure.

"Yeah, yeah. A hypothesis? Theorems? Questions?"

"Plenty of questions," Tony said. "Though I think we can pretty much exclude Kenny as Gordon's murderer. They're both dead. Someone else must have killed them both."

Harry grinned. "The guy in the orange hat."

"Orange hat?" Tony's eyes darted to Kate's.

She had no doubt that he remembered her asking Jed Dawson about it when they had dinner at the inn. "The other man who was with them the night Gordon was murdered. I don't guess you know who that was."

Tony frowned, shook his head. "Your illustrious police chief asked me the same thing. I do remember Lott was with a couple of people, but I didn't notice who they were. Claudine was too busy hogging the spotlight."

"She does kind of stick out." Harry grinned at him.

"Let me give you some manly advice. Stay away from women like Claudine Frankel."

"You don't like her?"

"I don't care one way or the other. She and Gordon are two of a kind—needy. You don't want to get involved with people like that. They'll drag you down."

Harry looked disappointed.

Kate just looked at Tony. Was he talking from personal experience?

"Now, about Mr. Orange Hat. No one has seen him and he hasn't come forward?"

"Nope." Harry whistled. "Unless he's dead, too. How weird would that be?"

"Pretty weird," Tony said. "But stranger things have happened. It's a real stumper," he added, fully into the spirit of investigation. "Kate filled me in on the details, but let me just make sure I've got this right. Gordon, who's a history professor and puzzle competitor, shot in the parking lot, not too long after midnight, since he was covered with snow. Kenny, a software and computer games developer, stuffed into a trunk in the boiler room with a head wound, but no weapon. Sounds a bit like Mrs. Peacock in the library with the wrench."

"And no watch," Harry said.

"That monstrosity Gordon was wearing Friday night? Someone actually stole it? Really, there is no accounting for taste."

"Unless the police found it on Kenny," Kate added. "Not that we'll ever know."

"I bet they didn't find it," said Harry. "I think whoever killed them has it."

"Logical," Tony said. "But why? What is it about a watch that would set off a murder spree?"

"Harry thinks that the watch is the key, and I have to admit, he's got a good case." Kate turned to Harry. "Do you mind if we let Tony in on our research? A fresh eye might have some different insights."

"Sure." Harry rolled himself over to the computer desk and opened up the AEGLT file. "Hey, you've added some stuff to it."

"After you left last night." Kate pointed out two new documents. "I did some more research on Isaac Walsh."

"Who's Isaac Walsh?" Tony asked.

"Kenny Revell's partner at MKD technologies. They develop video and computer games."

"Ah ha." Tony nodded, making the leap effortlessly. "And you think this watch is connected to some kind of research they were doing."

Harry logged onto the internet and typed in a web page. "I did some more research, too."

"Not during history, I hope."

"Of course not. I did it during English." He rapidly clicked through pages until he stopped at a photograph of several strange-looking watches.

"Spy watches," Kate said.

"Sure, why not?"

"I'm not following," said Tony. "You think Gordon was a spy?"

Harry rolled his eyes and clicked to enlarge one of the photos. "Look at this beauty. It's an old recording watch."

Kate and Tony both leaned in to get a closer look.

He clicked out of that page and onto another image. "And this ones contains a hidden camera."

"A bit cumbersome," said Tony. "And didn't the bad guys notice when a spy stuck his wrist in their face for a picture or a recording."

"That's beside the point."

"Technology has progressed a lot since the cold war," Kate added.

"Exactly," Harry said. "Now check this out. These are new models." Another click of the mouse. "You can take video with this one, view movies on this one."

The new watches were about the same size as current sports watches. The same size as the one Gordon Lott wore.

"Look familiar?"

Tony shrugged. "I really didn't pay that much attention. He was flashing it around in the bar the night after his loss, but it was dark."

Kate and Harry zeroed in on him.

"So he still had it that night after the competition," Harry said in sinister tones.

Tony chuckled. "You guys are good. Keep going. I'll catch on."

"But don't make any huge leaps without supporting criteria," Kate warned.

"Ah, there's the old Kate," said Tony.

"When I was a total geek."

Tony and Harry both grinned at her.

She heaved a sigh. "This is all very intriguing, but the importance of the information has to be based on certain criteria. We don't know that the watch is pivotal to the murders and not just the object of a burglary. Gordon might have put it in his pocket, or left it in his hotel room, or even lost it."

"He didn't," said Harry

Kate narrowed her eyes at him. "How do you know this? The chief didn't tell you."

Harry looked out the window.

"Harry?"

"Well, the chief is doing a lot of work at home. I think he doesn't trust me to be there alone at night. Like maybe I'm going to rip him off or something."

"More likely, he's concerned for your safety."

"Whatever. Anyway, he lets me use his old GR4, but not his new setup. It's really sweet—state of the art.

"Anyway, I was working on this dumb paper, and I look over and the chief is looking at a web page. This web page." He nodded toward the page that was currently on the screen. "Photographic memory," he added for Tony's edification. "Kate has it, too."

"I'm humbled." Tony put his hand on his heart and winked at Kate.

"But the chief has eyes in the back of his head. He caught me watching and clicked out of the page. Then gave me a lecture on obstructing justice—which I *wasn't*. I was just curious."

Tony laughed out loud.

"So later I just Googled until I found the same page. See? He's trying to figure out how the watch fits in, too, right?"

"Right," Kate admitted, "but you really shouldn't be spying on the chief."

Harry shrugged. "Just practicing."

Kate rolled her eyes. "I live in constant dread that the CIA will recruit him and I'll lose the best assistant I'll ever have."

Harry grinned. "I'm holding out for one of those top secret agencies that don't exist."

"Good for you," Tony said, grinning back at him.

Kate sighed. She could relate to Harry's need to know. It was the bane of a quick mind. She was afraid that it would be detrimental to the fragile male bond that was growing between Harry and the chief. And it could be detrimental to Harry's health if he got too cocky.

Tony was reading the specs for the video watch. "Hmm. For argument's sake, let's say that the watch is tied up with the reasons for murder. What do we know?"

"That Gordon kept looking at his watch during the competition." Kate frowned, searching her personal memory banks for an image of Gordon looking at the watch between sessions, but she couldn't pull one up. "But I didn't see him consult it during the breaks. Episodic, I know, but it does make you wonder."

"Suspicious," Tony agreed.

"Because . . ." Harry said, drawing out the word. "He wasn't using it to keep track of the *time*. There was a huge clock on the stage."

"To get information?" Tony's voice was incredulous.

Harry just smiled.

"You think someone was feeding him the answers through the watch?"

"How else could he have finished so fast?" Harry said. "Even Kate said it was impossible."

She hadn't said that exactly, but she wasn't going to quibble now. Not in the middle of a proof.

"Except that no one had access to the answers," Harry continued. "Kate locked them in the safe at the museum, and in her briefcase at the tournament."

"Unless Gordon used the watch to take a digital picture of the puzzle once it was in front of him," Tony said.

"That would work."

"Slow down, you two." Kate stood up, paced to the window and back. "Even if he managed to take a photo of the puzzle, he'd still have to be able to plug it into a PC and feed it into a Sudoku cheat."

"Revell designed video games," Harry said. "Companies always develop a cheat to test the reliability of the program. A Sudoku cheat would provide the correct answers and relay it back to the watch, which would display the solution."

"Incredible," Tony said. "All Gordon would have to do was copy down the numbers."

Kate shook her head. "It sounds good. But how could they pull it off? He couldn't sneak a computer into the competition, not even a Blackberry or a cell phone." Kate looked at Tony. "You caught him trying to take his cell into the Stamford comp."

Tony nodded.

"Even admitting that it would work in theory, he'd have to have access to a wireless system, which I'm sure the VFW Hall doesn't have."

Harry's forehead creased. "Maybe—"

Kate was on a roll. "Unless . . . the cheat was built into the watch. Shit!"

"Kate."

"Sorry. But the ramifications are staggering."

"Yeah, anyone with a wristwatch could cheat. I mean, *really* cheat," Harry said.

"It would cost a fortune to develop." Of course software companies spent fortunes on development, gambling on the returns. MKD was big enough to design something like this. Kenny Revell was probably more than capable. And Kenny Revell was dead. "Shit."

Harry didn't seem to notice this second lapse.

"And what kind of market would it have? Do you know any Sudoku players who would pay a fortune to cheat?" Kate aimed the question at Tony, who was following the argument in silent amazement.

"I never thought about it. What's the point of working a puzzle if you're going to cheat?"

"To win," said Harry. "People do it all the time. Some games come with the cheat built in."

"And," added Kate, "there's a hotline to call for clues to the *Times* crossword. Puzzle answers are given in the back of every Sudoku book."

"Gordon did care about winning," said Tony.

"I think we should check out Isaac Walsh," Harry said. "He might be the link we're looking for. He might be the guy in the orange hat."

Tony was beginning to look pensive. "It sounds far-fetched to me, but possible. Have you discussed this with the police?"

"No way!" Harry said. "He'll just get mad and tell us to butt out."

"He doesn't like to share the spotlight?"

Harry slumped down in his chair. "The chief's a control freak. Like nobody else has half a brain."

"That isn't fair," Kate said. "He's under a lot of pressure and nobody cooperates with him. He can't do his job if he's worried about us."

"I still think we should pursue the MKD connection. I bet Revell and Lott were in on some scam together. And they had an argument and—" Harry made a gun with his finger. "No, I forgot about Revell being dead, too. So it must be . . ."

"Harry, stop speculating."

"But we could solve this!"

Tony held up his hand. "Wait a minute. This is all theoretical, armchair detecting, right?"

"Right," Kate said.

"Right," Harry echoed.

Kate eyed him suspiciously. He'd acquiesced too easily. "*If* we do find anything important, we'll tell the chief what we know. We are *not* going to act under any circumstance. It's a mental exercise—that's all. It's just that we both . . ."

"Need to know," Tony finished for her. "You don't have to tell me. It's the bane of a puzzle nut. So as long as we're pursuing this *purely theoretical* investigation, what if it isn't about the watch?"

"It has to be," Harry insisted.

"That's because you have a spy mentality. It's skewing your ability to analyze without bias. What about jealousy or revenge or one of those classic motives?"

"I still think it's about the watch. I wish I knew where it was made." Harry glanced at the computer, then rolled his chair back up to the screen.

Tony stood up. "I hate to leave, but I have to meet Ginny Sue at the inn. Thanks for letting me join the team for a while. I can't remember when I've enjoyed an afternoon more. Good luck with your investigation."

Harry merely waved over his shoulder.

"I'll go downstairs with you," Kate said. "See if the mail has come."

"Remarkable boy," Tony observed as they made their way downstairs.

"Yes, but a handful."

"And he lives with the police chief?"

"Yes. He was the professor's apprentice and was living in a trailer with an abusive uncle. I sort of forced the chief into taking him on a emergency basis. Now the problem is getting the chief to keep him."

"Good luck. The chief can't be an easy man to live with."

"No. I don't think he would be," Kate agreed. "But I won't let him send Harry back to that cretin of an uncle and I won't let him go to foster care."

Kate handed him his coat and gloves.

"Very altruistic. But Kate, he's got more abstract intelligence than savvy. Don't let him fool you into thinking he's like us. He's still a kid."

"I know." Kate opened the door for him.

"Sure you won't have dinner with Ginny Sue and me?"

"Yes, but thanks. I really need to get some sleep. I'll see you before you leave."

"Excellent. Good afternoon, Alice."

Alice waved her fingers at him. "Lovely to meet you."

"Be careful, Kate. I would hate to see either you or Harry hurt." Tony kissed her cheek and left.

"Charming man," Alice said when Kate closed the door.

"Yes, he is." Kate just hoped he didn't break Ginny Sue's heart.

6					5			
7				8		5	2	1
4			7	2				
	6					7		
2		3				1		9
		5					8	
				3	7			4
1	9	7		6				5
			9					8

CHAPTER

FIFTEEN

KATE PICKED UP the mail and climbed the stairs to the office, a feeling of lethargy settling over her with each step. The last of the tournament participants had departed. Tony would be gone tomorrow and life would settle back to normal.

Kate felt out of sync. She knew it was the typical letdown after the excitement at the end of a long project. With the two murders, she hadn't even been able to savor the success of the weekend.

She wondered what her fellow think tankers were working on now. Of course they wouldn't be able to tell her; she no longer had security clearance. What she did have was her museum and a Sudoku tournament and a birthday coming up in a couple of months.

Thirty years old. Her party girl days would be behind her. Kate snickered. She'd never been a party girl. She'd always been a working girl. In school, at the museum as the professor's apprentice, in college, the think tank, now as owner and curator of the museum. Had she missed out on life?

She stopped at the office door to shake away her gloom. She had exhibits to arrange, a new docent program to organize, clubs to oversee, carpets to order, a heating system to update, and the future of a fourteen-year-old boy to worry about.

Harry was still sitting at the computer.

"Okay, Ace. That's enough supersleuthing for today. I want you to help me measure the storage room. I need more space to display some of the puzzles in storage."

"What are we going to do with the stuff in the storage room?"

"I thought maybe we could use some of the rooms on the third floor.

"No!"

"Harry, I don't mean all of it. Maybe just one area—"

"That's the professor's apartment. You *can't*. It isn't right."

Kate sighed. She'd known he would balk at the idea—she had resisted at first, too. But keeping a whole floor as a shrine couldn't be healthy. They both needed to move on.

Harry was typing furiously.

Time to let go of the subject for a while. She'd broached it in her usual inept way and gotten the reaction she deserved. "What are you looking at now?"

"This stupid MKD site. I know we can figure this out." Harry chewed on his lip. "I *know* we can."

"You're probably right. But if we can, so can the chief."

"No, he can't. Everybody is gone. He'll never be able to find the killer now."

"Then the police in other jurisdictions will find him." Tony's parting words came back to her. *He's still a kid.* Was Harry afraid that the killer would come back? "You know the chief wouldn't let anything happen to us."

"He would've caught him if anybody had cooperated. They think it's funny to ignore him, but it isn't. They're ruining everything. It isn't *fair!*"

"No," Kate said, trying to stay calm under the sudden onslaught of raw emotion. "That's why it's important for us to trust in him. And to cooperate."

"He's going to leave."

"Leave where?"

"Granville."

Kate took a sucker punch to the gut. "No, he isn't. It will take more than a few busybodies to make him quit."

Harry shook his head. "That cheat website isn't the only thing I saw on his computer screen. He's been looking at other police jobs."

Kate grabbed the desk to keep herself from reeling. He couldn't do that. Not to Harry when he was just getting used to having a stable home. Was that why he was going to ask Simon about sending Harry away to school: because he was planning to leave?

Kate tried to imagine life in Granville without the chief. It stretched like a bland, gray nebula in front of her.

Suddenly, in one of her rare—very rare—insights into human behavior, Kate understood that Harry wanted to solve the murders so the chief would stay. She rapidly blinked stinging eyes. She bet the chief didn't even realize how much he meant to Harry. He was as clueless as she was when it came to personal relationships.

"It doesn't matter."

Kate pulled herself together. "Well, it matters to me. And even if the chief does give up, which I doubt, you and I will still have each other."

Harry ignored her, just leaned into the computer screen like he hadn't heard.

Well, she'd just have to talk to the chief when he came to pick Harry up at six. He probably didn't realize that he was making big headway in Granville. The GABS had actually staunched rumors about Gordon's murder for him. Well, they'd done it because Kate had asked, but before they wouldn't have helped the chief even if Kate had asked. And they'd gone willingly to the station house to be questioned. So what if they'd finagled lunch out of him? That was a small price to pay.

She'd tell him so. Tonight.

But when the chief did arrive, twenty minutes late, Kate didn't have the heart to do it. He was moving slow. Dark circles framed his eyes; the deep chocolate color seemed abysmal in the lamp-light.

"Long day?" She knew it was a stupid question. It was obvious that he'd had a long week, a long year.

"Like all the others. Come on, Harry. Get your backpack. I'm afraid it's pizza again tonight."

"Pizza's okay," Harry said quietly and logged out of the computer before picking up his backpack.

If Kate ever cooked, she could have invited them to dinner, but cooking had never really interested her. Besides, Pru wouldn't approve of Kate having the chief to her house, even with Harry along.

It was time to talk to her aunt. Tell her to get over a year-old traffic ticket and start being nice. And encourage her friends to start being nice, too.

"What about the Bowsman Inn? "Kate asked. "My treat."

There was a spark of hope in Harry's eyes, before the chief said, "Thanks, but I have work still."

Harry's face fell.

"Well, what if Harry and I go and bring you take-out?"

"I'm okay with pizza," Harry said.

Kate was at a loss. It was almost as if Harry was afraid to have an opinion around the chief. Hoping that if he made himself agreeable, he could keep the chief from leaving? Or just wanting to spend every possible minute with him before he left?

Kate felt sad, then she got mad. Brandon Mitchell had a responsibility, too. So what if it was tough right now.? He had a boy who needed him.

Who you *foisted on him,* she reminded herself.

"Harry aced his history test today."

"That's great." The chief sounded like he was asleep on his feet.

Kate wanted to kick him. She didn't care if he was tired, he could show more enthusiasm.

"I always ace my tests," Harry said. "No big deal."

"It's great," the chief repeated.

Kate bit her lip to keep from saying something she would regret. This was stupid. She and Harry were walking around on eggshells. It didn't help them and it certainly didn't help the chief. Maybe if they solved this case, he could kick back and see how important he was to Harry. Or it was possible he just didn't care.

Brandon was watching her, but not with his usual laser-like intensity. Kate guessed that he wasn't really looking at her, but was miles away.

He seemed to catch himself. "If you're ready to leave, Harry and I will walk you to your car."

"You go ahead. I have to feed Al and lock up."

"Then come down and lock the door when we leave."

Kate saw them out and locked the door. Then she went down the hall to the kitchen to feed Al. She sat at the table watching him eat. When he was finished, he jumped onto her lap. While he cleaned his face and paws, Kate stroked his back. After a while, Al lost interest, jumped to the floor and disappeared into the dumbwaiter chute. Kate locked up and went home.

The next morning Ginny Sue called to say she was taking a personal day from school to drive Tony to the airport and would come by the museum that afternoon.

Kate sat at her desk, listening to water drip from the icicles along the eaves. It had finally gone above freezing for the first time since the snowstorm and water ran in rivulets down the curbs and into the gutters.

She ordered the carpet by phone, since she'd spent two months browsing through the squares at the local carpet outlet. She finally decided on a nylon with durable weave and an ornate pattern that would be good at camouflaging dirt.

She called Sam, since he hadn't called her since the morning they'd found Kenny Revell. She hoped he was just busy, but she suspected that he was sulking. And she didn't know why.

Her call went to his voicemail. "Just wanted to say hello," she said in a chipper voice that didn't sound like her at all. "Talk to you later." She hung up. She'd made the first overture, now it was up to him to come out of the sulks.

Ginny Sue finally showed up at one thirty.

Kate practically jumped on her. "Have you had lunch? No? Great! Let's go to Rayette's."

"Going a little stir crazy?" Ginny Sue asked as Kate propelled her down the slushy sidewalk.

"Yes."

Rayette met them at the door. "Where have you been? All I've been hearing is gossip. What's the real scoop?" she waved Holly, the lunch waitress, away. "I'll take care of these two. You'll still get the tip."

Kate and Ginny Sue ordered. Rayette dropped the order off at the kitchen and came back with a coffee pot and three mugs. "Okay. Give."

"I don't know a thing more than you do." Kate sipped her coffee. It was strong and black with a faint taste of hazelnut. "I only saw Chief Mitchell for a few minutes when he came to pick up Harry last night. He was tired and cranky, so I let it slide. Besides, I'm trying to stay out of it."

Rayette's eyebrows rose. "That doesn't sound like our Katie."

"You heard Jason. He called me a traitor."

"Oh, *that.*" Rayette dismissed it with a flick of her wrist. "It's just because it's winter and he has nothing else to do."

"I think Jason has a lot of nerve," Ginny Sue said. "People still treat him like an outsider sometimes and he's been here forever. You'd think he'd have a little compassion for Chief Mitchell's position."

"Ayuh," Rayette said, pouring more coffee. "But Jason bends over backward to make himself liked. The chief doesn't."

"Is that why you had him pay for lunch?"

"Just my way of helping out the investigation," Rayette replied with a small smile.

Kate considered that. "Why doesn't he try harder to be liked?"

"Maybe he doesn't know how?" Ginny Sue ventured.

"Or doesn't want to. Ayuh."

At the rate he was going, he would never learn to handle these people. *And your people skills are so stellar,* Kate chided herself. Still, she'd grown up here and even as a geek, she belonged. *In a sense.*

It seemed like Brandon would never be treated with anything but distrust. And that was partially his own fault.

"It would make his job easier," Kate said. "And my life." She put down her coffee. "It seems like whatever I do, it gets people's backs up."

"You should know this town better than that to take something like this personally," Rayette said. "If there's a side, someone will take it, and someone else will take the other. Remember the mall issue? And what about this past Christmas when that Evangelist church on the highway petitioned to have the secular decorations taken down from Granville Green? Half the town had been complaining about those tired old reindeer for years, but as soon as someone else attacked them, they hunkered down. Now we'll be stuck with those ratty old things for years to come.

"There's always something to set people off even if they have to make it up themselves. Especially in winter. Not much else to do."

Kate laughed—a little. Santa's sleigh had festooned the center of town for every Christmas that she could remember. "I guess you're right. We like a good fight. And it doesn't always matter which side we're on."

"That's better. You're the go-to girl. People can't bring themselves to help the chief, but most of them don't really want to hinder him. So they come to you."

It was true, Kate realized. People told her things they would never divulge to the chief. Even though they'd hired him, they still saw him as a confounded outsider. Still, their sense of fair play and ethics warred with their live-free-or-die motto. More and more they used Kate as a conduit to alert the chief to things they would never divulge to him in person.

Rayette stood up. "Gotta get back to work. Don't worry about things. Jason and Erik will get over it. Actually, I think they're enjoying the attention. Ayuh."

"Sorry," Kate told Ginny Sue when Rayette was gone. "I didn't

want to talk about all this stuff today." She smiled. "I really wanted the scoop on you and Tony. I mean, if you want to talk . . . I'm
sorry. . . it's none of my business."

"Sure it is." Ginny Sue beamed her large smile back at Kate.
"He's great, isn't he?"

"The best," agreed Kate. She was stuck after that. She'd never
figured out the fine art of girl talk—or any talk for that matter. She
made another stab, hoping it wasn't the wrong one. "Are you going
to see him again?"

"I think so. He said he'd call from Chicago." Ginny Sue reached
out and squeezed Kate's hand. "But it's alright if he doesn't. I'm not
expecting anything. And you shouldn't feel responsible or anything."

How did Ginny Sue know she felt responsible? "I did sort of
throw you two together, unintentionally."

"And I thank you for it. Now, don't worry. My heart won't break
if I don't hear from him again." Her face clouded over for an
instant. "Though it would be very nice if I did."

When Kate returned to the museum, Izzy Culpepper was chatting
with Alice over a stack of mail. It was clear that Alice had been filling him in on finding the body and the subsequent fleecing of the
chief the day before.

Kate put on a brave face. "Hey, Izzy."

"Afternoon, Katie. Alice here was just telling me you found
another body." He shook his head. Melted drops of snow flew from
his postal cap. "Never had murders here before."

Kate wanted to ask "before what," but she already knew the
answer. *Before you and the chief came.* She took the mail from Alice
and began looking through it.

"You ladies be careful." Izzy tipped his cap at them and hoisted his mailbag. "Maybe you should keep the front door locked until things get back to normal. If they ever do," he mumbled under his breath.

"Thanks, Izzy," Kate said, deciding to ignore the advice and the commentary. She turned to Alice. "Did we get any visitors while I was gone?"

"No, but the phone's been ringing off the hook. Everybody wants to know the gory details." Alice shook her head. "Never knew a nosier bunch of people in my life."

"Anyone complaining about the chief?"

Alice's eyes sparkled. "Every one of them. Sure don't know why the man sticks it out. Just stubborn, I guess."

Kate gave her an unenthusiastic smile. She just hoped his stubbornness lasted. What would Harry do without him?

Harry came in as usual at three fifteen, but after saying hello, he took his backpack into P.T.'s Place and shut the door. Kate let him go. She couldn't offer any assurance or advice. They would just have to weather the storm.

Her day brightened considerably an hour later, when the boy she'd seen Harry with at the tournament and another boy showed up at the museum asking for Harry. They invited him to go skiing with them that weekend.

Harry said he had to work.

Kate was more than willing to give him the day off, but when she told him so, he just said, "Don't want to," and went back to the interactive room.

After that, Kate didn't have much time to worry about him. Things got busy. The afternoon turned warmer, but stayed overcast, and the museum was a perfect place for a family outing. Especially if they thought they might pick up some tidbits about the latest murder; the museum had a steady flow of visitors.

When the chief picked up Harry that night, Kate was hurrying a last group through the Japanese puzzle box room. Harry stuck his head in the door to say good bye; Kate didn't even see the chief.

By Saturday night, Sam still hadn't called her back. Maybe he was fed up with her. Maybe he was going out with someone else. She considered calling Ginny Sue, but didn't think she would have the patience to sit through more encomiums about Tony. So she poured herself a glass of wine, turned on the television, and opened her Sudoku book.

She decided to sleep in on Sunday, but it was not to be. Pru called at eight o'clock to say she'd pick her up for church. Intellectually, Kate knew it was the right thing to do. She'd skipped last Sunday because of the tournament and Granville was a churchgoing town.

She really didn't want go. She knew Reverend Norwith would give a sermon on the murders, and that every eye in the congregation would turn to her.

Sure enough, the sign outside the Presbyterian church read "When Bad Things Happen to Good People." Kate gritted her teeth and followed her aunt inside.

She looked immediately for the chief and Harry. They were sitting in a pew two-thirds of the way back. People had given them a wide berth this morning and they sat isolated, surrounded by empty seats.

Kate smiled as she passed, but neither of them looked at her. Harry was staring at his hands clasped between his knees. The chief was staring into space, looking like a heathen among the chosen.

Kate had a overwhelming urge to sit down with them, though she knew the chief wouldn't appreciate it and it would cause tongues to wag. There'd be no question as to her loyalty if she did.

It would put her squarely in the enemy camp.

Instead, she followed Pru up the aisle to their regular pew and steeled herself for the next trying hour. The choir filed in and the congregation stood to sing "Onward Christian Soldiers." Kate sang along until they came to the stanza, "we are not divided, all one body we, one in hope and doctrine, one in charity." One body, one hope. Kate came to a decision: she would speak to the chief after the service. At church, in front of everyone.

If she had to choose sides, she'd side with him.

But when she scanned the faces of the crowded narthex, Harry and the chief were nowhere to be found. She was soon surrounded by people making small talk and wondering about the murders. She saw Elmira coming up from the choir room.

She stopped to say hello to Pru, but only nodded to Kate before joining another group of friends. Sam must have told her that they were on the outs, though Kate still hadn't figured out why.

Erik Ingersoll was a Methodist, but she saw Jason Elks across the room talking to two other museum board members. He caught her eye and turned away.

He was still mad at her. She knew, as sure as he was standing there, that he was using the "fellowship" hour to poison the board against her.

CHAPTER

SIXTEEN

KATE DIDN'T GO to the museum Sunday afternoon. She went ice skating. It had been a long time since she'd been on the ice. The pond was crowded with kids, and even a few adults had ventured out. Kate left them alone and they didn't bother her.

As she circled the pond, she watched the others. Everyone seemed to be having a good time, laughing and yelling and falling on their butts. Kate didn't fall but she also didn't have a good time. Maybe she should have called Harry. She would have called Sam except that he'd never returned her call, which meant he was still mad at her.

Ginny Sue might have come with her, but Ginny Sue would probably be sad now that Tony had left town, and she was afraid that instead of cheering each other up, they would bring each other down. So she continued her lonely orbit until her nose grew cold and her feet began to ache. Then she packed up her skates and left.

She swung by the museum long enough to feed Al, but someone had already left him food. Harry must have come in after church. She trudged upstairs but the office and P.T.'s Place were dark. Harry had come and gone and he hadn't even called her to see where she was.

Well, to heck with everybody. She went home.

The phone rang.

"I saw you come in with your skates. Did you have a nice time?"

"Yes," Kate said more snappishly than she intended. Having Pru constantly watching her from the window was getting oppressive.

"That's nice. Who did you go with?"

Kate let out a controlled sigh. "No one, just me. It was fun."

"Sam skates. At least he used to."

"That's nice," Kate said.

"You two shouldn't stay on the outs. You're better friends than that."

You could have fooled me. "We're not 'on the outs.' At least I'm not."

"Whatever you did, you should apologize."

Kate moved the phone from her ear. Why did Pru just assume it was her fault? She let it slide.

"Do you have plans for dinner? Simon and I are going out to the pancake house. Would you like to come along?"

"Thanks but I'm going to heat some soup and go to bed early."

"You're not feeling sick, are you?"

"No. Just tired. Have a good time." Kate hung up. She went to the kitchen, opened the refrigerator, closed it again. She picked up her Sudoku book, but didn't open it. Tapping it against her palm she wandered into the living room.

Why wasn't anything happening with the investigation? How

could anything happen, though, with the whole tournament populace dispersed? How could the investigation progress with no one in Granville cooperating with the police?

It snowed again during the night. Only a couple of inches, just enough to cover the frozen crust with a clean layer of powder, but enough to hide the icy patches.

Which was a negative way to think, Kate thought as she slipped and slid up to the museum walkway. She hurriedly dragged out the snow shovel and salt to clear a path before Beatrice Noakes arrived to take over the receptionist duties. As she finished pouring out the last of the crystals, Alice's head appeared above the snow-heavy hedge.

Kate slid down the walk to meet her.

"Bea's still sick. I told her I'd fill in for her today."

"You don't have to do that. I know you're busy. Harry and I can manage."

"The nice thing about being busy," Alice said, "is that you always have time to do just one more thing. But I've got to get to the beauty shop by three thirty."

"Thanks. Harry can man the desk after that."

It was an uneventful morning. They never got many visitors during the day when school was in session. Kate had been toying with the idea of opening later during the winter and staying open until eight two nights a week.

At the moment it seemed like too much work.

Harry and Izzy showed up simultaneously at three fifteen, Harry dragging his backpack through the snow, and Izzy bowed beneath the weight of the mailbag.

Kate told Harry he'd have to sit at the front desk.

"But I—"

"Harry, do you want me to miss my beauty parlor appointment?" Alice looked as stern as an octogenarian imp of steel could.

"No. . ."

"Get yourself something to eat first," Kate told him.

He merely grunted, dropped his backpack on the floor, and went back to the kitchen, which the GABs made sure was stocked for a growing boy and an absentminded curator.

Izzy pulled a rubber band from a stack of mail and separated the stack. "Hear there's more snow coming."

"It's winter," Alice said.

"Ayuh." He handed Kate the mail. "I'll see you to your door, Alice, since I'm going that way."

The two of them left, struggling along the sidewalk, Alice supporting Izzy as much as he supported her.

Kate flipped through the stack of envelopes. Invoices for the equipment rental, the hall rental, gas and electric bill, several circulars that she dropped into the wastepaper basket.

Harry came back with a triple-decker sandwich.

"What's that?" Kate asked as red oozed from between the slices of bread.

"A ketchup sandwich."

"I remember those. Wouldn't you rather have ham and cheese or peanut butter?"

"Nope." Harry sat down behind the desk and popped open a can of Coke.

Kate went back to the mail. At the bottom of the stack there was a letter from Jason Elks. *Why would Jason write to me?* She tore open the flap and unfolded an official-looking letter.

"Ms. McDonald: I'm writing in reference to a situation that has become untenable. Erik Ingersoll and I have been members of the museum board for nearly ten years. However, since you, as the new curator, do not trust our integrity, nor our veracity, and have betrayed what was said in confidence, we have no recourse but to resign from our positions on the board.

"Respectfully submitted, Eric Ingersoll and Jason Elks." It was cc'ed to Marian Teasdale, the president of the board.

Kate stared at the letter, dumfounded.

"What's the matter?" Harry's voice drifted toward her from far away.

"Erik and Jason have just resigned from the museum board."

"Why? Let me see." He dropped his sandwich on the ink blotter and hurried around the edge of the desk to look over her shoulder at the letter. "They can't do that."

"They just did."

Kate shook her head, wondering how things had gotten so out of her control. She didn't think Brandon seriously considered Jason and Erik as suspects.

The men she knew wouldn't be capable of one murder, much less two. They might be crack shots, she had no idea, but she knew for a fact that Erik could never sneak up behind someone to bash him on the head. Erik wheezed even when he was standing still.

Should she call them? Beg them to reconsider? Or were they really saying they wanted *her* to resign. After all, she was the low man on the totem pole. They'd sent a copy of their letter to Marian Teasdale. Had they tried to persuade Marian to oust her as curator? Another of those "her or us" situations?

They couldn't do that—Kate owned the museum. But they could make things very difficult for her. The board was responsible for the operation of the museum. Kate depended on them. She didn't know anything about running a museum except what she'd learned from them in the last few months. She needed them.

"What should I do?"

"I dunno. What do you want to do?"

Kate sank down on the edge of the desk. "All I wanted to do was help the museum. It seems like everything I do pisses someone off." She held up her hand before he could call her on her language. "I know. I think I have to buy the next pizza."

Harry gave her a lopsided smile. "We can run the museum without them."

Or they could run it without me. Just because she'd inherited it didn't mean that she had to be curator. She'd have to step aside.

Then what would Harry do? Would the new curator nurture him or would they just confiscate his key and say good riddance? A moot point, since Harry would be sent off to boarding school unless Kate forced the chief to keep him. She'd have to look for another math job. She might never see Harry or the chief again.

Her stomach knotted. "I think I'd better call Marian. I'll be upstairs."

Marian's housekeeper answered and it was a few minutes before Marian came on the line. "Hello, Katie."

Kate's stomach, which was already on self-destruct, started to burn. She plunged in without ceremony. "Did you get your mail today?" Kate didn't wait for her to answer. "There should be a letter from Jason and Erik."

The sound of rustling came through, then, "Yes. Here it is. What's it about?"

"They're—"

"Oh, dear," Marian said. "What on earth brought this on?"

Kate told her about their argument with Gordon Lott and how she'd told the chief about it. "I had to. I didn't think they killed Gordon. I'm sure they didn't. But the argument was bound to get back to Chief Mitchell and I wanted to make sure he didn't misinterpret their reticence." Kate sighed. "For all the good it did.

"If they'd just volunteered the information up front, instead of skulking around avoiding him, it would be over with by now. Instead, I'm out two board members and it seems like half the town is mad at me."

"Katie, you're exaggerating."

She was, which was weird. She never exaggerated.

"They'll come to their senses."

"And if they don't?" Jason and Erik might be curmudgeons, but they were puzzle buffs, and they cared about the museum. They donated a lot of their time to it. Kate wasn't sure she could find two new people who cared as much.

"We'll worry about that later. Everybody is edgy because of these murders. No one blames you. Both men were strangers. In all likelihood, they brought their murderer with them. The chief surely knows that. Everyone will calm down once he solves the case.

"Now stop worrying. Jason and Erik are upset and they have to take it out on somebody."

"Why me?"

Marian sighed. "Because you're an easy target. You don't fight back."

"I don't understand them."

Kate heard Marian's light laugh. "P.T. used to say the same thing."

"I'm letting him down," she said morosely.

"No, you aren't, but you need to stop letting people push you around."

"Do I?"

"Yes, my dear. You do."

"What should I do?"

"What would P.T. tell you to do?"

"Be patient."

"Of course he would," Marian said on a sigh. "He was a patient man."

"Once he told me to punch Darrel Donnelly in the gut."

"*No*. Did he really?"

Kate smiled reminiscently. "Only once, after Darrell had pushed me into a mud puddle. It was in third grade."

"Perhaps a metaphorical punch to the gut is just what some of the people in this town need."

Somehow Kate couldn't see herself as the town bully. Besides, she wanted people to like her.

"I think the best thing for you to do is let them stew in their own juices for a few days. Then, if they don't come to their senses, you can start kicking some butt."

Kate pulled the receiver away from her ear and looked at it. Had her proper, sophisticated board president just told her to kick butt? Amazing.

"Now, don't worry about them. You just concentrate on keeping the museum running smoothly."

Kate sat at the desk for a long time after she'd hung up. Had she brought all this angst on herself? She never had this kind of trouble at the think tank. At least not that she'd recognized at the time.

There was a soft knock at the door. Harry came in carrying a steaming mug. "I thought you might want tea."

Kate tried for a smile, just managed a twisted grimace. "Thanks."

Harry leaned against the edge of the desk. "What did Ms. Teasdale say?"

"That it was time I kicked some butt."

Harry's mouth dropped open. "Wow. Did she really say that?"

"Uh huh." Kate took a sip of tea. "And I'm going to start now." She snatched the letter off the desk. "I'm going out. Can you handle things here by yourself for a while?"

"Yeah, but . . . you're not going to do anything crazy, are you?"

"No. I'm going to demand some respect."

Harry followed her downstairs, watched anxiously while she put on her car coat and striped knit hat.

"I'll be back," she said and strode out the door. Marian was right. She didn't stand up for herself. She was tired of everybody putting her in the middle, then getting mad at her because it was easier to be mad at her than to deal with the real problems.

She wanted to be a people person. She'd left a job she loved to make a difference in the lives of the museum patrons. She might not be the best curator in the world, but she didn't have to stand by and be the brunt of everyone's ill humor. She had rights, too.

She walked the two blocks to Jason's house, a small white clapboard federal halfway down MacArthur Lane. She shoved the picket gate aside and strode up to the front door. But when she banged on the knocker, she suddenly hoped he wasn't home. She'd been so angry that she hadn't planned on what she would say.

The door opened. Jason Elks stared out at her in astonishment.

Kate swallowed, her mouth incredibly dry. She pulled the letter of resignation out of her pocket, unfolded it and smoothed it out as best she could with fingers hampered by nerves and her woolen gloves.

"Jason Elks, this is what I think of your resignation letter." She tore it into shreds and dropped the pieces into his hand. "Don't you dare try resigning again. And tell Erik the same thing."

She turned and marched down his walkway, forcing herself not to look back. She did get a peek at the door when she reached the sidewalk. Jason was still standing there, the paper pieces clutched in his hand.

There, she thought righteously. *One down, two to go. And that's just the beginning.*

Swyndon's Photography was a storefront shop on the west end of Main Street. Easels of family portraits stretched across the plate glass window display. Kate pushed the door open. A bell tinkled over her head and Sam came through a curtained doorway from the studio in back.

"Kate." He was obviously surprised to see her. He actually smiled before he remembered that he was mad at her.

She rushed straight into it. "I don't know why you're mad at me. And I don't know what you told Elmira. But if you have a problem with me, I'd appreciate it if you would tell me to my face, not make me find out from your aunt."

"I didn't tell her anything." He winced, looked chagrined. "And I'm not mad."

"Then why are she and Pru on my case?"

"I was . . . jealous."

"What? Of whom?"

"Chief Mitchell. Maybe I was wrong. But you do what he tells you, when you don't listen to me." Sam's face tightened like a pouting two-year-old.

"I do what he tells me because he's *the chief of police.* So get off your high horse—or not. It's up to you."

She marched out, leaving him staring after her. *Two down.* She continued along main street, turned right at Granville Green, and marched into the small police station.

Elmira looked up from the reception desk. Surprised, then delighted, then remembering that she was upset with Kate, her brows knitted.

Kate leaned over the desk. "I just told your nephew that he has no reason to be jealous. He's acting like a spoiled two-year-old. And I'm not going to put up with it. Now, I'd like to see the chief."

Elmira's frown transformed into a grin. "You tell 'em, Katie. Go on back."

Kate knocked on the chief's door and opened it before she lost her courage. She had a sneaking suspicion that she was burning her bridges, but if things didn't change, she'd be back at the institute anyway.

If they'll even take me back.

The chief looked up from a stack of papers. "Kate?"

"I have a lot to say to you, but first you're going to tell me how this case is progressing." She pulled up a chair, cleared off the stack of folders and deposited them on the floor. She sat down. "Go ahead."

The chief dropped the papers and leaned back in his chair. "It isn't. I have my ideas, but all the potential suspects have left my jurisdiction."

She hadn't expected this. Not so much what he said, but his appearance of acceptance.

"What about Jason and Erik?"

"What about them? There's no evidence to build any kind of a case against them."

"Then would you please tell them?"

"No."

"Why not?"

"Because that's not the way it works. They'll have to get over it."

"They just quit my board because they think I fingered them."

Of all the reactions she expected, it wasn't the one she got: he laughed.

"Where did you pick up talk like fingering? Been watching too many old movies?"

"I don't know. From Harry probably. You've corrupted him."

A frown passed over his face and Kate realized she'd blundered off the topic of the investigation and into his personal life.

"Enough."

She fell silent.

"Kate, I—just bear with this a couple of more months and things will go back to normal."

"Why? Do you have a lead?"

He shook his head. "That's when my contract is up."

"What does that have to do with it?"

"For a smart woman, you're slow on the uptake today. I'm not signing another one."

She stared at him. "You're giving up?"

"Three murders in six months? You do the math. This town will never accept me. I know when to cut my losses."

Her ears were buzzing. Even though Harry had warned her, she hadn't really believed him. She took a breath and found it hurt. "And what about the people who depend on you?"

This earned her an ironic look.

"Don't you dare abandon Harry. I'll never forgive you."

He smiled, but it was a sad smile. "You'll never see me again. Harry will get on with his life. But I'll ask you not to spread the word. I don't think I could stand the glee."

"I can't believe I'm hearing this. I thought you had more. . . more . . . *guts* than that. Stop wallowing in self-pity and solve this case. Then *you* can get over it." Her voice quavered and she knew she had to get out or burst into tears.

She propelled herself out of the chair, practically stumbling over the stack of folders as she headed for the door. It only took two tries for her to turn the knob. The chief didn't get up to help her. She had no idea what his expression was, but it was obviously too late to care.

She walked down the hall and straight out the front door, not even pausing when she heard Elmira call her name.

The cold air stunned her until she realized she was shaking from emotion, not the cold. She had either just failed miserably— or being "a people person" sucked.

She took the last half block to the museum at a run, slipping and sliding and not caring. As soon as she was inside, she shut the door and leaned against it.

Harry looked up, startled. He was holding the phone receiver. He slammed it down.

"I'm alright," Kate assured him. "Just a little crazy. Okay, a lot crazy. I hope you didn't hang up on whoever was on the phone."

Harry jerked his head, no.

"I'm sorry. I didn't mean to scare you. I can't believe what I just did."

Harry glanced down at the phone, then came over to her. "What did you do?"

She could kick herself for scaring him. His face looked stricken.

The telephone rang. "Probably your hang-up. I'll get it." Kate stepped to the desk and picked it up.

"Avondale Puzzle Museum," she answered, just as Harry cried, "No!"

7		8					2	
3					2	5		
	2				3		6	4
4			3					
		1				9		
					9			6
1	6		5				7	
		3	4					1
	5					8		2

CHAPTER

SEVENTEEN

KATE PUT DOWN the phone. "They hung up." Then she saw Harry's face. "What is it? Are you sick?"

Harry shook his head in quick staccato jerks. "Not sick. Just—"

He sucked in breath and Kate became really alarmed. "Then what? Tell me."

"I think I just really screwed up."

"Because of the phone call? No big deal. They'll call back."

"I think they just did. Oh shit."

"Harry, watch those swear words or you're going to be buying the next pizza."

"I don't care, I'm going to be in big trouble anyway." The color had drained from his face and he looked even paler than he usually did.

"You're not making sense. This can't be about that phone call."

"It is."

Kate didn't get it. "Listen, if they call back, just say you got disconnected and apologize profusely."

Harry swallowed, his Adam's apple bobbed. "They won't call back. They don't have to."

There was something going on here besides bad phone etiquette. "Okay. I'm completely lost. Why don't you just tell me what's upset you?"

Harry stood rigidly in front of the registration desk, his eyes focused on the roll of tickets that was sitting dead center.

He opened his mouth, but instead of telling her he asked, "Did they say anything to you?"

"No. I said 'Avondale Puzzle Museum' and they hung up. It was probably a wrong number."

But Harry had already started shaking his head. "How could I be so stupid?"

"About *what,* Harry? You're beginning to scare me." Had it been some kind of threatening call? Jason and Erik came to mind. Or one of their loyal friends who blamed Kate for getting them in trouble with the police? Only they weren't in trouble, unless the chief had been lying to her. "Who were you talking to when I came in?"

"Nobody," Harry answered in automatic teenage denial.

"Another hang-up?"

"No."

"Then what?" Kate was losing her patience. The professor had always pointed out that impatience usually caused more harm than good. But she couldn't help it. "Either you were talking to someone or it was another hang-up."

Harry didn't answer for a long time. She watched emotions flick across his face. Finally he said, "I was on hold."

Kate sputtered. "Sorry. It's obviously not funny, but after that buildup, it sounded like the punch line to a joke."

"It's not a joke. It might be awful."

"Then you'd better tell me. Sit down."

Harry slid behind the desk and dropped into the swivel desk chair. He took a few seconds to trace the edge of the desktop with his fingertips, and Kate didn't press him. He was getting his thoughts in order. At least he hadn't picked up a puzzle book the way the professor used to when he didn't want to talk. Kate gave him space. She knew he would tell her—eventually.

Harry shifted in his chair, but kept his head lowered. "After you left—to go out. I could tell you were upset, and the chief—he's cranky all the time, and I know he's going to leave, and I don't have anywhere to go except back to Buck—"

"I won't let you go back to your Neanderthal uncle. I'll take it to court if I have to."

"It doesn't matter."

Of course it mattered, but Harry was cushioning himself, preparing himself for disappointment. God, how often had she done the same thing? When the other kids taunted her for being a geek. When their parents were mean to her because she skewed the grade curve. When a teacher resented her intelligence instead of nurturing it. When her mother died. "Okay, but just know that you won't have to go back."

Harry shrugged. He still wouldn't look at her, but concentrated on rolling a pen back and forth across the ink blotter. "So, I thought if I could just help. . ." He pushed the pen away. It rolled onto the wooden surface and over the edge. They both watched as it hit the floor.

"I called MKD."

It took a second for Kate to understand. Then it all fell frighteningly into place. Harry had decided to investigate on his own. It was no longer an intellectual exercise, but a frantic effort to keep his new life.

"And it would have worked, but I thought you'd be gone longer, and when you came back I panicked and hung up."

"What would have worked?"

"I had this story worked out. I told the receptionist I was a student doing a report on computer games and asked if I could talk to the developers of Fight Squadron. That was the last game that Walsh and Revell worked on together—at least according to the MKD website."

Kate nodded gravely. "And how did you plan to work around to the subject of murder?"

"I wasn't going to. I really did have some questions. I've been working on this prototype."

"A prototype of what?"

"Of a computer cheat, sort of. But I got stumped on one of the steps and I thought if I asked Walsh if it was possible, he might give himself away."

"How? Admitting to murder? Or confessing to developing a cheat to fix live competitions?"

"That. Because if he answered right away, I'd know he'd been at least thinking about a Sudoku cheat. And if you noticed, there are no Sudoku games in the MKD catalogue."

Harry took a deep breath, forced it out. "I knew there was a chance they'd get suspicious and might try to star sixty-nine me. So I planned to answer the phone like I was a kid and not let them know it was the museum. . ."

"But I came back and foiled your best-laid plans," Kate finished. "I'm sorry. It was a valid option, but you shouldn't be interfering in an investigation."

"There is no investigation. The chief's hands are tied. I heard him tell the mayor. And when I asked him if the other cops were cooperating with him, he laughed. Not like he thought it was funny. He just said the cops in Hanover don't have a clue."

"So the chief isn't investigating at all?" asked Kate, distracted.

"Only what he can do around here. And everybody's gone home."

And the chief is going to leave at the end of his contract because he can't solve the murder.

Kate tried to relax. "No harm done. Maybe the hang-up was just a coincidence."

Harry gave her a look that said he wasn't buying the old coincidence argument.

"It could be the case. Did you recognize the receptionist's voice?"

"No, but I never got close enough to Claudine to have anything to compare it to. It could've been her."

"But it might not have been. This could be her day off, or maybe she doesn't answer phones, just directs visitors to the correct office. But, Harry, no more interfering."

"Are you going to tell the chief?"

She knew she should, but right now Kate cared more about Harry's state of mind and his relationship with the chief than she did about the ethics of the situation.

"I think," Kate said slowly, "that this is a spilled-milk situation. Normally, we would tell the chief everything. But thinking that the hang-up call was Claudine is pure conjecture, and you know how the chief feels about conjecture. I think we'll just keep it to ourselves."

Harry let out a huge sigh.

"But Harry, I mean it: *no more.*"

"Okay. Now do you want to see my prototype?"

Kate followed him upstairs, marveling at how resilient the teenage psyche was. One moment on the brink of doom, the next like he didn't have a care in the world.

He stopped her outside the closed door to PT's Place. "You didn't peek?"

"Nope."

He threw open the door. Spread out on the puzzle table were an assortment of electronics, modems, a camera, and a labyrinth of color-coded wires.

"Wow. So this is what you were doing all weekend. Does it work?" Kate asked, seeing immediately what it was.

"Parts of it. I had to scavenge most of it from the chief's garage. He was just going to recycle them. Sam loaned me the camera."

"That was nice of him."

Harry gave her a sardonic look. "Yeah, but I think he loaned it to me just to get back on your good side."

And she'd just let him have it. *Bad timing,* thought Kate. *So what else is new?*

She moved around the table to get a better look. A paper copy of the A Division puzzle lay in front of a computer screen.

"This is sort of how it works. Remember, this is just a prototype. Really primitive."

Kate nodded, fascinated.

Harry picked up the camera that fed into the computer. He took a picture of the puzzle, typed in a shortcut, and the puzzle appeared on the screen. "This is where I ran into trouble. Cheats are designed to solve puzzles programmed into the game chip. This puzzle isn't. So I had to manually feed the numbers into a blank grid on the game edition, but I'm sure it can be done electronically. It's just . . . I've only had access to a computer since I've been staying at the chief's, so I'm kind of playing catch-up when it comes to programming."

"I think you've done a remarkable job."

"So," Harry continued, "that took extra time, but I'm sure Revell could have it coded so that when the photo comes in, it's relayed to the cheat. Then the cheat fills in the numbers . . ." He clicked a button on the screen. The answers appeared in all the cells of the grid.

"Normally, this would be done in a split second, but this is very basic, remember."

Kate nodded. She thought it was brilliant.

"Once the numbers are entered, I e-mail the finished puzzle as a jpeg back to the watch, which I can't do since I don't have the watch. But I e-mailed it to myself and signed on as a guest on your laptop. I hope that was okay?" He opened the e-mail icon, attached the completed puzzle and pressed Send. He then opened the laptop and the e-mail appeared in the guest mailbox. He opened the attachment.

"And, *voilà!* There's the puzzle. All I have to do is copy down the answers and win."

"Wow," Kate said. "It's impressive. And complicated. And all that for what? A certificate and a plastic medal? You couldn't even enjoy winning because you didn't, the computer did."

"Stupid," Harry agreed. "But some people don't care about anything but winning."

"Sad but true. I just didn't think any of them were puzzlers."

Harry frowned. "I wasn't sure they could fit all these components into a watch. That's why I called MKD."

They were both staring at the screen when a large shape loomed in the doorway. They jumped guiltily.

It was the chief. And he was scowling. "Who the hell left the front door unlocked?"

Kate slapped her hand to her chest. "You scared us."

Harry looked quickly at Kate.

"I did it," Kate said, feeling like a chastised kid instead of the museum curator that she was. She'd been worrying about how she would react when she had to meet him again after her scene at his office. She shouldn't have bothered. She could tell he was going to hit and run without even acknowledging the confrontation. "Alice had to leave early and I got busy and just forgot."

"You should get a real receptionist."

"I will. Eventually."

"In the meantime lock the damn door."

Kate felt her cheeks heating up, damn red hair. She crossed her arms. "Another swear word from you and you'll be buying Harry and me pizza."

"I don't give a—" Brandon speared his fingers through his hair, the gesture of a man pushed to the max. Then he saw all the equipment.

"What's that?"

"Nothing," said Harry.

Obviously it was something, and the chief had a right to know. Hell, he should be ecstatic that they had come up with a plausible motive for murder. A falling out among thieves.

"What are you two up to?" asked the chief, stepping from the doorway. He stopped in front of the makeshift Sudoku cheat.

Kate stepped closer to Harry. "Isn't this incredible? Harry created it. You're going to be so impressed." *Or else*, her tone said.

The chief looked over the jumble of computer parts. "I recognize these."

"I borrowed them. I thought it would be okay."

The chief glanced at Harry, looked back at the prototype. "So what is it?"

Harry said nothing, but looked at Kate. Kate realized she'd just jettisoned them into dangerous waters. It was too late to go back.

She opened her mouth, but the chief had noticed the quick exchange of glances.

"If you two are interfering in this investigation—"

"We're not," Kate said. "Well, in a purely theoretical, armchair kind of way."

"Uh huh. And what does this *theoretical* investigating entail?"

Kate was hoping that Harry would take up the slack here, but Harry wasn't looking at either of them. "You remember I told you that Gordon's watch was missing."

Brandon nodded.

"Has it been found?"

"Not yet."

"Well, Harry . . . and I . . . were just theorizing about why someone would steal a watch and leave a wallet full of money."

"Saw that, did you?"

Kate ignored the question. "I mean the watch was ugly. So we were trying to figure out if there was something significant about the theft. Then we got to wondering how a person could cheat on a paper game, besides the obvious. That's why we have partitions between the individual players."

"Pure conjecture."

"I realize that. You don't see us trying to convince you to investigate, do you? We were just working our mental facilities. Brain gymnastics."

"Uh huh."

"So Harry put together this prototype—"

"Of what?"

Kate wanted to kick him. He knew what it was. He was just being obnoxious. "Of how the watch might allow Lott to cheat.

Harry will have to explain it to you. I have the basics, but it's over my tech-talk level."

Brandon turned to Harry. "Show me."

Harry looked apprehensive. Kate gave him an encouraging smile.

"Well. It's really simplistic, remember, and it might not even work, but, well, suppose Gordon Lott had found a way to use an electronic cheat on the puzzle? I mean, it could work, right?"

"Yeah," the chief said. "If you clear an existing puzzle and the cached solution, then enter the new numbers, the cheat would conceivably solve it. Did you run a search on Sudoku cheats?"

"Yeah, and I went on a couple of the blog sites about computer cheats. There's a way to do it. But I don't know stuff like nulling and coding and stuff like that."

"You'll learn. So. . ." The chief leaned over the camera. "This is the watch?"

"Yeah. I had to connect it to the old computer by USB. But it could have connected wireless, couldn't it?"

"Possibly. But don't worry about that yet. Show me the rest of the process."

Harry suddenly looked so proud that Kate's throat tightened, and she had to look out the window to keep from bursting into tears.

"I took a digital picture of an A-level puzzle, then downloaded the photo onto the desktop. But I had to use a blank grid and enter the same numbers manually, because I don't know how to override that stuff in the cheat. But let's just say, Gordon could do that, or—" Harry bit off the end of his sentence. "Or something."

Kate turned from the window. She was certain that Harry had almost said "or Kenny Revell could do it." Then they would have really been in trouble.

"A dex drive of some kind."

Harry and Kate looked at him blankly.

"Doesn't matter. It could be done. Go on."

"So then I sent it—e-mailed it—to Kate's laptop since I didn't know how to get it back in the camera without taking a picture of it and that would have been pretty near impossible."

He touched the keyboard of the laptop and Kate's tropical beach screen saver gave way to the completed puzzle jpeg.

"Once the puzzle was solved it could somehow be programmed to return to the watch face, like sending a picture to a Blackberry . . . or something." Harry shrugged.

The chief didn't say anything, just peered at the computer screen.

"And then, all Gordon Lott would have to do is lean on his elbow so he could see the watch face and copy down the correct answers."

"Except that he didn't."

Harry frowned.

"He made a mistake."

"Yeah, but—"

"And he would have to have a way to connect to a hard drive."

"Wireless?" Kate ventured.

"If there was an open system nearby."

Harry looked eagerly at the chief. "But it could work? Theoretically?"

"Yeah, it could work . . ." Brandon said slowly. He was looking intently from the camera to the computer screen and back again. "Or . . ." He turned to Kate. "You gave me a description of the watch, but tell me again."

Kate closed her eyes until she could picture Gordon consulting his watch. "It was big and clunky like one of those multifunction watches."

"Or a spy camera watch," Harry put in.

The chief hushed him and moved over to Kate's laptop. "May I?"

She nodded, uncomfortably aware of the AEGLT file icon on her desktop. Harry cut her a look. She considered lunging for the laptop, but the chief had only gone online. He typed in a website, then motioned for Harry to look.

Kate squeezed in, too. It was a patent page for a watch that was both a computer and a cell phone. "Doesn't mean it's been invented, but if it hasn't been, it won't be long."

"Wow," said Harry. "It really could work."

"We don't allow laptops, Blackberries, or cell phones in the solving area," Kate said. "But we never thought about watches. I mean what are the odds?"

Harry grinned.

"Don't answer that."

The chief gave Harry an appraising look. "Nice piece of reasoning."

Harry beamed. Kate could have hugged Brandon for finally making Harry feel needed. Of course, she didn't.

But as she drove away from the museum, she glanced in the rearview mirror and saw man and boy standing beside the chief's car and she thought things might just work out after all.

SNOW BEGAN TO fall just as Kate unlocked the museum the next morning. *Here we go again*, she thought. Nature was a lot easier to cope with in Alexandria and the mere thought of spending the day keeping the museum walk clear made Virginia seem like Eden. But she was here in Granville. She wanted to be here. She just didn't want to be shoveling snow and lugging giant bags of deicer around.

She should really hire someone to do this. Harry could keep up with things after school but that left a good eight hours for Kate to deal with every contingency. She supposed the professor didn't deal with things like snow. He just let things run their course, which was why the museum had been left in such a deplorable state.

Kate had made lots of progress since taking over the museum, and with the proceeds from the tournament, she would be able to make even more improvements. But her brain was tired from disuse. Scheduling and basic accounting didn't hold a candle to theoretical mathematics.

Even murder investigation paled in comparison to *epsilon chains* and *infinite discontinuity*. Besides, the investigation was out of her hands. It was even out of Brandon's hands. There was nothing to do but wait for the murderer to be caught or for the case to become cold.

That rankled. She hated loose ends, but life was like that, she was discovering. Full of tangles and loose ends, and no tried-and-true method for getting things right. Jason and Erik were mad, Sam was mad.

Harry and the chief, at least, had come to some kind of tenuous camaraderie, which could blow apart at any minute if the chief found out that Harry had called MKD. *Well, he will have to* not *find out*. Kate didn't like subterfuge any more than she liked unanswered questions, but she had no choice.

She'd done what she could do. She'd stood up for herself in the best way she knew how. Now she would just have to wait for the repercussions.

She did a lot of waiting during the day. There were no visitors to the museum in the morning. Alice, who was still filling in for the ailing Bea, had left the desk to polish all the glass cabinets. She made Kate lunch and they ate it in the kitchen while keeping their ears open for any patrons. None came.

By three thirty, Kate was staring out of the office window. Harry was late and so was Izzy. She leaned her head against the casement and watched the snow fall.

It had started to taper off when she caught sight of a flash of orange across the street.

She straightened up. Saw a man standing on the far sidewalk

between two cars. He appeared to be looking straight at her. He was bundled up in ski parka and gloves. A scarf was wrapped around his neck and covered his chin. But the orange jester's hat gave him away.

Kate froze, wondering what she should do. The phone was across the room. If she left her place by the window, he might be gone when she came back.

He lifted his chin toward her, then turned and started down the sidewalk. Motioning to her? She watched until he hesitated, turned around, and looked straight at the office window.

He wanted her to follow him. And she would. Kate bolted across the room and raced downstairs. "Call the chief!" she yelled to Alice as she yanked open the entrance door.

"Where are you going?" Alice asked, standing up from the desk.

"After the man in the orange hat. He's getting away. He's head-ed south down Hopper Street. Tell Chief Mitchell to hurry."

The man was half a block away, heading toward the center of the historic district. Kate sped toward the sidewalk. If she lost sight of him, he would be able to disappear into the warren of side streets and alleys that divided the large homes.

As she swung around the gate to the sidewalk, she saw Harry and Izzy walking slowly up the sidewalk from Main Street.

"Harry, it's Orange Hat! Call the chief."

"Wait! Stop!" Harry was already running.

Izzy trotted after him. Alice was standing in the doorway, call-ing, "Come back here!"

Kate slipped on the sidewalk, flailed her arms to keep on her feet. Then started off again. "Call the chief," she yelled over her shoulder.

The man turned the corner and Kate sped up, but by the time she reached the end of the block he was gone. Mounds of plowed snow obstructed her view of the street, but she knew he'd turned to the right. She stepped into the middle of the intersection, looked down the narrow street.

Three of the houses on the next block were still vacant from when their owners had sold to the mall consortium. There were no cars on the street, but neither had the sidewalks been shoveled. No one to help. And no orange hat. She started down the street more slowly, looking left and right.

She reached MacArthur Lane where Jason Elks lived and saw the orange hat. The man was standing in front of Jason's house. He didn't go inside and he didn't try to run.

Two cars were parked on the street. One was Jason's but that didn't mean he was home. He often walked into town.

And even if he were home, would he help her?

Orange Hat stood unmoving for a second, then turned and jogged toward the second car, which was parked in the cul-de-sac at the end of the lane.

Kate hesitated, sensing a trap. If she took time to knock on Jason's door, Orange Hat might get away. But if she went after him, how would the chief find her? She'd run out without coat or hat or gloves. Not only was she freezing, but she had nothing to leave behind as a clue.

Orange Hat began to run again. He might be planning to run over the frozen lawns and escape. Kate had no choice but to keep him in sight and hope that the chief arrived in time to stop him from getting away.

The only immediate thought she had was that she couldn't let him escape. But another part of her brain was already analyzing the situation. He must want her to follow him, or why show himself? Why wear the orange hat? And why wait for her at every turn?

What could he possibly want? She didn't know anything that could be injurious to him. She had no idea who he was. And the way he was bundled up, she wouldn't be able to identify him if they finally caught him.

She'd have to stay in pursuit, just not close enough to get hurt. Then she remembered that Gordon had been shot.

Kate stopped cold. He might have a gun.

She began to shiver so violently that she could hardly think. She wouldn't risk her life to catch Orange Hat, no matter what he'd done.

For a moment, she stood perfectly still, afraid to move, afraid not to move, while the sweat chilled beneath her sweater and turtleneck. Slowly, she began backing away toward the street.

Orange Hat reached the second car. He fumbled in his pocket, something fell to the snow, and instinct made Kate turn and run. She was still running when she heard the engine start up behind her.

She'd just made it to the end of the lane when she saw Harry rounding the corner. She waved frantically for him to move back.

The car sped toward her.

Kate leapt aside.

The car fishtailed in the street, the rear passenger side careered into her, and she flew into the air.

Kate landed in a bank of snow and lay there, stunned and numb with cold and fright. She heard Harry crying, "Kate!" Then he was kneeling beside her, his face almost as white as the surrounding snow.

"Did you call Brandon?" she stammered between rattling teeth.

"I told Izzy to. Are you okay?"

"I-I think so." Kate tried to move, but the cold or the impact of her fall or both made it impossible.

Izzy came huffing up behind Harry. He'd lost his mailbag and his face was twisted into a mask of horror. "Katie. Say something."

Kate looked at him and laughed. It hurt. Then she started to cry.

"I'll call an ambulance."

"No. Just give me a minute." She had to get up. The tears were freezing on her cheeks. The rest of her was a human ice cube. She steeled herself and pushed up to her elbows. It hurt, but not agonizingly so. She tested her arms and legs. She was pretty sure nothing was broken. She could see clearly. No concussion. Just cold. *Really cold.*

"I'm okay. Help me up."

"Don't move." Harry attempted to push her back down, which was totally counterproductive.

"Just help me up before I'm frozen stiff."

With Harry and Izzy's help, she struggled to her feet, bringing several layers of encrusted snow with her. She swayed and Izzy braced his whole body against her to keep her on her feet. The world righted itself.

"Did you call the chief?" she asked him.

"I told Alice to. Can you walk or should I carry you?"

Kate looked down at Izzy's small frame. "I can walk. Did either of you see who it was?"

Harry and Izzy shook their heads.

"We were too worried about you," Izzy said.

"The car?"

Harry frowned. Kate knew he was reconstructing the scene in his head. "White car. A Chevy. It had one of those gold parallelograms on the front. License plates. They were covered over."

Of course they were, thought Kate. He'd intended for her to follow him, but not be able to identify him.

Harry's eyes widened. "Do you think he planned to—Oh *shit.*

Sorry. I mean, why would he want to hurt you?"

Good question. Had he purposely lured her into that alley in order to run her down? Why not just shoot her? It would be easier. But why would Orange Hat want to kill her?

Kate's body jerked with a violent shiver. Harry unzipped his jacket and took it off. He pushed her arms into the sleeves and rezipped it up to her neck while Izzy tried to brush away the worst of the snow.

With them supporting her on either side, Kate made her slow and painful way back to the museum.

"Of course I called him," Alice said, after she'd recovered from the shock of seeing Kate being helped through the door. "I just hope the damn fool was listening."

"Alice!" Kate and Harry said simultaneously.

"Well, pardon me. Didn't mean to offend your tender ears. He is a damn fool. And what are you two heroes gawking at? Harry, run upstairs and build up the fire in the office. Izzy, you turn up the thermostat." She took Kate gently around the waist. "Now, let's get you upstairs."

It took a lot of work and several rest stops before Kate made it to the office. The fire was blazing. Harry had unearthed a couple of blankets and they were lying across the arm of her chair.

Kate eased into the wing chair. Alice tucked the blankets securely around her. Aloysius jumped down from the bookcase and climbed into her lap.

"Harry, honey," Alice said, "come over here and see if you can unlace these boots. If you can't, cut 'em off." She frowned at Harry's expression. "The laces, not her feet. But any longer out there in the elements, it might've been her feet. You take a lesson from that, young lady."

Kate shuddered. Harry appeared before her, holding a pair of scissors.

"Watch my pedicure," Kate said, eyeing the scissors.

Harry smiled weakly. He looked young and frightened.

Kate didn't watch as Harry tugged at her shoelaces, but Al hung over her lap and swiped at the scissors. When Harry finally cut through the knots, he pulled off her boots, then her socks. Kate drew her shriveled feet up and tucked them beneath her. Al let out a disgruntled yeow at being disturbed and resettled himself among the folds of the blanket.

Someone had just tried to kill her and she couldn't even begin to guess why.

The front door buzzed. *Thank God*, Kate thought.

"Ms. Hinckley? Kate? Harry!" The chief's voice. It was thunderous and was followed by the thud of footsteps on the stairway. *The carpet isn't down yet*, Kate thought idly. *The stairs are wet. And slippery. He'll break his neck. . .*

Then he was standing in front of her, holding Izzy's mailbag. He dropped it to the floor, looking down with sheer rage in his eyes. "What the hell happened?"

Kate blinked up at him.

Al gathered himself up and growled, his claws gouging Kate's thighs in the process.

"Damn it. Tell me what the hell happened."

You buy the pizza, she thought. *That's your third swear word. You have to buy the pizza.* But she didn't say it. Her lips wouldn't move. None of her would move.

"Stop yelling at her." Harry tried to wedge himself between the chief and Kate. The chief brushed him aside, then leaned over Kate and reached for her. She shrunk back. Al sprang. Kate just managed to catch him before he became airborne.

"Hold the damn cat."

Kate pulled Aloysius close as he started a low rumble, his eyes fixed on the chief as the chief leaned past him.

"Hold still." In one movement, his thumb was on her eyelid. He pulled it up and peered in her eye, did the same with the other. She twisted her head away.

"'M okay," she managed.

Something whistled.

"The tea," Harry said and slid away.

The chief straightened up, stood looking down at her. Harry put a cup on the table and took Al out of her lap.

Kate took the cup in both hands. "I was looking out the window." She sipped at the tea. It was too hot to drink. "And there he was across the street. The man in the orange hat."

The tension emanating from the chief was so intense that for a moment Kate was afraid to go on.

"Let me guess. You followed him."

"No . . . yes." A shudder passed over her. "He started to leave and I was afraid he was going to get away. So I ran downstairs and told Alice to call you—"

"Which I did," Alice pointed out. "Which is why you're here instead of missing the whole thing."

The chief's jaw tightened.

"And Harry and Izzy were coming up the street. I told them to call the police. . ."

"Don't you give her that look," Alice piped in. "Izzy yelled at me to call the police and the two of them took off after her. And it's a good thing they did. Because there sure wasn't any policeman around when we needed him."

Kate hurried on before it became a free-for-all. "The man turned at the corner and I lost him behind all the snow. Then I saw him in MacArthur Lane. He was just standing there, like he was waiting for me. And before you yell at me. No. I didn't go down there. I waited near the street for Harry and Izzy. But—but then I heard a car, and when I turned around, it was aiming at me." Her voice broke. She bit her lip to keep it from trembling.

"Jesus." The chief knelt down, finally on her level. "Did it hit you? Are you hurt?"

"No. I mean, I'm not hurt." *Too much.* "I jumped out of the way, but it clipped me. And knocked me down."

"You're going to the emergency room." He stood up and flipped open his cell phone.

"No. I'm okay. And don't call Aunt Pru."

He gave her a look.

"Please."

Slowly, he closed his phone. "We'll discuss this later. Can you describe what he looked like, the make of the car?"

Kate told him. "Harry said the car was a white Chevy."

Brandon turned to Harry. Harry looked ready to bolt, but he nodded quickly. "I couldn't see the plates."

"He tried to *kill* her." Izzy's voice was strident. His mailbag was still on the floor, *his delivery forgotten.*

"Why?" The chief's question was so abrupt and so unexpected that Kate jumped. He zeroed in on her. "What have you been doing, what do you know that you haven't told me?"

"Nothing." Her eyes filled with tears. Why was he mad at her? She hadn't done anything but try to act intelligently.

"Don't give me that. You must have done something—found out something. You—" He stopped. Took a breath. "You can't seem to learn to leave things to law enforcement like a reasonable person would, and it almost got you killed. Now tell me."

Kate could only shake her head.

"Stop yelling at her. It's my fault." Harry stepped toward them, still clutching Al. "My fault."

"Don't," Kate warned. *Not when things were going so well between you and the chief.*

The chief turned on Harry. "How so?" His voice was modulated, but no one could mistake the controlled anger beneath.

Al's fur was standing on end. Alice moved instinctively toward the boy as if she could protect him, which was ludicrous. A septuagenarian and a cat. But it was so like them both.

"Just tell me the truth."

Harry's bottom lip began to tremble. "I called MKD and they traced the call."

Kate tried to get out of the chair, but she was hopelessly entangled in the blankets.

"You don't know that," she said, her eyes on the chief. "If I hadn't answered the phone—"

"Quiet."

Silence fell over the room while currents of emotion eddied like a whirlpool, threatening to suck them under.

Kate watched the chief's chest swell as he took a deep breath, slowly let it out. More quietly, he said, "You almost got her killed."

"I know. I'm sorry." A tear slipped from Harry's eye. He whirled around, nearly knocking Alice over, and bolted out of the door, clutching Al to his chest.

"You big bully," Alice cried. "And him just a *boy.*"

Kate wrestled with the blanket. "Go after him. It isn't his fault."

"He jeopardized your safety. He can stew in it. Don't leave that chair. Izzy, show me where this happened."

Izzy snapped to attention, but eyed the chief with disgust before he followed him out of the room.

Kate grabbed at Alice. "We have to find Harry."

Alice patted her shoulder. "You sit like Chief Mitchell told you to. Don't want him getting any more riled up. I'll go find Harry."

When she came back a few minutes later, she was alone. "Nowhere. I looked in every room, even the kitchen. He's gone."

Kate finally got her feet untangled from the blanket and stood up. "I'm going to look for him."

"Not now. He's probably hiding somewhere, crying his heart out. You wouldn't want to embarrass him."

"No, but—"

"He'll come back. It's too cold to stay out for long."

Kate wasn't so sure. He'd run away before. And he was already afraid that the chief was going to send him away. He must be certain of that now.

Kate sniffed. "He didn't have to be so mean."

"Well, he *is* from Boston." As if that explained everything. "Maybe the boy went home."

To the chief's house? Kate didn't think so. "I wish we knew for sure." But they didn't and they could only wait until Izzy and the chief returned, so Kate could try to make things right again.

The minutes ticked by: five, ten, fifteen, eighteen. Finally, after twenty-two minutes, Kate heard the downstairs buzzer. She steeled herself. No way was she going to let the chief abandon Harry. It wasn't Harry's fault; it was hers for letting them investigate, even theoretically.

"Did you find him?" Kate asked as soon as the chief stepped into the office, Izzy right behind him.

"He's long gone by now."

At first Kate didn't understand. "Not the orange hat. *Harry.*"

"No," the chief's tone was ice. He reached in his pocket. "But I did find this."

He held an evidence bag. He took it to the desk and opened it over the blotter. A gold medal secured by a wide purple ribbon rolled onto the felt blotter. A 2002 Grand Master Award. And the 2002 Grand Master was Tony Kefalas.

"Do you recognize it?"

Kate shook her head. It couldn't be. *Not Tony.*

"Don't lie to me."

"What? Oh. I recognize it. I'm sure you do, too. But it wasn't Tony."

"Because he's your friend?"

"Yes. But also, because he's in Chicago. So it couldn't be."

"Are you sure?"

"Ginny Sue took him to the airport. He had a tournament there. Call them," she added rashly. She knew it couldn't be Tony. "And besides, he only wore it when he was emceeing. He . . . took it off at the inn last Saturday night when we were having dinner."

The chief's eyes flickered. Belatedly, Kate remembered that he'd also been there—with Claudine. "He put it in his jacket pocket." She paused while she replayed the scene. "It must have fallen out and someone found it."

"Or it fell out when he was just now trying to run you down. He lured you to that alley. Premeditated."

"It's obviously a plant."

The chief barked out a dry laugh. "Everybody's an expert."

Kate closed her eyes and imagined the man standing at his car. *Reaching into his pocket for his keys . . . something falling out on the ground.* She thought again. *Not falling.* "He dropped the medal intentionally. When he was getting his keys out of his pocket. He *wanted* me to think it was Tony. But why?"

"Don't even consider trying to find an answer to that question. You're going to wait here for constable Curtis and he's going to take you to Valley General to be checked out. Then he'll drive you home. Alice can lock up." He slipped the medal back into the evidence bag. "Don't argue."

"Where are you going?"

"To catch a murderer."

"Find Harry first."

"Harry can take care of himself."

"You are so wrong," she said, but he was already gone.

CHAPTER

NINETEEN

KATE WENT TO the emergency room, sitting in the back of the squad car. In the front seat, Paul Curtis and Dickie Wilson talked in low tones, but their mood seemed almost festive. Kate didn't blame them. Triage was probably more fun than staying with the investigation and being the brunt of Chief Mitchell's impatience.

During the ride, Kate took the time to call Harry's cell. He didn't answer, but she didn't think he would. She left a message begging him to call her. She wanted to call the chief, too, but not in front of his patrolmen. So she sat and listened to the hum of the conversation and wondered how soon she could get away so that she could look for Harry.

By the time they arrived at the emergency room, she'd started worrying about more than finding Harry. She knew for a certainty that Tony hadn't tried to hit her. He would never hurt anyone. But he did know about their armchair investigation. He'd even joined in. It *couldn't* have been Tony. He was her friend.

Both officers accompanied her inside. They'd been ordered to wait until she was either released or admitted.

"Just have a seat," the admitting nurse told her after she'd taken Kate's insurance information. "I'm afraid there's a wait. Always busy after a snowstorm—falls and heart attacks from too much shoveling."

Kate took a seat in one of the brown molded chairs. Curtis and Wilson stood by the entrance, chatting in low tones and drinking coffee out of Styrofoam cups, prepared to stay as long as necessary. They straightened up when Kate passed them heading for the outside door. She lifted her cell phone for them to see. No cell phones in the waiting room.

She stepped into the cold and tried calling Harry again. Still no answer. She left another message, set her phone to vibrate, and went back inside.

"Katie McDonald. What are you here for? Nothing serious, I hope."

A harried looking woman was sitting two chairs down from Kate. She noticed Kate and her face puckered with concern. "Are you sure you're okay? Your cheek is bruised. Did you fall down?"

Kate touched her cheek and winced. She must have hit it when she fell. She had no idea how bad it was.

"I hope nothing's broken."

"No. Just a precaution," said Kate, trying to remember the woman's name.

"Fell on the ice, did you? Happens even to us seasoned New Englanders."

"Yes. I fell. Thanks for asking . . ." The woman's name came to her. "Mrs. Renquist."

"Larry, too. He's my youngest. Fell off his sled. Dave's in there with him." She shook her head. "Pretty sure his leg is broken. Last summer it was his collarbone. Skateboard. These boys, just don't seem to stay out of scrapes."

Kate nodded, then shook her head. She checked her cell. Harry was in a scrape and he didn't have a mother to take care of him. He had her and the chief. And the chief didn't seem to care.

Mrs. Renquist glanced over to the two officers and raised an eyebrow at Kate. The blood rushed to Kate's cheeks. She'd been brought in by the police, and it would be all over town before the six-o'clock news. *God, it's not even six o'clock*, Kate realized; it just felt like midnight. She hurt everywhere.

"I fell and they were nice enough to drive me here."

"You were lucky they were nearby."

"Yes."

Finally Kate's name was called. A tall, lanky resident smiled and nodded, and decided x-rays were unnecessary. He sent her home with a sample of pain pills.

The officers drove her back at the museum. The museum was dark. Alice had closed up, but Alice's porch light was on. She'd have to go over and ask Alice if Harry had returned.

Officer Wilson nixed the idea. "The chief said I was to drive your car home and we're not to let you go back to work. Sorry, Katie."

Kate didn't argue. She wouldn't add to their troubles by defying the chief. So she sat in the backseat of the police cruiser while Dickie Wilson followed them home in the Matrix.

Both officers accompanied her to her front door. It was a bit of overkill and Kate suspected that at this point they'd surpassed the chief's orders and were merely procrastinating.

The bungalow's porch light was on as well as the rest of the house. Aunt Pru must have heard about her accident. Hopefully, that was all she'd heard.

Kate thanked the officers and was looking for her keys when the front door opened and Pru, wearing a black-and-white running suit, peered out at them.

"Thank God you're alright. I would have come to the hospital, but Alice said these two nice young men were taking care of you, so I made chicken soup. Is that you, Paul Curtis? How's your grandmother?"

"Much better, thank you."

"So glad to hear that. You'll have to bring her to dinner some evening."

Kate rolled her eyes. Fortunately, she was standing behind Pru.

"Good night, ma'am. Katie." Paul tipped his cap. Wilson did the same and they jogged back to their car.

Pru led Kate inside. "Lovely boy. Oh, you poor dear. Let me help you with your coat." She tussled Kate for her buttons, then gasped. "Katie, your *face*. Did they give you some arnica? I have some in my medicine cabinet. I'll just—but first, let me get the soup. You crawl into bed and I'll bring your dinner on a tray."

Kate was momentarily distracted by looking into the mirror over the credenza. She had a shiner. No wonder Mrs. Renquist had been so curious. "I'm really okay. I'll have soup in the kitchen. I'm starved."

Kate barely had time to grab her cell phone before Pru had her out of her coat and was helping her down the hallway. "I don't know what's happening to this town: murder, and people trying to run over good citizens."

Kate knew where this was going: Pru managed to lay every ill at Chief Mitchell's feet. And tonight, for once, Kate was ready to agree.

Pru sat her down at the table and placed a steaming bowl of

soup in front of her. Kate breathed in the heady aroma. When Pru said she'd made soup, she hadn't meant she'd opened a can. The soup was homemade with big chunks of chicken, celery, carrots and wide egg noodles.

Kate took a cautious spoonful of hot broth. "This is wonderful."

"That's what families are for. Would you like a glass of milk?"

"No, this is plenty thanks."

Pru sat down opposite her and watched her eat. "Paul Curtis is such a lovely young man. . ."

"He can't be a day over twenty-three," Kate counted. "He was in middle school when I graduated from Valley High."

"I read in a magazine that older women–younger men relationships are the newest thing."

Kate paused with spoon half way to her mouth. "I'm not that old." She blew on the spoonful and slowly sipped.

"You're almost thirty."

How many times were they going to have this same conversation? It had escalated in the last month or so. Soon Kate would turn thirty and it would become "you're *over* thirty. . ."

Kate was aching and tired, and she needed to find Harry. "Pru, Paul is nice. But I'm not going to marry him, or even go on a date with him. He's a kid."

"Then you should apologize to Sam. There are more women in this town needing husbands than men needing wives."

"I didn't do anything to Sam. I don't know what he's mad about."

"You should ask him, then apologize."

"What if it's not my fault?"

"Apologize anyway; men have their pride."

Tell me about it, Kate thought, picturing Brandon Mitchell. "I have mine, too."

"If you're not going to see Sam anymore—which I think is a big mistake—then you should be nice to Paul. It's obvious that Norris Endelman isn't going to pop the question. These divorcees are always skittish."

Kate's head was pounding. Her nerves were frayed. "Aunt Pru, I know you mean well. But right now I have more urgent things to think about."

"If you worried about that hit-and-run driver, don't be. I'll stay here with you. I should have had Paul and the Wilson boy stay. Why didn't that police chief post a guard? Someone just tried to kill you." Pru's hands flew to her cheeks. "I'd almost forgotten. How awful. Someone tried to kill you and I'm worried about you going on a date."

"No one tried to kill me. I was standing in the street and the car fishtailed into me."

"That's not what Alice Hinckley told me."

"Alice wasn't there."

Pru pursed her lips.

"Really, you don't have to worry." Kate stood up. "I appreciate the soup. I'll put everything away. Right now I have to make some calls."

"At this hour? After what you've been through?"

Kate glanced a the kitchen clock. Eight thirty. Would this day never end?

"Harry's missing."

"What do you mean 'missing'?"

"He and the Chief Mitchell had words. The chief sort of blamed Harry for what happened."

"That so-and-so. I *knew* it was a bad idea to have the poor boy live with that man. What does he know about raising children?"

Kate didn't confess that it had been her own idea, one that neither the chief nor Harry had been fond of at the time. But things had been going so much better. Until recently. "Maybe you're right, but right now I need to find him. He ran from the museum and I haven't been able to get him on his cell. I'm really worried."

"Do you think he went back to his uncle? Not that Buck Perkins knows any better how to raise a boy. A nasty kind of mean. But he is family."

Harry would never go back. But Buck might try to kidnap him. Harry's trust fund would be a strong incentive. Harry wouldn't have a chance against him because Buck was more than nasty mean; Kate thought he might be pathological. "I have to find him."

"Did you try calling him?"

"Yes, and the chief. I just got their voicemails."

"Hmm," Pru said.

"I'm going to look for him."

"You can't go out now."

"I have to. It's still early."

"Absolutely not. You should be in bed. And it's too dangerous."

"I'll lock my doors and I won't get out, but I have to look."

"Then I'll go with you."

"No. I mean, I'd like you to stay here in case he calls. Tell him to come here or call me and I'll pick him up."

"You'll stay in the car?"

"Yes."

"I think that snot-potty police chief ought to be out looking for him."

"He might be, but I don't think Harry would let the chief find him. He was pretty harsh."

"Humph."

"Please understand. I have to look for him."

"I do understand. Doesn't mean I approve."

Kate leaned over the table and kissed her aunt's cheek. "You're the best family anyone could have."

"Humph," said Pru again and began clearing the dishes.

Kate drove straight to the museum. She hurt everywhere but she was glad she'd decided against taking the prescribed pain pills. She'd need all her wits to drive and look for Harry. She had no illusions about just coming across his shadowed figure running through the streets, but there was one place that she thought Harry might go.

She remembered something the professor had told her when everyone else thought Harry had run away. The professor knew better. He said, "Harry wouldn't run away. He'd run here." And that time he'd been right.

Kate parked in front of the museum. Except for the new security lights, the museum was dark, just as it had been when they'd picked up her car. That didn't mean Harry wasn't inside. As she let herself in the front door, a frisson of remembered fear skittered up her spine.

She quickly turned on the entrance hall lights and looked around. Empty. She headed back to the kitchen, looking into each of the exhibition rooms as she went. The kitchen was empty. The back door and cellar door were both bolted.

She retraced her steps and climbed the stairs to the second floor, turning on lights as she went. He wasn't in the office, and neither was Al, which was odd. Normally, by now he would have come out to see what was going on and beg for food.

He might be outside on a nocturnal prowl. Al came and went as he pleased, using laundry chutes and dumbwaiters and chinks in the house they'd never found. They'd long ago stopped being concerned about his whereabouts. Kate just hoped he was with Harry.

She opened the desk drawer. The ring of spare keys they kept there was gone.

Please let this mean he's here, she thought as she began to climb the stairs to the third floor. The professor's living quarters were on that floor. She'd never been inside them until after the professor's death. She rarely went there now. It had been the professor's inner sanctum and since his death had become a kind of shrine.

Maybe it was also a place of refuge for a lonely, hurt teenaged boy.

When she reached the third floor, she tiptoed across the landing. She saw no light coming from beneath the apartment door. She paused for a moment, wondering if she should knock or take him by surprise. Or if the door was even locked. She refused to think that she had been wrong and Harry was long gone.

She tried the knob. It didn't move, but she had her own set of keys. She found the correct one and fit it to the lock, then quietly turned the knob and opened the door a few inches.

"Harry?" she whispered.

No answer.

"Harry, I'm coming in." She opened the door wider, felt along the wall until she found the overhead light, and flicked it on.

"Yeow," Al protested. Kate slumped with relief.

Harry was curled up on the professor's big bed, with the patchwork quilt pulled over him so that only his head and the arm that encircled Al stuck out. He was fast asleep.

She tiptoed toward him. Al's ears pricked up as he watched her. *Warily*, she thought.

"It's okay, Al," she whispered. "Don't wake him up."

Al wriggled, Harry's arm slipped away, and Al rolled over on his back, all fours splayed as he waited for a rub. Kate stroked his stomach, deliberating on whether to wake Harry up or let him sleep. She decided on the latter. She crept back to the hall and called Pru to tell her she'd found Harry, but they were going to stay at the museum for a while and that Pru could go home.

Pru didn't like the idea, but she acquiesced.

Kate considered calling the chief, but didn't. He might not even be worried. He might be so absorbed in his case that he'd forgotten all about Harry. Maybe he didn't care. *To hell with him.*

There was a settee by the window. Kate made her way toward it and eased herself painfully onto the cushions. She felt a flicker of annoyance at not being in her own comfortable bed, but quickly checked it. This wasn't just a case of teenage selfishness. This was a case of Harry needing a place in the world and belonging to people who cared about him just as if he were family.

Kate knew she felt that way about him. She just wished she knew if the chief felt the same way.

She'd just found a comfortable position when her cell phone rang. She grabbed for it and turned it off.

But Harry stirred and sat up, blinking sleepily. Then his eyes widened and he began to shake his head.

"It's okay," she said quickly. "I'm not going to make you leave. I was just worried about you." She saw that his eyes were swollen, not just from sleep but from crying. She had a hard time not bursting into sympathetic tears herself.

"I was . . . just . . . saying good-bye to the professor. Then I'll leave." He pushed the quilt away. Al rolled off the bed and landed on the floor with a heavy thump. "You should put him on a diet. . ." Harry's lip trembled.

Kate forgot her own aches and pains and crossed to the bed. "*You* can put him on a diet."

Harry shook his head and a fresh tear splashed onto the sheet. He brushed it away with his sleeve, then yanked the covers over his head. "Go away."

Instead, Kate sat down on the bed. He rolled away from her.

"You don't have to leave. I want you to stay."

A muffled reply. She tugged the quilt down. Harry hid his face in his sleeve.

"Harry."

"Why did he have to die? He liked me to be with him."

Kate didn't have an answer. She couldn't have answered if she did have an answer. Her throat was tight and stinging. Then she thought, *what the hell,* and gave way to her own buried grief.

She wasn't even aware that Harry had turned back and was watching her.

"It sucks," he said.

Kate nodded, letting her tears flow. "It really sucks."

So they sat for a while, the rest of the world closed out. Then Kate finally pulled herself together and gave Harry a watery smile.

"You wouldn't desert the professor, would you? He meant for you to carry on his collection."

"He left it to you."

"Only because you're fourteen. It will be yours after—"

"Stop it. I don't want to hear."

Kate stopped, then started again. "He meant for us both to protect what he loved best. You're not going to walk out on that, are you?"

"It won't matter. He'll send me away to some foster family who only wants the money or make me go to some dumb boarding school so he won't have to keep me."

It took Kate a second to realize the "he" was no longer the professor, but the chief.

"He only thinks that you'll be more challenged at a private school."

Harry snorted.

Kate sighed. Maybe Brandon did just want to get rid of him. He had to be a huge responsibility. So where did that leave them?

"I'll petition the court to have you live with me."

Harry stared at her incredulously. "You almost died because of me."

"That is so much bullshit."

"*Kate.*" Harry's reminder was even more painful. Kate hadn't realized it before, but the game of whoever swears three times buys the pizza had become a ritual between Harry, Brandon, and her. *Like having tea by the fire with the professor.* They were building their own family.

The thought was shocking. They weren't anything like a family. Were they? "Look, why don't we go to my house? You can stay there for the night. I'll call the chief and tell him you're okay. We can figure this out in the morning."

Harry's bottom lip protruded. It made him look so young that Kate had a hard time not laughing. "Please? Pretty please."

"I'd rather stay here."

"I know, but you can't stay by yourself. And I can't sleep on the settee."

"You can have the bed."

Kate gave him a look. "Aunt Pru made chicken noodle soup. From scratch."

Harry unconsciously licked his lip. He looked around the room as if it were the last time he'd ever see it.

"And when you're eighteen, or whatever the legal age is, you can move in here."

Harry stared at her, his expression stuck between defiance and hope. "I thought you were going to make it into a storage room."

Kate shook her head. "We'll find more room someplace else. Deal?"

Still he hesitated. Then finally, "What's going to happen between now and when I'm eighteen?"

"I don't know. You'll have to trust me."

"Okay."

		3				9		
	2		3		6	8		7
	4			2	9			
1	3				4			
7		5				4		2
			5				6	9
			9	6			7	
9		4	1		7		5	
		8				6		

"I CALLED MY Aunt Pru to tell her you're okay. She was worried about you. And I'd better call the chief."

"No, not him."

"He'll be worried, too."

"No, he won't. He'll be glad to see the back of me."

Kate didn't argue. She'd get him settled, then call Brandon in private. She turned her phone back on and saw that she had three messages. All from Ginny Sue. Either Pru had called her and she wanted to help look for Harry, or the chief had been asking her questions about Tony's whereabouts.

She pressed the call button.

Ginny answered on the first ring. "Why haven't you called me back? I've been calling and calling."

"Sorry. My phone was off. I just saw the list of missed calls. What's the matter?"

"The matter? Chief Mitchell has arrested Tony for murder!"

Kate was silent, too stunned to think of anything to say.

"You've got to do something. It's all your fault!"

"Wait a minute. You're not making sense. Tony's in Chicago."

"No, he isn't. He's here."

Kate could tell Ginny Sue was close to tears.

"He finished on Sunday and came back yesterday. I picked him up in Boston. And now he's in jail. I'm going over there now. You've got to come and make Chief Mitchell listen to reason."

Harry had come over to the settee and was mouthing, "What?" at her.

Kate glanced at Harry. "I'll meet you there, but it will take me about twenty minutes."

"Hurry!" Ginny Sue hung up.

"What?" Harry asked out loud.

"Ginny Sue said they've just arrested Tony for murder."

"He's in Chicago."

"That's what I thought. But Romeo seems to have made a surprise visit. Now he's in the Granville jail."

"For what?"

"Hit and run? Murder? I have no idea."

"Not Tony."

"I know that, and you know that, but that fathead—"

"He's not a fathead."

Kate flinched. In spite of all Brandon had done to him, Harry was still sticking up for him. "No, you're right—he isn't. That was just my exasperation talking. I'm sorry."

"I don't care."

He did. And it was Kate's fault as much as it was Brandon's. She'd been the one who forced them together. Now, they were all paying the price for her interference. Unfortunately, she was about to interfere again. "I'm going to the station. I don't suppose you want to go with me."

He shook his head.

"I don't blame you. I'll drop you off at my house."

"I can stay here."

"No, you can't. Now, no more arguments. And no more running away. Promise?"

"I guess."

"Good." Kate called her house. "Aunt Pru? I'm bringing Harry home. Can you stay a little longer?"

"Of course," Pru said. "Poor boy."

They locked up the museum and drove to Kate's house where she handed Harry off to Pru. "He's hungry. And he's staying the night."

"Where are you going?"

"To the police station."

"What for? It's after ten. Don't tell me that snot—"

"*Pru.*" Kate cut her eyes to Harry.

"Come along, Harry. Dinner's waiting in the kitchen."

Kate pointed her finger at Harry. "You be here when I get back."

She gave Pru a quick hug, whispering, "Thanks, you're the best."

As Kate backed out of the driveway, she saw Pru and Harry standing at the screen door, almost the same height, and both looking bewildered. She felt a stab of contrition for dumping the two together without easing them into the relationship. She could only cross her mathematical fingers and hope for the best.

The Granville police station was a block off Main Street, opposite the courthouse. It was a small two-story building, normally quiet. But tonight, light came from several windows. Two sconce lamps lit up the entrance.

Elmira Swyndon was sitting at the station desk. Her eyes widened as she took in Kate's bruised face. "I heard about your accident. Are you alright? Thank goodness you were able to come. I was just about to leave for the day when the chief brought in that nice Mr. Kefalas. And Ginny Sue is here crying her eyes out. Is it true he murdered those men?"

"No!" Ginny Sue's wail made them both jump.

"Ginny Sue?" Kate hardly recognized her mild friend. She sat crumpled onto the wooden bench that ran along the front wall of the visitors' area. Her hair was tousled and her eyes were wild.

"It's all your fault, Katie. Chief Mitchell would never have arrested him if you hadn't—" Ginny Sue shook her head, buried her face in her hands and sobbed.

Kate wondered, *If I hadn't what?*

"I'll get some water." Elmira pushed herself out of her chair and hurried to the cooler.

Kate sat down beside Ginny Sue and put her arm around her shoulders. Ginny Sue shrugged away. Kate manage to hear a muffled, "Your fault."

Elmira returned with a paper cup of water. It gave Kate a start. She'd been here before. Last time it was Kate who was getting the water and she was suspected of murder.

"Now, now," Elmira said and handed Ginny Sue the cup.

Ginny Sue gulped it down. Her face was blotched, her expression helpless and frightened. "He didn't do it."

"I know," Kate said in what she hoped was a soothing voice. Why did she always have to be the voice of reason? *Because you are a scientist, and no matter how much you try to be like other people, you'll always be the rational one.* She finally admitted to herself that maybe that's where she belonged. In the rational world, not this place of sloppy emotions.

But Ginny Sue was her friend and she tried again. "I didn't even know Tony was in town. I told the chief he was in Chicago."

Ginny Sue sniffed. Elmira dug a Kleenex out of her dress pocket and handed it to her.

"Tony called me from Chicago. He had a few days before his next job and said he wanted to come for a quick visit. . ." She faltered. "He was so sweet. I mean, I really like him, but I didn't really expect to see him again. Nobody's ever done that before. . . want to visit me." This set off a new round of tears.

Elmira patted her back and said, "Now, now."

Kate thought it was sweet, too. She didn't think anyone had ever gone out of their way to visit her, either. She felt a little envious. Not about Tony but . . . She joined Elmira in the back patting.

"And now you've ruined everything."

Kate drew her hand back. "Because I recognized Tony's medal on the ground? The chief recognized it, too. Anybody would. Over three hundred people saw him wearing it during the tournament. I had no idea that Tony was back. You could have told me."

"Why should I?"

Over her head, Elmira pursed her lips, shook her head.

Kate was stymied. She'd have never expected that Ginny could turn on her this way. Ginny Sue wasn't mean to anybody. She liked Kate. Until tonight anyway.

"Does Tony have an alibi?"

At last Ginny Sue looked at her. "What do you mean?"

"Where was he when I was getting hit by a car?"

Ginny Sue seemed to notice her bruised face for the first time. Her eyes widened, but she only said, "How dare you imply—"

"I'm not implying anything." Kate could hear her voice rising. She couldn't stop it. "I just asked where he was at three o'clock today."

Ginny Sue crushed the empty paper cup. "With *me.*"

Kate rolled her eyes. "Then tell the chief." She was tired and aching, and no one was cooperating.

"I told him. He just gave me one of his looks. He doesn't care. He'll just make Tony a scapegoat."

"He would never do that," Kate snapped. "He won't stop until he finds the real culprit. He's too honest to do anything less."

"I hate him." Ginny Sue broke down again. It was hard to take. Ginny Sue was the most congenial, optimistic person Kate had ever met. Always supportive. Dependable. A friend. Now, all that was gone. What was wrong with people?

Ginny Sue had to be overreacting. Brandon couldn't seriously believe that Tony dressed up in an orange hat and tried to run her down. He didn't even have a car here, though he could have rented one. Claudine had had to rent one when she drove hers into a snowbank.

The chief appeared in the hallway that Kate knew led back to Room C, Granville's version of the hot seat. Tony was standing beside him, pale and a little shell-shocked.

Ginny jumped up from the bench and ran to them. She threw herself into Tony's arms. The chief stepped away, looking sardonic. It was all really embarrassing. What if Tony was just amusing himself? Ginny Sue wouldn't recover easily. And it would be even harder for her to face the town after the way she was acting now.

Elmira scooted closer to Kate. "Don't mind her. Being in love makes people a little crazy sometimes."

Love? How can Ginny Sue be in love? She'd only met Tony a week and a half ago. If this is what love does to you, Ginny Sue could have it.

Kate sat back on the bench and tried to relax. Ginny Sue's anger had left her shaken. She wanted to leave before she had to face more of Ginny Sue's accusations. And before she had to face Tony. Elmira could tell the chief that she'd found Harry. She had no reason to stay. But she couldn't seem to move.

She watched Tony and the chief exchange a few words. Then Tony trundled a sagging Ginny Sue across the waiting area and out the front door. He hadn't even seen Kate. But the chief had. One eyebrow lifted then snapped back into place.

Kate automatically smoothed back her hair. She'd lost her hair clip at the emergency room and she knew that she must look half-crazed, with all those curls loose and corkscrewing around her face. Why hadn't she gotten up and left when she'd had the chance?

The chief strode toward her. Kate saw the shock register on his face. She must look really bad. He didn't look so hot himself. The skin was drawn across his cheekbones, his eyes were opaque with fatigue. Even his shoulders slumped, something she'd never witnessed before.

As if reading her mind, he straightened up, his tough-guy façade firmly back in place.

Elmira hurried to stop him. There was a brief, silent standoff. The chief won and Elmira returned wordlessly to her desk.

"When was the last time you slept?" Kate asked before she could stop herself.

"Around here? Seems like never. What are you doing here?"

She shrugged, which was stupid. She'd come because Ginny Sue had called her. She wanted to tell him that she'd found Harry.

"If you're going to give me grief about questioning your friend Mr. Kefalas, don't."

"You can't really believe Tony was driving that car."

He opened his mouth, but shut it again without saying what

he'd been about to say.

"Should I call Simon?"

"He doesn't need a lawyer, yet. I haven't arrested him, much to my chagrin."

"You didn't arrest him?"

"Jesus! He just walked out the door."

"I thought maybe he'd arranged bail or something."

"I brought him in for questioning. His medal was found at the scene of the crime. Physical, tangible evidence. That's how an investigation works. Not guessing. Not disregarding a suspect because you can't *imagine* him doing it. Of all people, you should understand that."

"I do." But she hadn't been acting like it. She'd been running on pure adrenalin for the last few hours, had been reacting instead of thinking. "But I told you it wasn't Tony."

"Tautology. Don't go there."

He was right. She was just repeating herself. "I also came to tell you that I found Harry."

Neither the chief's posture nor his expression changed. "Where?"

"He was upstairs in the professor's apartment. I took him to my house. Pru's with him. I think it will be better if he stays the night."

"That might be best. In the morning, I'll contact—"

"You will not contact social services. You are not sending him to a foster home. He needs a real home."

"And just where do you expect him to find that?"

"With you. He needs a good male role model. Someone whom he can look up to, depend on, someone who can teach him how to be a good person. If you can't be bothered, he can live with me." She slammed down on her words. Fatigue was making her imprudent.

Why was he being so obtuse? Why couldn't people just act intelligently. Predictably. *Patience. Patience,* she repeated to herself, the same words that the professor had offered her so many times: when she was the brunt of kidding, when she wasn't invited to the prom, when Mrs. Tolliver accused her of plagiarism because she didn't believe an eighth grader could write so intelligently. *Patience.*

The chief was obviously trying to hold on to his own temper. A muscle jumped at his jaw line. His eyes had deepened until they were almost black.

"I'd better go." Kate realized that she'd stood up somewhere during their confrontation. She nodded curtly and headed for the door.

"It's not going to work."

Something in her snapped and Kate turned on him. "Not if you don't want it to. And you obviously don't want it to. You push people away when they care about you. You antagonize people who are trying to help you. Make false accusations—"

"I didn't accuse good old Tony of anything."

Kate knew both of their voices were rising. She was past caring. "You alienate a boy who only wants your love and respect. He needs you. We—the whole town needs you. But you aren't going to stick, are you?

"You want to know why Harry made that contraption, why he contacted MKD? Because he knew you were going to leave. He saw you looking at the websites. He thought if he helped solve the murders, you would stay."

"Kate—"

"But you don't care. So go ahead. Run away when things get tough. But it's just going to be the same in the next town. And the next. Because anything worth having doesn't come easy. And that's the only way you want it."

She heard Elmira gasp. They'd be the major topic of gossip the next day. Maybe for a whole week. It didn't matter. He was leaving. Everybody was mad at her.

"So just—just go *fishing.*" She felt a bubble of hysterical laughter rise to her throat. She bolted toward the door, irregardless of how crazed she must look. She was afraid she was going to be sick. She hated Brandon Mitchell for coming here, for letting her down, for giving Harry a glimpse of what life could be and then snatching it away from him.

Well, to hell with him. She'd find a way to keep Harry. She'd clear Tony's name. She'd had enough.

The cold air hit her hard, knocking her back on her heels and clearing her head. She stood on the sidewalk panting, but not able to get enough oxygen to her lungs. Gradually, sanity returned, and she was horrified at what she'd done. She'd dressed down the chief in front of the whole station house. At the very least, Elmira had witnessed it. They probably hadn't even known he was looking for a new job.

If people knew he was leaving, they'd make his last few months a living hell, and have fun doing it. Well, good for them. It was no more than he deserved. He'd never fit in here.

And maybe she didn't either.

She'd thought that getting back into the mainstream of life would be fulfilling. It was awful. If her position at the institute hadn't already been filled, she could have gone back to it. But she'd been replaced and it would be a long time before there would be another vacancy.

She'd have to stay for the museum's sake. *But no more dealing with people.* For the first time, she understood why the professor had been a recluse.

"Kate? Are you okay?"

Tony's voice. She looked around. He was getting out of Ginny Sue's car. Had they stuck around to give her more grief? She started walking away.

Tony caught up with her and took her elbow. "You look weird."

She didn't say anything. She couldn't because now that the adrenalin rush was over, she thought she might burst into tears. She never cried at the institute. At least not often.

"Listen. I really need to talk to you. Not tonight, tomorrow. At the museum? Eight o'clock. Ginny Sue will have left for work by then."

Now what? wondered Kate, only mildly interested. Fatigue was rapidly taking over.

Tony squeezed her arm. "I know Ginny Sue's kind of upset right now."

"With me."

"Don't take it to heart. She's just a little overwrought. She's not like you. She doesn't understand that mathematicians make rational decisions, ones based on logic, not emotion. She'll come around."

Maybe Ginny Sue will come around, thought Kate, *but what about me?* He'd made her sound like a machine.

"Now, don't give it another thought."

Kate went back to her car, so tired now that she could hardly make it over the mound of crusted snow at the curb. She drove home with the windows open just to stay awake.

Pru and Harry were both asleep. Kate turned off the lights and tip-toed back to her room. She undressed in front of the mirror in her bedroom, taking stock of her battered body. Not only were her left eye and cheek an unsightly combination of blue and black, there was a huge bruise on her hip bone and several more along her leg.

She stared at her image, the full import of how close she had come to being killed finally sinking in. Someone had lured her out of the museum in order to run her down. It seemed perfectly obvious now. And she thought she was being so smart for not following him down MacArthur Lane.

A bath helped ease the physical pains and strains, but it couldn't do anything for her state of mind. She'd burned her bridges tonight by talking to the chief that way. And she'd burned Harry's, too. She put on her old flannel nightgown and tiptoed back to her room.

Harry's voice came from the darkened guest room. "Kate?"

She sighed, then went to his door.

Only the night light shone in the room. Harry sat up on one elbow. Kate recognized a pair of her father's pajamas. He looked muzzy from sleep, his hair rumpled. "Did the chief arrest Tony?"

"No. Just asked him some questions and let him go."

"Good."

"Good night—"

"Kate?"

She stopped. She knew she wouldn't get away without having to answer the most important question.

"Did he? You know. . ."

"I told him you were staying here tonight and I'd get you to school in the morning. Where you will stay all day, and then come directly to the museum. Just like always. It's going to be fine," she added in an attempt to make things seem normal.

They were anything but and she dreaded having to tell Harry what had really happened between her and the chief. Tomorrow would be soon enough. He deserved at least one more night with people who cared.

KATE AND HARRY were both bleary-eyed when she dropped him off at school the next morning. He was wearing the same clothes from the day before and a sullen expression.

She knew he was still hurting from the chief's anger, unsure what his future would hold, and embarrassed for letting Kate see him cry.

Kate was totally out of her element, but she guessed—a thing she hated to do—that a bit of tough love might help him keep on the straight and narrow until she could figure out what to do about him.

"Stay at school," she ordered as she stopped the Matrix at the circular drive that ran in front of Granville Valley High School. "Do not skip class, do not think about running away, and be on that bus after school."

Harry gave her a brusque nod and opened the car door.

She watched him shuffle up the sidewalk to the front entrance, his shoulders slumped as if he had the weight of the world on them. And he did, at least the weight of his world.

It wasn't fair that a boy should have been through so many bad times. Even her childhood seemed like paradise by comparison. Of course she'd had a loving mother and father to cushion her from a cruel, teasing world. After her mother died, she had her father, Pru, and the professor.

She'd been hoping that the chief might step into the professor's shoes. But it was obvious now that the chief didn't want the responsibility. How could he not love Harry?

He was leaving. And not just Harry, but her. It was stupid to feel that way. She had done nothing to warrant his staying and she'd thrust Harry onto him, another thing to add to the list of grievances against her.

She'd never thought when she left her job in the institute that life in the outside world would demand so much emotional energy, would be so sloppy.

She wanted coffee, but she was afraid to stop at Rayette's in case word of her argument with the chief was already on the grapevine.

Tony was sitting on the museum steps waiting for her. She'd almost forgotten about him.

He stood up and watched as she stiffly navigated her way to the entrance. "Wow," he said when she was a few feet away. "That's some shiner."

Just the tip of the iceberg, thought Kate, forcing a smile that hurt her cheek.

"Come in. I'll make coffee."

She led him down the hall to the kitchen. Al was sitting expectantly on the floor where he knew his food dish would appear shortly.

He eyed Tony, then hauled to his feet and padded across the linoleum to do figure eights around Tony's trouser legs.

Tony leaned over to pick him up, which Al allowed him to do. "He weighs a ton."

"We had him on a diet. Some expensive dry food that looked like strips of cardboard. He hated it and let us know about it. And he's so good at hunting and begging, that it did absolutely no good."

Kate put his bowl, a Willow pattern china soup bowl, on the floor. Al let out a "Yeow," and wriggled out of Tony's arms.

Tony walked to the window while Kate filled the coffee carafe from the sink.

"A maze?"

"Yes," Kate said. "It was completely overgrown when I first moved back. But we had it pruned and now it's a favorite with kids and adults alike."

Tony smiled at her. And she knew that he would never hurt her.

He turned his back to the window and scanned the kitchen. Kate was uncomfortably aware of how shabby it was. There was still a lot of work to do and since they'd relinquished their equity loan, they'd fallen woefully behind with the renovations.

"I love this kitchen. It reminds me of my grandmother's. The whole museum is amazing."

Kate agreed with him about the museum, but the kitchen was in desperate need of some TLC.

The coffee finished dripping and Kate placed two mugs on the table. Tony sat down in front of one of them and focused on his cup, which he pushed in a counterclockwise circle with the tips of his fingers.

"Did Ginny Sue go back to work?"

"Yes. She wanted to take more time off, but I didn't want her to jeopardize her job over me. She asked me to apologize for her until she could come over and do it herself. She knows she was out of line last night."

"It doesn't matter."

Silence fell between them.

Kate sipped her coffee and waited. Why didn't he just get to the point?

She was trying to think of a way of drawing him out, when he said, "Are you happy?"

Kate nearly dropped her mug. Of all the topics of conversation she'd expected, this wasn't one of them. "Well, yes. I guess. I mean it's really different from what I was doing before, but . . ." she shrugged. "It's home."

"I was raised in Westchester. New York," he added for Kate's edification.

"I know where it is."

"I never got to sit in our kitchen. Only when I visited my grand-mother."

"Tony, why don't you just tell me what you have to say?"

Tony gripped his mug with both hands, looked up at her from under long, dark lashes. On a woman it would have been coy, on Tony it just looked lovable. "That noticeable, huh?"

"Meaning that even Kate, the math geek, picked up on it? Yeah."

"You don't give yourself credit. You're good with people."

"Ha."

"No, seriously—"

"Tony, get on with it."

Tony took a huge breath, then let it out slowly. "Okay, but first you have to promise not to divulge what I'm about to tell you."

"Tony, you sound like an old spy movie. Just say it and get it over with."

Though by this point Kate wished he wouldn't. She was impatient and wary and the two didn't sit well with her. It was evident that whatever he was going to say was going to be bad. "If it has something to do with the murders, I can't promise."

"It doesn't. At least I don't think that it possibly could."

Kate braced her elbows on the table. "Spill."

"Remember me telling you about confiscating Gordon's cell phone?"

"At the Stamford tournament?"

"Yes. There was a little more to it than that. I . . ." He hesitated. His eyes darted around the room and finally came back to rest on his coffee mug. "The fact is, I had a one-nighter with Claudine right before that. I didn't know she was with Gordon. She certainly didn't act like it. She came on to me in the bar after the opening ceremonies.

"You know how it is. Well, maybe you don't. But I'm on the road a lot and I don't get much time for, um, developing relationships. And there are always single people at these things, and—"

"I get it," Kate said, not wanting to hear any details.

"When I stopped Gordon from entering the puzzle area with his phone, he accused me of trying to get him kicked out for personal reasons."

"Claudine."

Tony nodded. "Of course that was totally bogus. I had no intention of ever seeing her again. But he made a big stink and threatened to go to the organizers and file a complaint.

"I backed off, not because his accusation was valid, but to spare the tournament any more headaches than the ones inherent in that kind of gathering. Gordon, being who he is—was—thought he'd one-upped me. He went around the rest of the weekend acting slimy and superior. Needless to say, we were not friends."

"Did you tell Chief Mitchell?"

"No. That was then and this is now. I didn't see any reason to muddy the waters with past history."

"He'll find out."

Tony's shoulders sagged. "It was years ago."

"He's tenacious."

"I noticed. But you'd really have to stretch to turn that little incident into a motive for murder."

"Then why didn't you tell him?"

"Mainly because I didn't want Ginny Sue to know. She's a nice girl and she might not understand."

"The chief wouldn't tell her, unless it was necessary for the investigation."

"Which it isn't," Tony insisted. "But Ginny Sue told me about life in Granville. About the Granville grapevine. She said there are no secrets."

Kate thought that was a pessimistic attitude. Surely not everything made the rounds. *Then again . . .*

"And if it got back to her—"

"I think she'd understand that it was over long before you met her."

"But it would be so embarrassing for her to be the object of that kind of gossip."

"So tell her first. Explain that it was just one of those things you mentioned and that it is in the past. Tell her the truth."

Color speared across Tony's cheekbones.

"Tony. It *was* in the past, wasn't it?"

"Yes. I don't know what made me take Claudine up on it in the first place. She's not a very nice person."

But a very hot one, thought Kate. *Who loves to be the center of male attention.*

"The thing is, the night we all had diner? Ginny Sue left soon after you did. I would have liked her to stay, but she's local and I didn't really know how she'd react." Tony's color deepened. "I can't believe I'm telling you this."

Neither could Kate and she was sure her cheeks were just as red as his.

"Anyway. Claudine caught me as I came back into the inn after seeing Ginny Sue to her car."

"Wait a minute, Claudine left with the chief."

"He was gone when I saw Claudine."

Kate wasn't sure she should be feeling the sense of relief that hearing that gave her.

"She started coming on to me." Tony stopped and rubbed his forehead. "She—she pulled me into the cloak room. She was all over me and I was feeling frustrated, because I'd sent Ginny Sue home. And—"

Kate closed her eyes. "Please tell me you didn't sleep with Claudine."

"I didn't. But we got all the way upstairs and to my room before I came to my senses. She can be very persuasive."

"I'm sure," Kate said dryly.

"I didn't let her in. But she had me out of my jacket and tie and was working on my shirt buttons when I stopped her. I mean we were in a hotel hallway. The realization cooled me off pretty damn quick, I can tell you."

"Did anyone see you?"

Tony shook his head. "That's the first thing I did—look around to make sure we were alone. We were. Claudine was pretty revved by then, and I was freaked. So I extricated myself, picked my jacket and tie off the floor, and opened my door. She would have come inside, but I shut it in her face."

"Oh, Tony."

"I know, I know. But I realized while we were going at it that I really didn't want to screw up this thing with Ginny Sue in case it was going somewhere. Plus how would it look? Gordon was dead and—I didn't know how else to get rid of her."

"Tony. You idiot. Don't you dare toy with Ginny Sue. She's my friend even if she's mad at me and I'll never forgive you if you hurt her."

Tony smiled, which Kate thought was an odd reaction. "That's the second threat I've received in less than twenty-four hours. "

"What kind of threat? I didn't threaten you."

"That you'd never forgive me if I hurt Ginny Sue? Granted that was mild compared to the other one. Chief Mitchell told me that if any harm came to you and he found out that I was the perpetrator, he would personally tear me limb from limb."

"Brandon really said that?"

"Yes. And he meant it. He's got a mean streak, your police chief."

"Not mean, just tough." Did he really care about her or was it just macho posturing? Kate suspected that he cared for all the citizens of Granville, whether they wanted him to or not. *So why is he planning to leave?*

Tony was watching her. "Kate, Kate, Kate. . ."

"What?"

He merely shook his head.

Kate let it pass. The important thing was to get Tony to tell this to the chief. It might give him something to go on, besides orange ski hats. And— "Damn! How dense are we?"

"You've thought of something?"

"Your jacket. It was on the floor."

"Yeah, she stripped it right off my back."

"Tony, think. Jacket. Medal in the pocket. Tussle with Claudine. *Jacket on the floor.*"

Tony sucked in air. "You know, I didn't even think about that. It could have fallen out and Claudine took it. It would be just like her. Kate, you're a genius."

Kate gave him a sour look.

"Sorry, but you are. Embrace your brain." Tony grinned. It fell almost immediately and his brows snapped together. "But how does that help? She could have tossed it in the nearest trash can, or left it at the front desk where anyone could pick it up."

"Or, it might not have been her at all. A totally unknown person could have found it," Kate added.

"And we're back where we started from."

"Exactly," Kate said.

Tony sipped his coffee and tilted his head at her. "I still don't get why someone would want to kill you."

Kate could think of a few reasons if the drama at the police station last night was any indication of how people felt about her. "Maybe they didn't. Maybe they just wanted to scare me. Or it might not even matter who it was, as long as the medal was found. The fact that I was chosen as the victim could just be convenience. Maybe they're really after you."

"Why?"

"I don't know. You tell me."

Tony looked blank. Then, "You mean do I have any enemies in the puzzle world? That's ludicrous."

"Do you?"

"No. Well . . . Gordon didn't like me but he was already dead."

"What about Claudine? Do you think she would want revenge because you, uh, spurned her advances?"

"Very quaint," Tony said with a glimmer of a smile. "But I imagine, to Claudine, one man is as good as another. I wish I'd never met her."

"I really think you need to tell Chief Mitchell everything."

"And drag this out even longer? No way. I've got to be in Texas this weekend. I'm conducting a training session for judges."

Kate thought he was being optimistic about making the trip, unless Brandon found new evidence in the next twenty-four hours, which didn't seem likely. "You might have to make contingency plans."

"I can't cancel at this late date. I have a reputation to think of."

"I'm sorry, Tony. About everything. You agreed to emcee as a favor to me. Don't deny it. I know I couldn't offer you the same fee as the established tournaments do."

Tony waved it away. "It was my pleasure. And I've enjoyed myself immensely, except for the murders and being accused of hit and run. Ginny Sue is really sweet and I'd like to see more of her, but . . ." He shrugged again. "I don't know. It's just too complicated."

"So what? You're just going to fly off into the sunset? Never to be heard from again? That's hardly fair to Ginny Sue." Then again, Brandon was about to drive off into the sunset. And that wasn't fair to anyone.

"Wouldn't it be better to tell her the whole truth and let her decide?" Though she was hardly the person to be giving advice. Every time she tried to tell the truth, it seemed to bite her in the butt. But she knew it was the right thing to do.

"You think she'll understand?"

Kate had no idea. "I'm sure she will."

Tony left after that. Kate and Al followed him to the door. "Please think about what I said," she told him before she closed the door.

It was out of her hands now. She'd done her duty. Henceforth, she would no longer be cooperating with the police. A spy for the chief. A *traitor*. She'd been called them all. She'd tried to help and made everybody mad at her in the process. Well, she was finished with that. No more.

She stepped into the mechanical puzzle room. She didn't spend much time here. It would have been better named the miscellaneous room, since it was a catchall for puzzles that didn't belong in any of the other collections. *Sort of like me*, Kate mused.

One of the display cases held a variety of interlocking puzzles. Three-dimensional puzzles whose various parts combined to sustain the puzzle's particular shape. There were route-finding mazes and dexterity puzzles. Tangrams, Magic Squares, Pentominoes, Strung Cubes, Optical Illusions, Burr Puzzles, Falling Marbles, Soma Cubes—all created to challenge one's ingenuity and patience.

All solved by the correct logical procedure and attention to detail, while keeping the larger picture in view. They could all be maddening, but that was because of the solver's inability, not a shortcoming of the puzzle.

She stopped at the display of Rubik's Cubes. These had once been the professor's favorite puzzle. And hers. They'd worked them for hours, sitting before the fire in the office. Later, the Cubes were supplanted by Sudoku, and if the professor had lived, they might have made a new puzzle discovery together.

She ran her finger along the glass top of the display case, wondering if she could absorb some essence of the professor, like Harry had tried to do in the professor's apartment last night. But she felt no transforming power. Just quiet, except for the squeak of her finger across the glass.

"Tell me, professor. What do I do now? Display patience as you always taught me? Or should I take Marian's advice and stop letting people push me around?"

There was no answer. The room didn't become suddenly cold. No eerie murmurs drifted on the air. Just silence and the tick of the case clock down the hall.

The buzzer rang, letting her know someone had entered the museum.

"Just me," Alice said when Kate stepped into the foyer. "You're here early." She bustled past Kate, looking pinker and daintier than ever. She hung up her coat and hat in the closet and came back to the desk.

Kate picked up her purse from the desk where she'd dropped it on her way in with Tony.

"Alice, could you handle the museum alone, maybe until Harry gets here? I'd like to go out."

"Certainly," Alice said. "Don't worry about a thing. It's about time you took a day off."

Yes, it was, but not today. Today she was going to start fighting back.

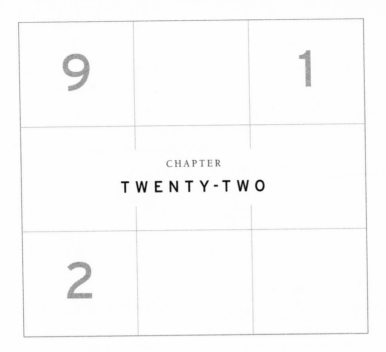

CHAPTER

TWENTY-TWO

KATE DROVE TO Manchester with no clear idea of why or what she thought she would achieve; but she was determined to do something. And since she'd been a potential victim of Mr. Orange Hat, she felt pressed for time.

She'd come to the conclusion that the Revell-Claudine-Lott connection had to have something to do with the two murders. Nothing else made sense. And the sooner Kate figured out that connection, the sooner suspicion would lift from Granville and from Tony.

Manchester was the largest town in New Hampshire, and like most growing towns, it was a combination of old and new. The downtown business district consisted of offices occupying Victorian gingerbread houses, steel high-rises, and everything in between.

Kate took I-93 south, which cut across the northeast section of town and looped down to sprawling industrial parks before continuing south all the way to Boston. Which made her think of Brandon and how angry he would be if he found out she was investigating on her own.

She wasn't exactly investigating. But if she happened to find a clue to the murderer while she was *not* investigating, surely the chief couldn't complain about that.

She knew he was frustrated because the possible suspects had left his jurisdiction. But she wasn't constrained in that way. And it was imperative that something be done.

She also knew that having preconceptions about the outcome of a problem was not the most valid way to go about finding a viable solution. She'd done enough studying, analyzing, and comparing the situation to have valid reasons for believing that the watch/possible cheat connection between Lott, Revell, and Claudine Frankel was the most likely path to solving the murder. She, like any good mathematician, was obligated to follow a proof as far as she was able.

And besides, she was mad as hops.

The only wild card was Mr. Orange Hat. It seemed likely to Kate that he must work at MKD, too. Possibly Isaac Walsh. If she were wrong, she'd only taken a day off from work.

MKD was in a complex right off the exit ramp at the back of a winding access road. It was a two-story gray building and she almost missed the nondescript sign that stood in the strip of grass outside. There was a parking lot across the street and beyond it another gray, bland building.

Kate had no intention of going inside or even being seen. She turned into the parking lot and cruised the aisles looking for a white Chevy sedan. Among the thirty or so cars parked there, there was only one white Chevy and it was a truck.

The Chevy had probably been a rental. She wondered if Brandon had done a search for it. Or it could have been borrowed, or even stolen for that matter.

Okay, she had come here half-cocked. Which wasn't a wholly bad thing. But it was a very un-geekish thing to do. Geeks always had a plan.

She pulled into a slot at the end of one of the rows, where she could see the entrance of the building. It was eleven o'clock, too early for lunch—if the employees even left the building for lunch.

She didn't want to miss any action at MKD. Not that she really expected any. But it *was* the day after her attack, and someone was getting desperate or they wouldn't have come after her.

She'd made the connection between the principals, but what she couldn't figure out was why they'd come after her. Did they think she knew something she didn't? Did she have something they wanted? She'd wracked her brain far into the night but had come up with zip.

Except that she'd been attacked the day after Harry had called MKD from the museum. It had to be directly related. And she was going to find out what it was so they could get back to normal life. In the back of her mind she knew she was hoping, like Harry, that if she solved the case, the chief would change his mind about going away. It was foolish and yet still she hoped.

She turned off the engine, put on her sunglasses, took a Sudoku book out of her bag, and settled down to wait for something to happen. Within five minutes, the heat had dissipated, her fingers grew stiff, and her nose was cold to the touch.

She spent the next two hours alternating between running the heat and shivering with cold. In between she wondered if Brandon had called social services. If Harry would even be there when she got back to the museum.

Surely Brandon would give him a chance to say good-bye. Maybe she should just go home and consult Simon Mack about the legalities of adopting Harry instead of sitting here shivering, waiting for nothing.

By the next hour, she had completed four advanced Sudoku puzzles. Only two men had gone into the building and no one had come out. At this rate, the case would go as cold as her nose. And where would that leave them? Always looking over their shoulders. Except it would be Kate looking over her shoulder—Harry and the chief would be gone.

Time to apply drastic measures. Harry's call had prompted the attempted hit and run. Another call might get things moving again. She picked up her cell. Dialed the number for MKD.

She did feel a prick of conscience that she might be screwing up someone's investigation. Though it wasn't clear that anybody was still on the case.

She got a recorded directory. Deliberated for a second whether to get transferred to an operator or punch in Isaac Walsh's extension. She wished she'd asked Harry who had talked to him before he'd hung up.

She pressed zero. A woman's voice asked how she could direct her. Kate listened closely. Not Claudine Frankel.

"I'd like to speak with Isaac Walsh, please."

"Just a moment. I'll connect you.

A series of clicks as the exchange went through. And she suddenly knew how Harry had felt waiting for Walsh to pick up.

"Development," said another female voice.

This time Kate recognized it. She took a calming breath. "Hi, I'd like to speak with Isaac Walsh."

An instant of silence. Had Claudine recognized her voice, too? "Whom may I say is calling?"

Here it was. "Kate McDonald . . . of the Avondale Puzzle Museum in Granville." *What do you say to that, Ms. Frankel?*

Claudine had nothing to say. For a long moment. "And this would be in reference to what?"

Playing dumb. Not a stretch for Claudine, thought Kate's cattier side. Now she needed to make a decision—quick. She plunged in. "I'd like to meet with him about creating a Sudoku ch—tutorial. Today if possible. I have a bit of work to do here at the museum, but I could drive down and be there in about two hours."

"Please hold."

Kate's hand was shaking, but she didn't hang up. This time she wouldn't be the victim. She had no intention of meeting the man. Just prod him into action if he was guilty.

It seemed forever before Claudine came back on the phone. "I'm sorry, Mr. Walsh has gone home with a cold."

"Oh, that's too bad," Kate said, feeling ridiculously relieved. "Perhaps, next week, when he's feeling better."

She waited to see if Claudine would identify herself or ask her to call back, but heard only the click of the phone as Claudine cut the connection.

Kate tossed her own phone on the passenger seat and flopped back against car seat. As soon as the adrenalin rush began to subside, she started thinking again. If Walsh had gone home, wouldn't she have seen him come outside? There was no parking lot behind the building. She'd noticed that as she wound her way through the park.

So Claudine must be lying. He was either still in the building or he hadn't come in today. Was Claudine on the phone to him right now, warning him that Kate was on his trail? Or—

The door to MKD opened and a man hurried out, in a black parka and a bright orange ski hat. How dumb was that? Even if they thought that Kate was miles away.

Walsh hurried across the street and got into a car several rows away. Kate alternated between watching him and watching the front door. When he pulled out of the lot driving a beige Taurus, Kate started her engine.

It was thrilling—the chase. It was also stupid. She knew she should just drive away and call Brandon to tell him she'd found the owner of the hat. But he would be furious. And she'd had just about all of his anger she could take.

And besides, she was just going to follow Walsh to see where he went—if he'd panicked and was making his getaway, or just heading home to decongestants and bed.

Either way, she'd come too far to pull back now. She'd just have to be very careful.

Walsh turned right out of the parking lot, but instead of taking the ramp to the highway, he continued on the street that cut beneath the overpass. Kate waited several seconds, then followed.

It was a wide two-lane street, lined with snowbanks that were black with car exhaust. On the other side of the highway, it became a busy four-lane thoroughfare, and it was easy for Kate to keep from being seen.

A few long blocks later, Walsh turned right again. The soot-covered snow changed to white and a block later they entered a suburban neighborhood. The houses were mainly split levels and ranches with large lawns, many dotted with snowmen and sled tracks.

Kate hoped that he wouldn't be met at the door by a wife and several cute children. That would be awful.

Get a grip, she told herself. *It's a school day. And even if he has a family, he's the man in the orange hat.* And a possible murderer.

He turned again. It was harder not to be spotted now and Kate fell back to what she considered a safe distance. She passed a park with a frozen pond and a sign that said Skating Today. Several young children were falling on the ice, their nannies or mothers chatting at the side of the pond. Two golden retrievers chased each other in the snow. Beyond the play area, bare tree limbs made a tracery across the blue sky.

She was so busy admiring the view that she almost overshot Walsh as he turned into a neatly plowed macadam driveway. He lived in a split level. There were no sleds or snowmen, no wreath on the door. Kate began to feel better.

She parked at the curb next to the park. There were already several cars, minivans, and SUVs parked there. Her Matrix would fit right in.

Walsh left the car in the driveway and went in the front door, which seemed strange since there was an attached garage and probably an entrance there. *Unless he's planning to leave again. . .*

And if he didn't? How long would she have to wait to see if he made a run for it? The fact that he'd left MKD right after her phone call might be a coincidence. They did happen, though Kate didn't like them.

She began to feel foolish. And wished she'd stayed at MKD to watch for Claudine. *Patience,* she told herself, just like the professor would have done. Then she smiled. *Be patient and then punch him in the gut.*

She was deliberating on whether to stay or go when a car passed and pulled into the driveway behind Walsh's Taurus. A red, sporty Honda. Kate sat up. Claudine Frankel got out and went up the front steps.

Eureka. Patience pays off. But what was she going to do about it? Certainly nothing physical. That had just been a metaphor. She hadn't punched anybody since third grade.

Someone tapped on the window. Kate jumped and let out a squeak.

Her first response was flight. She reached for the keys, still in the ignition, but he was already around the front of the car. He yanked opened the passenger door and Kate gave up all hope of escape. She pulled her hand back from the keys.

He slid into the car and closed the door behind him. "What the hell do you think you're doing?" asked one big angry chief of police.

"I, uh—how did you get here?"

"I was questioning Claudine Frankel. Tony came to the station this morning and confessed."

"Tony confessed? To what?"

"His real relationship with Claudine. Dumb f—man. So I came to get Claudine's side of the story. Imagine my surprise when I come out of MKD and see you driving off after Isaac Walsh. Are you crazy? These people are dangerous."

"I thought this was out of your jurisdiction. You're not in uniform."

"And I'm driving my personal car. No jurisdiction. Just a guy asking questions. Not my fault if she doesn't understand the finer points of the law."

The chief was bending the law? Kate was speechless.

He, however, had plenty to say. "What are you doing? Jesus, I could kill you myself."

"Watch it. You're one swear word away from a pizza."

"*Kate.*"

"Okay, I'm sorry. But everything is all messed up. Ginny Sue hates me. Jason and Erik have quit the board. Sam isn't speaking to me."

"He isn't?"

"No. Two men are dead. Someone tried to kill me yesterday and you're about to send my apprentice into the system. And there's not one damn thing I can do about any of it!"

"Kate—"

"I'll pay for the damn pizza! Harry and I tried to help you solve this case. Harry even figured out how Gordon could have cheated. But all the brain power in the world isn't worth beans if you let everyone down. Go away and let me try to fix this."

She turned away from him and concentrated on looking out the window and trying not to cry. She was tired of being on this emotional roller coaster. It accomplished nothing and made her look like a fool.

"Is that what you think I'm doing? Letting you and Harry down?"

Kate's head snapped toward him. "You? No, I . . . I meant me." She sniffed. "But yeah. You are, too."

He lowered his eyes. "I know you think I don't care about Harry, but I do. I just don't have time to give him what he needs. He should live in an environment where there's no violence—even peripherally—in a house with steady hours and people on call twenty-four seven. He needs stability."

"He needs *us*."

He looked at her, curious.

Heat rushed up Kate's neck and suffused her cheeks when she realized what she'd said.

He reached over and touched her black eye gently with the tips of his fingers. "Go home. Let me do my job."

Kate averted her face—and saw the door to Isaac Walsh's house open.

Claudine came out and hurried toward her car, carrying a suitcase.

"It's Claudine. She's running away."

Brandon opened his door. "Go home. I mean it." Then he was out of the car and racing back along the street, past the other parked cars. Kate had just enough time to hide her face before Claudine passed by.

Near the back of the parked cars, a black SUV pulled out, made a U-turn, and sped after her.

What did he think he could do? And what about Isaac Walsh? He was the one with the orange hat. He was the person most likely to be involved in the Sudoku cheat. And now the chief was chasing a blonde in a red car and the possible murderer was right across the street.

Kate slumped back in frustration. *"Go home." Right.* There wasn't much else for her to do. Surely Brandon knew something she didn't or he would have stayed to watch Isaac Walsh. She'd wasted all this time and energy for nothing. She turned the key in the ignition, checked the rear view mirror before pulling out into the street . . . and saw the orange hat appear at the front door.

Isaac Walsh ran toward his car. Kate didn't know whether to laugh or cry. Now what should she do? *Call Brandon.* She pressed his speed dial number. It went straight to his voicemail. Which meant he'd either turned it off or he was on the phone. Calling for backup, hopefully? She couldn't be sure. And if she didn't get through, Brandon might be trapped between two fleeing fugitives.

And a partridge in a pear tree. This was insane.

Walsh drove past without a glance in her direction. Kate waited for a few seconds, then did just what the chief had done: pulled a U-turn and joined the chase.

They backtracked through the neighborhood, but at the main road, instead of turning right toward MKD, Walsh continued straight.

Kate kept after him. The road became narrower and began to twist through stands of trees. She caught an occasional glimpse of water. Where the hell were they going? The airport was in the opposite direction. That's where she would go if she were a murderer.

This road seemed to be some kind of scenic route around the lake. She began to feel scared. What if Walsh were leading her into a trap? She speed-dialed Brandon again. Got his voicemail.

"I'm behind Isaac Walsh who is on—" She looked for a street sign, found none. No cross streets either. "On the road that runs by the lake, going south. I'm afraid he's behind you. Let me know that you got this message."

She hung up. Walsh's car rounded a bend, fishtailing wildly. The road was plowed, but there must be patches of ice on the asphalt. She slowed down to take the turn, saw the back of the Taurus as it rounded the next bend. She was falling behind, but it didn't matter. There was no way to go but forward.

Kate took the next curve and saw all three cars parked at the side of the road. She slowed to a crawl. Claudine's Honda was nose down in a ravine of white. The chief's SUV was pulled in behind it. And the beige Taurus had stopped behind it. She didn't see Walsh or the chief. But she saw Claudine standing halfway down the slope, pointing toward the ravine.

And she heard the shot as it echoed on the clear, crisp air.

7					4		9	
		9	8			5		2
					3		7	
9		1	3	2				
				4	7	1		6
	1		4					
3		2			8	4		
	9		1					3

CHAPTER

TWENTY-THREE

KATE PRESSED ON the brakes. The Matrix began to slide, which answered the question of why Claudine had skidded off the road—black ice. Kate spent a harrowing few seconds regaining control of the car and managed to stop with her passenger side just inches away from the beige Taurus.

Claudine swung toward the Matrix and Kate saw she was pointing with a small pistol. She bet it was a .38. No sign of Brandon or Walsh. They must be down in the ravine—

Good God. No! Kate prayed that Claudine's first shot had missed the men.

For a heart stopping moment, the two women stared at each other. Then Claudine swung the gun back toward the ravine. Taking advantage of the moment, Kate ducked down in the seat, popped the trunk, then opened the car door. She rolled out of the car with only one thing on her mind: *Stop Claudine.*

She crouched low. Keeping the car between her and Claudine, she slid her way to the trunk and found the only thing she could possibly use as a weapon—a tire iron.

Gripping it in one hand, she scooted around the edge of the car, and peered around the bumper. She could see the chief and Isaac Walsh rolling in the snow at the bottom of the ravine, locked together like in a television western. Claudine stood above them, ankle deep in the snow, waving the pistol between them.

She was too far away for Kate to be able to disarm her. There was nothing between her and the other woman but air and snow.

Brandon landed a hit on Walsh's jaw and the man fell back. Claudine raised the pistol.

Kate yelled "No!"

Claudine turned, her gun now trained on Kate. Kate lunged to the side, but her feet slid out from under her. Instinctively, she curled into a ball to break her fall and hopefully give Claudine a smaller target. Snow sprayed out around her, the earth seemed to shift beneath her, and a second later she was sliding down the hill. Straight toward Claudine.

A bush slapped at her clothes and yanked the tire iron from her hand as she careened past it. In desperation, Kate stuck out both legs, but it didn't slow her down.

Claudine stepped back, raised the pistol.

Kate was going to die. Then suddenly, one of Claudine's feet sank into the snow; she lost her balance. The gun jerked upward and another shot reverberated in the air.

Kate's ears rang. She plowed into Claudine. The woman grunted and the pistol flew out of her hand, arced across the air, and sank into the snow.

Kate rolled on top of her and pinned her down in the snow. Claudine grabbed Kate's hair, bucked and scratched, thrashing her arms and legs like a demented snow angel. Kate hung on with everything she had.

She didn't know what had happened to Brandon, if he was alive or dead. She was afraid to look and risk losing Claudine. She could only watch the clouds of her own panting breath until someone grabbed her from behind. She'd forgotten about Walsh. She lashed out, twisting and pummeling him with her fists.

"It's over. Stop struggling."

She could barely hear, because of the ringing in her ears.

"*Kate*. Stop."

Brandon's voice. And the ringing was sirens. He pulled her off Claudine and lifted her to her feet. She slumped back against him. His arms closed around her waist and two uniformed men dragged Claudine to her feet.

"The police . . . ? How? I tried to call you. . . How did they get here?" She was talking to air. His grip was so tight, she couldn't turn to face him.

"I know you said to leave. I was, but then Walsh came out, and I was afraid—"

"Kate, be quiet."

"I didn't want you to get shot."

"I know . . . just . . . be quiet."

She snapped her lips together. A tremor passed through her.

Another policeman was picking his way through the snow toward them. He wasn't dressed for the elements; he was wearing street shoes and a suit. His winter coat was unbuttoned as if he'd just had time to throw it on before getting out of the police car.

Kate thought he must be a local detective.

Brandon didn't let go of her. Maybe he thought she'd fall or bolt, because Kate knew she was in for it. He was breathing hard from the fight. Her body moved in tandem with the rise and fall of his chest.

The detective stopped in front of them. "Mitchell, you got clearance to *talk* to the Frankel woman. That was all."

"That's all I meant to do. Things got out of my control."

"I'll say." The detective looked sourly over the scene. Walsh was sitting in the snow at the bottom of the bank, looking dazed as two officers hauled him to his feet.

Another officer held a struggling Claudine while his partner handcuffed her.

"Who is this?" the detective asked, lifting his chin at Kate.

"An innocent bystander," Brandon said and increased his hold on Kate, letting her know to keep quiet.

"You know, Mitchell, your reputation precedes you. You better not have screwed this up."

Kate felt Brandon flinch. *What reputation?* Had someone from Granville complained about him? Of course they had, but to other law enforcement agencies?

"I think you better come in to the station and give us a statement. You too, miss. Are you okay to drive? You can go in one of the squad cars and I'll have someone drive your car over."

"Good idea," Brandon said. "She can ride with me."

The detective narrowed his eyes. "I don't think so."

Brandon tensed almost imperceptibly. Kate couldn't understand why the two men were so hostile. *We're all on the same side, right?*

"Fine." The chief let go of Kate and she nearly lost her balance.

Two officers passed by with Walsh stumbling between them. One of them had pushed the orange ski hat back on his head and snow hung in hardened globs off the end of each point.

"I had nothing to do with any of this," he protested.

"Yeah, yeah," the detective said.

"I didn't. I just saw the two cars and stopped to help. I thought he was attacking her. I didn't know he was police—"

"You knew who I was," Brandon corrected him. "It's on the official log, our little talk."

"I didn't recognize you." Isaac Walsh hung his head. "I just wanted the watch back, I didn't kill anybody. I swear."

The two officers pulled him away.

The detective raised his eyebrows at Brandon.

"Maybe," Brandon said. "But Frankel had a thirty-eight. It's in the snow somewhere. My guess is ballistics will link it to Gordon Lott's murder."

"It wasn't my fault," cried Claudine, fighting her two guards. "He killed Kenny. I *saw* him. He would have killed me!"

Walsh strained against his guards. "You're lying! I wasn't even there."

"Not *you*, stupid. Gordon." She was still struggling, but half-heartedly. "He knocked Kenny down and dragged him inside the VFW hall."

The detective glanced at one of the officers, who nodded slightly. "She's been Mirandized.".

The detective turned back to Revell. "So you waited for him and killed him."

"I just wanted the watch. I hate this stupid job."

Brandon sighed. The detective rolled his eyes.

The officers pulled Claudine away.

The detective helped Kate up the snowbank while Brandon stood where he was, watching them. The rest of the team had already begun to dig in the snow looking for the .38.

They had to walk past the disabled Honda to get to the road. As they passed, Kate caught a patch of orange on the backseat. She stopped, looked inside. Looked back at Walsh, whose head was being pushed down for him to enter the squad car. He was still wearing the orange hat.

"There were two," Kate exclaimed.

The detective stopped. "Two what?"

"Orange hats."

"What about orange hats?" he asked, clearly not amused.

"A long story," Brandon told him. He looked into the Honda's backseat and shook his head. "I'll fill you in at the station."

It was a long drive. Detective Clark, after finally introducing himself, fell silent. Kate knew he was trying to figure out how she fit into the investigation, but he was saving his questions for the station.

They drove north on what Kate learned was Lake Shore Road and cut through town until they at last arrived at the Manchester police station, a two-story, no-frills, brick and concrete building. She only saw Brandon in passing as he accompanied Detective Clark down a hallway and through a door at the end.

Brandon didn't even acknowledge her. She began to feel uncomfortable. Was he angry with her for butting in? She was only trying to help. But that's what happened when you dealt with people—they were always misconstruing your motives.

Maybe Brandon had the right idea after all. Move on. The institute might not need her, but there were other jobs. . . . She was appalled at the thought. She couldn't leave.

Who would take care of the museum and Harry? And besides, she didn't want to leave. She was building a *life* in Granville. A real, adult life. What was really bothering her was trying to imagine that life without a certain police chief.

A female officer came for her and led her back to an interview room, where her statement was taped. Detective Clark was present, but beyond looking like he'd sucked on a lemon, he let the other officer ask the questions.

She started with the tournament, the deaths, the snow storm, skirted the issue of why she was following Isaac Walsh, though she guessed Brandon had filled him in. She didn't mention Harry, or Ginny Sue, or how the people in Granville felt about the chief. She answered only what was asked, and tried not to get flushed when she admitted to not following the chief's order to go home a few hours earlier.

Brandon was waiting for her when she was finished. "I'll follow you back to Granville. Go straight to the museum. Call Harry. He's probably worried about you."

Kate merely nodded and let him open the door for her. True to his word, he followed her all the way to the museum, forty-five minutes of staying well within the speed limit, which gave Kate a perverse satisfaction since she was pretty certain the chief didn't always feel compelled to obey the law—for all his talk.

Harry met them at the door of the museum. "Where have you been?" He searched Kate's face, his eyes worried. He didn't even glance at the chief.

"Manchester," Kate said, and gave him a surreptitious wink.

"Wow," he mouthed, then cut himself short.

"Sorry I didn't call. We got kind of busy."

Harry nodded. "That's okay." He stood back while they came inside, then sat down at the desk where several books were open.

"Homework," he said. Kate thought he sounded defiant and she ached for him.

Brandon followed her to the office. Harry didn't look up, much less follow them, like he normally would.

As soon as the door was closed, Brandon tossed his jacket over the back of the wing chair and turned to Kate.

"Don't," she said, not feeling up to being chastised.

"I was just going to thank you. For probably saving my life."

She stared at him. "For slipping on the ice and rolling down a hill of snow? You're welcome."

"It might not have been graceful, but it was effective."

She didn't want to smile. There were too many things to feel bad about.

"Did Detective Clark let you in on any state secrets? Ones you can divulge to me?" she added hurriedly.

"Buzz Harry. Tell him to come up."

She started shaking her head. "Not now, Brandon. Please."

He looked taken aback, then said, "I just thought he might be interested in hearing the outcome."

"Oh." She pressed the intercom. "Harry, can you come up?"

There was no answer. She shrugged at the chief, but after a few seconds she heard his footsteps on the stairs, and then a soft knock before the door opened. Harry looked about as miserable as a person could look.

Kate smiled at him. "They arrested Claudine and Isaac Walsh, and the chief thought you wanted to hear the details."

Harry's face lightened briefly, then shut down again. He was already in protection mode. "Sure," he said, trying to be casual. He sat down on the edge of the desk and crossed his arms.

"Here's the upshot," the chief said, as careful not to look at Harry as Harry was not to look at him. "According to Walsh, he and Revell were working on a computer Sudoku software and a companion video game. Naturally, they developed a cheat for testing it.

"They contacted Lott to run the tests for them. Evidently they'd used him to run tests before. This was about a year ago, according to Walsh. Then Revell started tinkering with the design and came up with the wristwatch version. Walsh claims he didn't know about the camera and what they intended to use it for until he found out that they were going to test it at the tournament.

"Being the fine upstanding citizen that he is, he came down to the tournament to try and talk them out of it." Brandon laughed.

Kate shook her head. "If that's the truth, he could have just told *me* about it."

"And you would have disqualified Lott, and Revell and Walsh would have looked like crooks."

"They are crooks."

"Well, yeah—"

"So he killed them?" Harry couldn't keep his interest at bay any longer and he leaned forward eagerly.

"He says no. Just that he walked with them out of the Granville Bar and Grill but since it had started to snow, he decided to drive straight back to Manchester."

"So who killed them?"

"And where is the watch?" added Kate.

"Claudine had the watch when they arrested her. She'd been trying to sell it back to Walsh."

"Jeez—"

Harry and the chief both looked at her.

"That's not a swear word. So who tried to run me over the other day? Claudine or Walsh?"

Harry frowned.

"There were two orange hats," Kate explained.

"That was Claudine. Walsh has an alibi."

"So did she kill them?" asked Harry.

"Claudine killed Lott. She kept the thirty-eight." Brandon shook his head. "Amazing, the stupidity of criminals."

"So who killed Kenny Revell?"

"Gordon Lott," Kate said. "At least that's what Claudine said. Do you think it's true?"

The chief shrugged. "Not that we should be discussing this, but yeah. I think the DNA test will show two blood types on Lott, his and Kenny Revell's."

"Wow," Harry said. "Over a game."

"My guess is they had bigger plans."

"But it didn't even work."

"Let's see." Brandon reached in his shirt pocket and pulled out a folded piece of computer paper. "The answers were still saved in the watch. When the police computer expert downloaded it, I convinced him to give me a copy." He handed the paper to Harry. "Check it out."

Harry took it over to the computer and pulled up the Level A puzzle. "Wow. These answers are identical to the answer sheet. It doesn't make sense."

"Sure it does," Brandon said. "In his rush, Gordon must have copied down the numbers incorrectly. Pure human error."

"Amazing," Kate said.

Brandon took the paper and tore it into pieces. "I expect both of you to keep this in strictest confidence."

Harry nodded seriously.

"And the detective told you all of this?"

"Pretty much. We'd been exchanging information."

And then it struck her. "Are you transferring to Manchester?"

"Good God, no."

"But are you staying here?" Harry mumbled, barely loud enough to be heard.

Brandon didn't answer right away, and Harry turned away. "It doesn't matter. I'd better get back to the desk."

"I thought maybe Kate would give you the rest of the afternoon off."

Harry shot a panicked look to Kate. But what could she do? It was cruel to keep dragging this thing out. "Sure."

"Go get your stuff."

Harry's lip trembled but he turned and went out the door.

"Brandon. You—"

"See you later, Kate."

And he left, just like that. As if they both hadn't almost been killed that afternoon. As if the fate of a boy's life didn't hang in the balance.

Kate stayed at the museum long after closing time. She was half expecting Harry to seek sanctuary there. She considered calling Simon Mack, but knew that the court would not look favorably on a twenty-nine-year-old single woman trying to adopt a fourteen-year-old boy.

She made a cup of tea and sat down in her wing chair, not bothering to light a fire. She worked one puzzle, then another, trying to conjure up the professor or even Harry sitting silently beside her. She couldn't do it. There was only her, her Sudoku, and a cup of tea.

The buzzer rang. *Harry*, she thought sadly. She stood up, braced herself for good-bye. Listened to his footsteps on the stairs. Recognized two sets of footsteps. The chief obviously wasn't letting him out of his sight.

Her mouth twisted. She'd have to put a good face on this for Harry's sake.

She was smiling when they came in, but she couldn't look directly at either of them.

"I'm taking a few days off," Brandon said.

"Why?" She hadn't meant to ask, but she couldn't stop it.

"To teach Harry to ski."

Kate looked up.

Harry was smiling. "The chief's decided to give it another year."

Kate felt faint with relief. She looked at Brandon.

His features were expressionless. "But there are going to be some changes. . ."

Kate braced herself.

"I'm not working round the clock. So don't get involved in any more murders. I came here to have a normal job and I'm going to stick to that."

"And fish and hunt," added Kate.

"And ski." His face relaxed. "Can you believe Harry has lived here all his life and never learned to ski?"

Kate smiled, but didn't comment.

"Do you want to come, Kate? It'll be fun."

"Thanks, Harry, but . . ."

"I can't guarantee any thrills until Harry gets the hang of things, but you're welcome to join us."

"And watch me on the bunny hill," Harry groused, but he couldn't keep the excitement out of his voice.

"Well," said Kate. "If I come, that's where I'll be."

Brandon looked from Harry to Kate. "You don't ski, either?"

"I was too busy doing puzzles and homework."

"I can't believe it. Some of the best slopes on the East Coast are less than an hour away."

Kate shrugged.

Harry grinned.

Brandon let out a heartfelt sigh. "Then we'll pick you up at six a.m. Rain, sleet, or shine." The slightest smile crossed his lips. "Wear long underwear and your funny hat. It's going to be a long day."

ABOUT THE AUTHOR

Shelley Freydont is a past president of the New York/ Tri State chapterof Sisters in Crime, and a member of Mystery Writers of America, Romance Writers of America, New Jersey Romance Writers, and Kiss of Death RWA chapter. She is the author of five books in the *Linda Haggerty Mystery* series, and writes romance novels under the name Gemma Bruce. An avid lover of puzzles—Sudoku, crossword, jigsaw, and others—she lives in Ridgewood, New Jersey.

Please visit her at www.shelleyfreydont.com.

SOLUTIONS

PAGE 6

2	4	9	7	1	6	5	3	8
6	3	8	4	2	5	7	1	9
1	5	7	3	9	8	6	4	2
4	8	2	5	3	9	1	6	7
5	9	3	1	6	7	2	8	4
7	6	1	2	8	4	3	9	5
8	2	6	9	7	1	4	5	3
3	1	5	8	4	2	9	7	6
9	7	4	6	5	3	8	2	1

PAGE 70

5	2	1	6	8	3	4	9	7
8	3	9	5	4	7	6	2	1
4	7	6	1	9	2	5	3	8
6	9	5	4	7	8	3	1	2
3	1	8	2	6	5	7	4	9
2	4	7	9	3	1	8	5	6
9	8	2	7	5	4	1	6	3
7	6	4	3	1	9	2	8	5
1	5	3	8	2	6	9	7	4

PAGE 84

9	8	3	4	1	6	7	5	2
7	6	4	2	3	5	8	9	1
1	5	2	8	7	9	6	3	4
6	9	7	1	2	3	4	8	5
8	4	1	5	9	7	3	2	6
3	2	5	6	4	8	9	1	7
4	3	9	7	5	1	2	6	8
2	1	8	9	6	4	5	7	3
5	7	6	3	8	2	1	4	9

PAGE 170

2	7	5	3	1	6	4	8	9
6	4	3	8	9	2	5	1	7
9	1	8	4	7	5	2	3	6
3	6	1	7	5	8	9	2	4
8	5	7	2	4	9	1	6	3
4	2	9	6	3	1	7	5	8
1	8	6	9	2	4	3	7	5
7	9	2	5	8	3	6	4	1
5	3	4	1	6	7	8	9	2

PAGE 196

6	2	1	7	5	3	9	4	8
7	8	5	9	4	6	3	2	1
3	4	9	8	1	2	6	5	7
9	7	4	5	8	1	2	6	3
1	3	8	2	6	4	5	7	9
5	6	2	3	7	9	8	1	4
2	9	7	4	3	5	1	8	6
8	1	3	6	2	7	4	9	5
4	5	6	1	9	8	7	3	2

PAGE 216

6	2	8	1	9	5	3	4	7
7	3	9	4	8	6	5	2	1
4	5	1	7	2	3	8	9	6
8	6	4	3	1	9	7	5	2
2	7	3	5	4	8	1	6	9
9	1	5	6	7	2	4	8	3
5	8	6	2	3	7	9	1	4
1	9	7	8	6	4	2	3	5
3	4	2	9	5	1	6	7	8

7	4	8	9	6	5	1	2	3
3	1	6	7	4	2	5	9	8
5	2	9	8	1	3	7	6	4
4	9	5	3	8	6	2	1	7
6	3	1	2	7	4	9	8	5
8	7	2	1	5	9	4	3	6
1	6	4	5	2	8	3	7	9
2	8	3	4	9	7	6	5	1
9	5	7	6	3	1	8	4	2

8	1	3	7	4	5	9	2	6
5	2	9	3	1	6	8	4	7
6	4	7	8	2	9	5	1	3
1	3	6	2	9	4	7	8	5
7	9	5	6	8	1	4	3	2
4	8	2	5	7	3	1	6	9
2	5	1	9	6	8	3	7	4
9	6	4	1	3	7	2	5	8
3	7	8	4	5	2	6	9	1

7	2	6	5	1	4	3	9	8
1	3	9	8	7	6	5	4	2
8	4	5	2	9	3	6	7	1
9	6	1	3	2	5	7	8	4
2	7	4	6	8	1	9	3	5
5	8	3	9	4	7	1	2	6
6	1	8	4	3	9	2	5	7
3	5	2	7	6	8	4	1	9
4	9	7	1	5	2	8	6	3